"Who first played the Society game—putting it up as a barrier between us! Yet, I bested you in that, did I not?

"Showed you what fools all these Society people be. And still you run after them, ignoring me throughout this visit, turning away." And his voice softened as he continued. "Nay, Charle, I could not injure you one quarter as much as you do me by merely looking away."

Charlette stared back at his whitened face. "Shall I believe you are in earnest? Or are we playing one more grand game . . . whose loss for me shall be a loss indeed."

"Play the game out," he urged. "One more challenge! Come, Charle, have the courage to reveal your feelings for me. But I shall dare first. I'll jump first into the sea and wait for you to come along?"

Charlette took a deep breath, hesitating, tottering on the rail . . .

A Captain's Lady

Helen Argers

DIAMOND BOOKS, NEW YORK

A CAPTAIN'S LADY

A Diamond Book / published by arrangement with
the author

PRINTING HISTORY
Diamond edition / November 1991

ISBN: 1-55773-618-9

Diamond Books are published by The Berkley Publishing Group,
200 Madison Avenue, New York, New York 10016.
The name "DIAMOND" and its logo are trademarks
belonging to Charter Communications, Inc.

PRINTED IN THE UNITED STATES OF AMERICA

10 9 8 7 6 5 4 3 2 1

Prologue

❧ ═══════════════════════════════ ❧

ACROSS the room they stared at each other. Darrel Huntley, a sea captain, was surrounded by young ladies at the ball. His head was visible, yet appeared out of place, rising, as it did, from the center of a cluster of ruffled and laced ball gowns circumferencing him. Indeed, he appeared to one particular lady, with a very observant eye, to have donned a ruffled screen, for with every step he took it followed. At one point, he took a rather larger step and almost shook away one or two pink encumbrances, only to be attached on the other side by a créme muslin and a yellow crepe.

Overlooking his phalanx of ladies, Captain Huntley was determined to catch the eye of that special lady of his acquaintance. She was Charlette Varrick, an heiress from the Isle of Wight, where his father had been a sea captain for Mr. Varrick's ships. It was not difficult to pick out Miss Varrick. Wherever she was, she had always stood out—whether on ship, running with him on the beach or standing with the other young ladies of the main Society of the island. And now, here, almost seven years later, amidst the pale parade of young ladies, she was like a subtly glowing emerald. Blue or green, she always wore, Darrel remembered, for the sea she loved as much as he.

Actually, Charlette Varrick, once having spotted him, was attempting not to meet his glance. Rather, she lifted her green fan and partially covered her face. Then, realizing the idiocy of that, she dropped her fan against her green silk and gauze gown. Green silk was not proper attire for a young girl having her first Season in London. White or pastels in muslin or crepe was the thing. But with Miss Varrick's outstanding coloring—golden-red hair and blue eyes of a brilliance not ordinarily observed—she tended to choose bolder shadings to equal hers. The ladies of nobility

1

whispered that her choices, not to mention her enthusiasms, demonstrated a shameful forwardness that could not be condoned— very near to tying her garter in public.

But Captain Huntley's instant surmise had been right on the mark. Her predilection for blue-green selections stemmed rather from her love of the sea, wanting always to be reminded of the ocean surrounding her Channel island home.

London Society preferred she forget her island, however, and certainly a lowly captain would be first on the list of prohibitions. Charlette had no intention of permitting the old connection between herself and Darrel to revive, calling to heel her attention whenever it showed the lack of good sense to wander toward him. But throughout, she felt the Captain's sights set permanently on her.

Unable to withstand the intensity of those dark grey eyes, Charlette once again covered her face with her fan, and then quickly dropped it, refusing to allow him to control her actions. Of a sudden, she sensed rather than actually saw, him smiling, as if he had guessed both the reason for her lifting the fan and for subsequently dropping it. Defiantly, she looked fully at him. He *was* laughing. Alas, he had seen and guessed all.

With her flaming hair, she did not need the addition of a blush; and she was almost forcing her flushed face to cool down. She thought of the sea, but that reminded her of Darrel and herself sailing together, sharing their love of the sea as children, and, through that, of each other.

How dared he press his attentions on her so! No gentleman would have presumed on a previous acquaintance with a lady, unless the lady in question had given him leave to do so by first acknowledging him herself! And that she had refused to do throughout the night. Yet, his constant staring was a deliberate attempt to reestablish their old communication. Truthfully, they had always been able to know what the other was thinking. She recollected one such time, sitting in her carriage next to her father; when Darrel was down on the ground with the other children of her father's crew. While distributing Christmas gifts to all, Charlette had secretly met his glance, and they silently laughed at the separation between them. Afterward she had given him his real present: a sexton he had always longed for. But he had gone her one better by giving her his prize shell, which he'd risked diving for in a wild storm.

Across the room, she saw him making a diving motion.

Heavens! he had picked up her thoughts of the shell. No, he was merely gesturing. Impossible that they still could have that connection. Thankfully, a young lady with an overly spangled dress claimed his attention, freeing Miss Varrick from his fixed stare at last.

The spangled girl was acting oddly, jumping up and down before Darrel. Whatever could be the matter? Was she just being overly illustrative of a point in discussion, or was that her reaction to the Captain's proximity? Yet, now the girl's mouth was gaping, making her appear prodigiously like a fish out of water. Why didn't Darrel take pity and throw her back in?

He made the gesture of a fisherman reeling in a fish, and Charlette caught her breath. Impossible that he had felt her thoughts! Obviously, he was describing some fishing event, and the young lady had been overcome by the excitement of it, and that explained the jumping. Really, Charlette decreed, she had to stop giving him the honor of her conjectures.

A few moments more and Charlette was prepared to make her departure. Almost reflexively, she turned for a parting glimpse of the Captain. Relieved of his female entourage at last, he was free to devote himself fully to catching her eye, and her view of him was finally unblocked. He seemed darker than she recollected— sun-warmed, and his dark brown hair worn a bit longer than fashionable. Taller, more muscular, more of a presence. Indeed, there were so many changes that went along with a boy becoming a man that unconsciously Charlette was edging for a closer view.

Their glances met. He mimicked throwing shells, their old signal for meeting alone, and then he continued toward the starboard balcony. Charlette stood, unmoving. Then slowly, almost as if he were drawing her after him—reeling her in, indeed—she followed him through the crowd, evading this one and that. Following.

Turning, just before stepping out, he saw her coming after. And he smiled.

Chapter One

❦ ══════════════════════════ ❦

THE last time he had thrown shells at her window, Charlette Varrick was twelve years old and had awakened early one morning with her usual anticipation for the new day.

The smell of the sea came through her balcony's open doors, and she stepped out, breathing deeply, the elixir of the sea coursing through her veins, preparatory to her climbing down the tree. She had devised a sensible style out of her long skirt, merely taking the back hem and pulling it through her legs and fastening it to her high waist with a heavy leather belt. Thus, she could climb and run, and modesty need not blush for her. Although, Darrel had often pointed out with a grin, she looked like two flounders, side by side. When they had an outing planned ahead of time, she wore her full disguise: breeches and her hair braided and tucked beneath a cap. But for spur of the moment meetings, this outfit did well enough, she assured herself, while climbing down from balcony to tree, then swinging out and catching the trellis till she reached the second balcony below. To jump over that stone banister into the rose garden was simplicity itself, and then she was off across her property into the adjacent forest, through the trail she and Darrel had made, and to the top of the chalk cliffs, below which was the beach and sea.

But this time Darrel was waiting below the second balcony, and, hand in hand, they ran to the forest. There, turning breathlessly, she spoke to him.

"What have you got under your shirt? 'Tis making the oddest movements."

"I'll show you when we get to the beach," he said, pulling her along.

"Ease up, there. Why are we . . . running! No one is after us,

I daresay! All the gardeners know I meet you regularly. They are
my friends and shan't say a word to father. You know that! Darrel,
don't pull so hard!"

But Darrel had a relentless grip on her hand, as he jumped her
over a boulder in their path, and then a fallen tree, to shortcut their
way. At last, her skirt beginning to come out of her belt, her hair
flying every which way, Charlette pulled away from him.

"I refuse to run like this till I'm told *why* I'm running!"

"Cut line, Charle! Beggin' your pardon, Miss Varrick! But we
is running because I am challenging you to a race, and I'll wager
I make it to the beach afore ye!"

"You shall not!" Charlette exploded, readjusting her gown with
a fervor, racing after, now more than keeping on a level. All she
ever needed was a challenge!

The dangerous part of their run always came when they went
sliding and skipping down the white chalk cliffs on the rough-
hewn steps made into the very chalk rocks through the years by
ancient fishermen. These perpendicular masses of Undercliff were
not only attractions for visitors to the southern part of the Isle of
Wight, but served in good stead as a shield from the rougher
winds. So it was always soft weather there, amiable to flowers
even in December, and always to children who climbed the chalky
cliffs. Those prominences rose up to seven hundred feet, like
huge, fully rigged ships, becalmed. But these halflings, knowing
and treating the cliffs as pets all their lives, scurried down,
unafraid of their height or danger of slipping. The race was all that
counted as they even jumped the last foot.

When the two hit the beach they were still neck and neck, and
were delighted to declare themselves joint winners. Laughing
from the exuberance of the race, and the fun of the challenge, and
just in general good spirits, both were ready to hug each other
when Darrel stepped back and exclaimed: "I'm bloody well all cut
up!"

"From what? Did a branch get you? Darrel! What, in heaven,
is that under your waistcoat? Oh! Oh! The darling! The little baby
darling! It's crying! How could you shake it up like that, you
moonling!"

And bending down she helped Darrel remove a tiny black baby
kitten, almost newborn, from its nestling place at Darrel's
scratched chest.

Shaking and mewing, it cuddled in Charlette's arms. She

looked up at Darrel, standing above, and gave him one of her dimpled, dazzling smiles that always had him blinking.

"Is it for me?"

"Naw. What would a grand lady want with this bit o' fluff? I brung it so you could watch me drown it in the sea."

Charlette laughed. "That's pure gammon. Only a proper muttonhead would swallow that plumper. *You* who even takes care of sick squirrels, and swam out last year to release that dolphin stuck in the net."

Darrel grinned. "Righto! Not about to drown the mite, but I'll go bail that's what was going to happen to it, Charle. Mrs. Franklin said her cat had too many kittens, and she was going to get rid of this batch in a bag! Had to stop Mr. Franklin on his way to the pond. Told him I'd save him the trouble. People always like it when you save them trouble. Took the bag right away, oped it, and there they were. Three of the sorriest bundles of black fur. All almost exactly alike. Me mom's keeping one. I took the prettiest one for you. And I got the third."

The kitten was licking at Charlette's hand. "He's hungry, I bet. How can I feed him? He won't lap at his age!" Charlette's eyes were worried, and Darrel leaned across her bosom to stroke the kitten. The two were together, stroking the shaking little thing, enjoying the physical pleasure of being so close and giving warmth to each other and to another creature.

"I daresay they're older than they look, 'cause they drink from a bowl, if held up."

The kitten opened its pink mouth in a yawn almost as large as himself.

With a whoop of laughter, Darrel said, "Pardon us for boring you, mate!"

But Charlette took it seriously. "Well, we best entertain him, then. I expect a song shall do it. You sing to him. You know all the sea chanties! Can't you see, this is obviously a sea cat."

They sang to it, and petted it and talked of the sea to it—until it stopped shaking and relaxed against Charlette.

Of a sudden the rising sun took their attention, gradually lighting the chalk cliffs with so much reflected radiance, it seemed an immense pearl. A circumference of lumina, and they in the center, and here and there, a wild blue wave crashed forth, interrupting the expanse of white, yet the waves too ended in white foam.

Day now fully established, Darrel reluctantly stood up, for now he must tell her.

"I'm giving you the kitten," he began ominously, "and takin' the other with me."

The red-gold head beneath him did not move. She was absorbed with the kitten. He reached out and touched her hair that was softer than even the kitten's. Instantly, she looked up at his gesture.

The two locked their stares, until as was oft the case, she read what he was going to say. Jumping up, Charlette almost dropped the kitten, and then caught it up and went running.

He ran after. "Charle! Charle! Be good, me girl. You knew it would soon come!"

Charlette was determined to escape the words. For so long of late, she had feared he would follow his father's footsteps and go to sea. But when he had passed the age of cabin boy, and, indeed, spurned the thought of sailing off in that lowly position, considering how much he knew about sailing, she thought there was a good chance that they would have at least another year together.

There was a defiance in the girl—she was the richest heiress of the island, and although kindhearted, she was accustomed to having her wishes obeyed. Actually, most people were delighted to give her whate're she requested—before she even put it into words. Her father's wealth was partly the cause, but also it was Charle herself. First, she was such a lonely little girl, without a mother's good influence and a father who rarely stayed at home. Then too, she was such a sparkling child, interested in all the sights and people about her, that rarely could one bear to put a damper on her. None of the staff of the Sea Castle would ever betray her outings with an island boy—although a good many, the housekeeper, Mrs. Glasgow and Mitchen, the butler, especially, bemoaned that Charlette would never become a true lady if she continued to rub against her inferiors in life! That she could never see anyone as inferior was why the common islanders claimed her as one of their own, dubbing her "Our Sea Lady." Even Darrel's father, the stern Captain Huntley, who treated his son with affectionate discipline, succumbed to Charle's blue-eyed admiration and was willing to share his sea knowledge for hours on end. His second-in-command, Jem Barker, now retired, never tired of telling both Darrel and herself the grand sea tales. But the one who most succumbed to Charlette's every wish was her father. So much was she his lone delight that in the infrequent times he came home to the white stuccoed-and-shelled Sea Castle he'd built for them, he could not bring her enough gifts.

Of them all, only Darrel dared to order Charlette around. And even he felt himself rather daring for doing so. Yet, she was a reasonable girl. If one would but explain why she could not have what she wished, she was prepared to explain why it was imperative that it be granted.

Recollecting that she had superior powers of reasoning, Charlette stopped running and decided to resort to them, saying with her Miss Varrick tones, "But you must not go to sea. Later, perhaps. But now, you recollect, we are going to sail to the Needles and climb Freshwater Cliffs for the eggs again. We agreed to do so. Besides," she pouted, reverting to a child again, "if you go to sea, whom shall I have to play with, read with, sail with!"

"If that don't beat the Dutch! I'm not going to spend my life being your playmate! Just because your father practically rules this island, he don't rule me. I'm going to rule the seas!"

"I know you are! I'm going to sail the seas with you! We've always said so!"

"That was pure twaddle. You know *you* can't go to sea. By Jove, you're, after all, a girl. You can't change that. Just as neither of us can change our growing up."

"And that's why you brought me this!" Charlette exclaimed in horror, dropping the kitten on the sand abruptly. "Well, I don't want it. I don't want anything in exchange for you."

"You beastly little girl," Darrel admonished, picking up the frightened cat. "I'll take it along with its brother to sea with me. I meant us both to have a twin cat; I thought we'd both call it by the same name, Sailor, or some such, so when we saw it, we'd think that somewhere the other Sailor was with . . . my friend. But if you're not enough of a sport for that, I'll take him back."

Darrel was walking off with the kitten, and Charlette was in a quandary. He alone had the capability of making her feel as if she had not lived up to his expectations. And although she was still furious with him for leaving, she could not disappoint him or herself by allowing them to part thusly.

"You are not to take the kitten from me," she cried out and ran after him.

He stopped his jaunty walk away and with a smug smile handed the cat back.

For a moment the two stood together patting the kitten between them, and then their eyes held and they shared their feeling of sadness. "You are a game girl," he assured them both, "ain't you, Charle? You'll write to me and wish me well."

"I'd wish you at the bottom of the sea, if you weren't going to take Froth along."

"Froth! The name's Sailor."

"I like Froth better. If yours has the same white splashes on face, chest and paws, it's a dash sight more apt. Besides, can you see yourself standing on the poop deck, yelling, 'Ahoy, *Sailor*,'— half the mates aboard will come running."

"You know I ain't going to be anywhere near the captain's poop deck. And I should rather call out, 'Ahoy, Sailor,' than 'Ahoy, Froth.' With all the mates staring, I should look nohow!"

Charlette giggled, and then sighed, recollecting they were parting. "I should have listened to my governess and spent my time becoming a grand lady, instead of your companion. You're sailing off to have grand adventures, leaving me here waving at an empty sky."

"That's the position of all ladies," he said in obnoxious self-satisfaction.

"Not this lady!" Charlette exclaimed indignantly.

"All women must remain ashore while their men go off to sea. Me mom has never been aboard a single ship, for all the grand ones Dad's been captain of. And she don't even go to the harbor when he comes. She bides at home, and he comes up the walk with some surprise for her, depending on the cargo. He once bought her a silk wrap from China and called it a kimono, but Mom said it weren't decent; still, she keeps it in her chest and looks at it whenever he be at sea. I'll bring *you* a kimono if we sail to China, or some spices if we go to the South Seas. But that won't be for awhile, because I'm not sailing on your father's ships."

That last bit of information stifled Charlette's retorts in her astonished mouth. "But where are you going, then?"

"Your father and mine fixed it up between them. N'one asking me how *I* felt. I'm to be a midshipman on His Majesty's vessels. They got me set for the blasted navy!"

Charlette was not surprised at the bitterness of his tone. She knew well enough what he thought of the sailing prowess of the navy. Not to mention the cruelty to their crews. Tales of flogging through the fleet that left a man's back stripped to the bones before mercifully dying had the merchant sailors glad of their lot. But Darrel would be going in as an officer. And from there he could find his way into Society—which Charlette knew was Captain Huntley's wish. And part of her rejoiced at his chance to rise in the world and become her equal. But she was wise enough to say naught of that to him. One obstacle occurred, and she said gleefully, "But you're not of age to be a midshipman. You're not yet seventeen."

"No help there. Your father don't know that, and my father don't want me to tell. Says I look a proper giant, with my height, and all."

Unable not to attempt lifting his spirits, she said with false cheer, "Think on 't—you'll be learning to ship the carronades and locking the gun carriages. And always hauling, reefing and rigging! Maybe you'll even order the firing of the guns! That should be jolly!"

"There's that," he admitted. "But we're not battling Napoleon now, so it's all blockading. Tame stuff. While a merchant ship sails across the seas, and there's the Sailing Races to port, and all the prize money. And the navy promotes only gentlemen of influence, so I'd ne'er make captain. Who wants to be a lowly officer all my life, when I can be Captain of the Seas? Who would settle for a small brig or frigate rather than a full-rigged merchant ship like your father's, especially when racing!" Suddenly, the cat's movement got his attention. "I say, let's call him Racer. No, Rigger. Or even Froth wouldn't be amiss, for a racing ship rides high on the waves! What say there, cat, which do you fancy? Nod when you hear the proper one. And mind now, you're choosin' for your brothers as well!"

The black kitten was feeling safe against Charlette, climbing up occasionally to look her in the eye. But she held him down firmly against her softness. He experimentally let his paws scratch her green silk spencer, fastening onto a gold button.

"Pay attention," Charlette demanded imperiously, shaking the cat a bit out of his absorption on her button. "Is it to be Rigger? Or Sailor? Or *Froth*!"

At the last, the kitten nodded its entire body, in a definite indication of favor.

"You're such a fraud," Darrel hooted. "You not only said the last name louder, but you shook him while saying it. What Flummery! 'Flummery-Blummery—Bound to end in a Nunnery!' All you gentry are alike—always makin' certain naught's fairly left to chance—tipping things your way!"

"I didn't!" Charlette exclaimed hotly. "And I'm glad you're

going away, and I hope a tack block falls on your head, and a great big wave washes you off deck in the middle of the biggest storm and you, you never come up . . . and you drown-dead!"

Darrel, laughing at her vehemence, skipped alongside her as she climbed back up the cliff's chalk steps. At the top they paused unconsciously for the usual sighting of the world of white at their feet and nodded at its still being there.

"No point wishing me to drown, you know," he said, making her sit next to him on a conveniently jutting edge. "You know I never sink. Who pulled you safely to shore when that old sailboat we fixed up finally sunk beneath us! You may rule here on the island, but I rule on the sea! I am blessed by Poseidon, you said so yourself. You'll be a grand lady, while I'll be a grand captain, somehow. I noa be begrudging your fate, why not wish me well—now that we're parting . . . perhaps forever."

At that, the young girl's words stuck in her throat, but she rose to the occasion, while rising from the rock, and said instead, "I do wish you well and good sailing weather . . . and a life of calm seas and bright horizons." And turning on her heel, with the green ribbons in her bright hair standing up like a ship's kite, she sailed off toward the woods.

Coming on a run after her, Darrel caught her by the skirt-pants. "Don't play the grand lady yet, you have all your life to do that. Say good-bye to me, proper-like, we'll naught be seeing each other for years. Come on, Charle, stop being so tottyheaded. You know your father barely allows you to nod to me. Why else do we have to sneak about! I must make me way in the world—for us both. Give me a hug. Put down that blasted bit of fur, and wish me well. I'm going to miss you sore."

"Froth," Charlette inserted, but putting it down.

"Well, Froth, be it," he laughed, and hugged her tight. And then as they hugged, he put his hands in her hair and lifted her face and kissed her for the first and perhaps last time.

They both stood apart, in shock at their feelings.

Then slowly they began walking through the woods, ignoring the happy notes of bright anemones and primroses in their path. The sweetness of a beginning hyacinth floated up, but neither stopped to sniff. The two youngsters had become accustomed to all the beauty of the island. Yet it lived always in them as an undercurrent to their days and thoughts and being. Islanders were to beauty born and never could quite understand how others could accept living in ugly, dark, closed-in cities. Yet at this moment

they were concerned rather with the beauty they felt within—
suffusing all through, as holding hands they slowly walked toward
their parting.

"I shall miss you all my life," Charlette whispered at last, "and
envy you all my life. For I, too, would go to sea."

"Aye, you'd make a fine sailor," Darrel acknowledged graciously. "*I* know that, if no one else does. And I've said as much.
Aye, 'tis a blasted shame you were born a girl," he added,
protesting that fact too much in face of their recent feelings. But
she was pleased, so he continued, "We could have gone to sea
together! We could have had such larks!"

And Charlette agreed wistfully, "Actually, I cannot understand
why God made me a girl when I hate everything girls have to do!"

"So far you've even gulled God," Darrel exclaimed with a bark
of laughter. "Never do a thing girls do that I can see! With your
father's deep pockets, not likely you'll ever have to! You sail your
own sailboat. You drive your own curricle. You ride a horse like
the blazes. You don't sew. Or attend teas, like Lady Fralet. You
dress half the time like a lad! All you can't do, by gad, is go to sea
on one of your own father's ships. Not likely I'll fret meself into
ribbons o'er you. Got everything you wants, it seems t' me."

"But the only thing I really want is to go to sea . . . with
you."

"Aye, you want that, 'cause you can't have it. You always ask
for what is held away from you. You'd find life at sea a bad loaf,
Charle. Won't be anything like when we're playing and climbing
to the ship's crow's nest, and looking out on a fine morning. At
sea, it's jumping at orders all day, and at night no rest, for the
cabins being so close and foul."

"Not on *my* father's ships."

"On all ships. Especially of a storm, down below the waterline,
where I'll be stowing my gear and the bilge water runs through."
She started to object but he spoke over. "See! Always ready to
pluck a crow! No one argues at sea! You say, 'Aye, aye, sir'—no
matter the order. A sailor's life is no game."

"You say all that to me, but in your heart you'd not be
anywhere else," Charlette concluded with finality.

And he could not deny that, nor did she have to be told that he
was looking forward to his life beginning. He bent down and
kissed Froth on his nose, and then kissed Charle. "From Froth to
you," he whispered gruffly. And there on the edge of her property,
he turned quickly, stepping back into the woods, waving once

more before the trees covered him up. Charlette let her tears fall
unchecked now. Froth, feeling one on his face, objected, then
climbing to the source, licked Charlette's face.

"You mean to console me, do you?" She laughed a bit. "Thank
you, but I am heartbroken, and you're awfully small to take the
place of such a large lad."

Froth adjusted himself in Charlette's arms contentedly, as if to
say he'd do his best, winking his eyes closed, preparing for a
snooze, while Charlette made herself respectable, loosening her
high-waisted belt so that her skirt fell to proper modest length, and
brushed her wild golden-red curls into a semblance of order.
Then, cat in arms, face properly licked clean, the richest young
girl on the island, entered Sea Castle and made her way past
footmen and butler up the marble stairway to her room. Even as
she raced to her balcony and looked, seeing just the woods, she
acknowledged never again would she be climbing down, as she'd
done just a few hours ago. She'd more than lost her childhood
companion, Charlette realized. She'd left her childhood back
there on the beach with him, and had only a lady's future ahead on
her horizon. And yet, yet, she had this bit of froth still with her,
and a memory in her heart.

Chapter Two

❀ ━━━━━━━━━━━━━━━━━━━━ ❀

SEVEN years since Froth had come into her life, Charlette had to compliment her cat that he wore his age rather well. Certainly, she herself had changed prodigiously, no longer being the hoyden that had run around unsupervised on the island. Now she was a lady, dressed in a most becoming cream muslin gown, topped by a velvet spencer, decorated with military epaulettes, and cream half boots for travel. To complete her toilette, there was a green velvet bonnet with the high poke featured in the periodical *La Belle Assemblée*, as well as a silk cream ruffle within its brim framing her eager face.

For the last two hours while approaching London, she kept her bonnet, not worn during the ride, at a ready. Necessarily, during the stops at the several posting establishments while the horses were changed, Froth had had to be restrained from roaming. A constitutional he must have for the delicacy of the interior of the chaise, but exploring was not allowed. Still, in view of the views, Froth heartily objected to being enclosed. Within, he had a fondness for her ruffled bonnet, forcing Charlette to put it high above her seat, keeping temptation out of his reach.

"I must look somewhat presentable when I make my appearance at my aunt's," she explained to the disappointed Froth. "After I have made my first appearance, you may have the bonnet to carouse in. However, you would not wish me to give them a disgust of me? I am already thought of as 'that island girl'—not equal to the London ways. So both of us must strive to be up to the rig. I doubt we shall quite equal my aunt and cousin, who—I have been assured by no less authorities than themselves—are of first stare as well as of first consequence. But we must at least attempt to appear presentable."

In response, Froth's yellow eyes closed, and he nodded off.

"Very well, apparently the entire responsibility for upholding the Isle of Wight's fashionability shall rest with me." Yet, after a short cat nap, Froth was in a more cooperative mood and quite willing to lick his white-speckled paws into some semblance of order.

Charlette laughed in delight. "Thank you, Froth, dear. That is much appreciated."

Yet as she and Froth neared London and Lady Bridingsley's house situated at fashionable Regent's Park, Charlette was not overflowing with her usual merry expectancy. For she'd left her island before and been prodigiously disappointed. Shortly after Darrel had gone to the navy, she had herself been sent to Miss Smidgeon's School for Young Ladies of Virtue and Position, where they were to be taught to use the former to achieve the latter. As for Miss Varrick, whose father could be classed as a merchant, she had the dubious pleasure of meeting the daughters of nobility in all their unvarnished hauteur—fledglings in snobbishness who had not yet learned to temper their disdain with civility. Even the mistresses felt only the titled ladies were entitled to their respect. Actually, if it were not that her aunt was Lady Bridingsley, Miss Varrick would not have been allowed in the school. Francine, her cousin, had attended it before being sent to Switzerland, and Lady Bridingsley, without ever having met Charlette, had written her brother that he must send his daughter to that school if he had any hopes of her ever becoming a lady. Her father, reluctantly, had agreed. Without his saying as much, just by his silence, Charlette knew he did not approve of her spending time visiting Darrel's mother at her cottage or sailing on her own. And indeed, she had moped about the island long enough to give even herself a sense of disgust at her performance.

Yet if she had known what a humbling of her proud spirit awaited her at school, Charlette would never have agreed to attend. Instantly it was decreed she lacked the essentials, or the social graces. Even her posture was deplored. Had she never made judicious use of the backboard? She did not even know what that was, but soon, alas, discovered. In order to develop that straight, rigid posture that was hoped to be a model for their morals, several of the more backward girls, such as herself, had to spend at least two hours each evening with their shoulders tied to a painfully hard board. Charlette endured that by imagining herself tied to a mast, and reading her favorite sea tales. The prime one was

Defoe's *Robinson Crusoe*, which she had already read with Darrel. Or she would daydream of being shipwrecked on an island with Darrel as the only other survivor.

As for Darrel, she did receive one or two of his letters in the beginning, mentioning with disdain the punishment ordered for him by a second-in-command who apparently knew as little about the sea as the lord who had recommended him. He had nearly laughed in the officer's face when sent to the masthead to remain there for a full hour. Charlette and he had oft climbed up there and stretched themselves along the cross-trees for several hours at a time!

But his letters came less and less, until Charlette had to make up for the lapses by graciously writing his letters in her head and answering them in the same fashion. But soon she stopped writing both to him and from him. For what could one say about lessons in pouring tea! Oh, the indignity of such a tame life!

All her attempts to make friends with the ladies failed, and she first attributed that to her father's being *in trade*. Although when they went on to whispering behind her back, something more had to be the cause. For every time she turned round, there would be a cutting off of a remark. Without doubt, she was their prime topic of conversation. Then, confronted by so much face-to-face incivility, Charlette, with a grin, came up with what was admittedly a face-saving conclusion: Rather *they* be talking of her than she be forced to the highest boredom of talking about them . . . or worse yet, *to them*! Following that came another startling decision: She should make *learning* the objective of her time at school. Her pushing the mistresses to their limits in the scholarly subjects further shocked the ladies, even more than when Charlette had insisted on keeping Froth. "But I need a model for my sketching, and he is the most patient of subjects," she had insisted. A suitable additional payment by her father bought Froth's permission to be educated as well.

Nevertheless, despite Froth's endless posing, Charlette never could learn to sketch. Nor, indeed, could she tat, nor sing nor play the piano—all essentials in a lady's repertoire. Obviously, Charlette was falling shockingly short of being truly accomplished. Only the dance master was complimentary about her performing all the figures of the quadrille. In response she showed him several village dances, such as the Sailor's Jig. She and Darrel had become quite proficient in all its intricate turns and breathless pace, and always been wildly applauded by all who watched. But the dance master had pronounced it lacking in all elegance, and he suggested, as did all the others, that she forget her island's memories.

Another island memory ebbing was Darrel himself. At the end of the first year, during her vacation time back at Wight, she discovered Mrs. Huntley refused to talk about her son anymore. Jem Barker, who had taught both Darrel and herself the sea's ways, was similarly reluctant. Yet, when pressed, he explained, "Bolted from the King's navy, the boy has. It be thanks to God, he no be seventeen on signing up."

Planning to leave the navy, Darrel had taken advantage of the loophole of his not being seventeen when signing up and deserted a week before that fateful birthday. Absenting himself a day after the legal age would have opened him to a court-martial.

"To hear the scuttlebutt round the harbor, he took up with our enemy—that America—we be at war with! He be seen on those American schooners. Man an' boy, I trained him, an' if the lad be swopin' down on our fleet, I'll cut him," Jem had told her. Then, shaking his head sadly, he walked away, groaning, "But it noa bear thinking on't."

Charlette had assured him that Darrel would never attack a British merchant ship! And further, further, that he was justified in leaving the British navy, for he'd always been meant to be a captain of a fast merchantman, rather than imprisoned in a tiny frigate, and treated like a novice, when he could have sailed circles round the entire fleet!

"That he could. Knew more'n his pappy, afore being full growed. And ye no be a bad sailor, though ye be a lass!"

Though it was some time ago, Charlette could still remember that compliment with a blush of delight. A further pleasure was Jem's prediction that Darrel would return someday. "He be of this island, and ye never can quite leave it. Comes to a body where'er ye be—the sight of it in its mist, telling ye to come back home. No need to fret, the lad will come back to us."

And six years after leaving, Darrel had come back. Yet as fate had it, he returned while Charlette was still away in her last year at school; not notified, she went off, after graduating, on a hiking tour of Scotland with a former governess. Back at Wight, and hearing she'd long missed Darrel's homecoming, all her scenic descriptions died in her mouth. But her father had words aplenty for Darrel.

"The blasted ne'er-do-well, after shaming both his father and me by deserting, had the effrontery to claim he'd been a captain of an American schooner and even sailed round our waters. What cause does an American schooner have to be in our waters, if not *pirating*! The French keep an open door to the Americans, with the understanding that they wipe the seas clean of our dominance. Many a British merchant ship has gone to the bottom at the hands of a so-called American schooner! Well, let him stay in America and live off his ill-gotten gains there. We need no traitors returning here spreading their booty to buy their respectability."

"What did he wish to buy . . . here?" Charlette asked in a strained voice.

"A partnership with me, would you believe! Wanted to invest with us! Sail for us! Told me he was giving me *first choice*! The gall! I told him he couldn't use a childhood friendship with my daughter to wheedle his way into my firm."

"Did he do that? Mention me?"

"No," her father admitted. "There was no point. I'd turned him down." Though she asked no further, he continued defensively. "Only interested in those who'd profit him. In a lick, he was negotiating with those blasted Bates brothers. Mainlanders come to Wight to cut into my trade. No one else would even sail for them. To get the Huntley name, they made a most obliging offer. He put down a mere pittance for a full partnership with them! If his father were alive, he would have stopped him. Lad arrived too late for the funeral, but in time to try to be the death of me. For his first move was to sail forth to take over their only decent ship, the *Lark*, racing home from China. Which shows what he's after. By Jove, he's after my London Prize!"

That, Charlette did not even attempt to deny. The London Prize, given to the first ship to port with its cargo of tea, was an honor Darrel had wanted all his life. But she kept her tongue between her teeth, for never in her young life had she seen her father so beside himself. Darrel had often set up Mr. Varrick's hackles, even as a youngster. It was always brought about by Darrel's quiet assumption that he had certain rights. She recollected his often saying, "When I take over my father's place and become your main captain, Mr. Varrick, I'll name my first ship *Charle*, what say?" and her father had said he bloody well would *not*, and who had said he would even be offered a place in his line? "Have to earn your way, my boy, I play no favorites—just because of your father's record. You have to make your own."

Well, now it appeared Darrel was out to make his own record,

on his own, in his own shipping line. She'd gone to Jem Barker
for his view and heard that while at Wight, Darrel had delighted
in taunting them all, offering not the slightest apology for his acts.
He'd just grinned and hinted he *had* taken British prizes, after all.
"Got a bit of my own back for the floggings," but then, next
moment, he would deny that, and there was no proof. And a
fortune has a way of quieting the most ardent objections. Indeed,
the island had apparently accepted him as their prodigal son
returned, and since he brought his own fatted calf, they were all
prepared to feast on it with him. He went about hiring away some
of Varrick's best hands at double wages, which could not help but
win favor with the sailing folk. His next act, not so approved, was
to move from his Undercliff cottage into a castellated manor house
near Cowes, where the Bates brothers were headquartered. That,
everyone agreed, was flaunting himself far above his station.

Yet, after listening to all that, Charlette had only one question.
And the answer was that Jem did *not* have a message for her. Nor
had a letter been left either with Mrs. Glasgow, the Varrick
housekeeper, or with any of Darrel's old friends at the village.
Yes, she had lowered herself to ask.

So be it. Her father was correct about him. He had changed
beyond remembrance—not to even remember her. Actually, upon
reflection, she concluded this new Darrel Huntley was a stranger
and seeing him would probably put her to a blush, recollecting
how close they had once been. Therefore, when time came for her
to leave, she did Darrel the courtesy of considering him as little in
her plans as he had considered her and hers in his.

An elegantly lettered note from her cousin Francine, added to
Lady Bridingsley's invitation, encouraged Charlette to hope her
Season would be agreeable, after all. Her cousin's phrasing was
rather formal, but that could be the result of her education in
Switzerland. And though two years older than Charlette, due to
her time at the Swiss school, Francine had not had her Season in
London either. Now they were to have it together.

"And I shall be footing the bills for both. Rather crafty of
Priscilla," Charlette's father had chuckled, quite willing to send
along the required amount.

"But surely, Lord Bridingsley as a nobleman must needs be
quite plumb in the pocket. They would not need funds from us!"

"Probably not," her father said, quickly covering up his gaffe,
not wishing his daughter to feel she had bought her way into that

house. And if she did not wonder why a connection should be sought, after years of inattention, he would not spell it out.

Actually, Lady Bridingsley saw no reason to discriminate against her brother and not allow his name to be added to the list of people she was beholden to, including friends, acquaintances, tradesmen, even servants. For her lord was a dedicated gambler, sometimes losing as much as ten thousand pounds a night at his various clubs, agreeing with Lord Alvanley's, advice not to "muddle away his fortune in paying tradesmen's bills." Hence, Lady Bridingsley was left to manipulate the butcher and poulterer, while her husband strode off in a new pair of boots from Hoby's to join friends at White's. Recently, Beau Brummel, one of his fellow gamblers at that club, had been forced to flee to France to avoid debtor's prison. As a lord, that was not a possibility for Bridingsley, but a closing of credit all round had at last made it impossible for Lady Bridingsley to present her daughter to Society in the manner befitting her worth. It was amazing how when pushed to the limit, one can remember a hidden asset of someone else's that could be put to good turn. Or Charlotte. If the girl were allowed to have her Season concurrent with Francine's, the entire cost would be credited to Mr. Varrick. And she could claim the invitation for the island girl was out of the goodness of her heart. It would not be believed, either by Society or her brother, but it would be accepted.

If only Charlette was not obviously coarse! Thankfully, she had advised Miss Smidgeon's school, and so should not have to totally blush for her. Considering Miss Varrick's mother, there would be enough gossip about her as it was. At least her father, Thomas Varrick, came from good stock—Lady Bridingsley's own, being her younger brother. Their father was a gentleman, whose estate was used to improve his life, rather than his life being used to improve his estate. It was subsequently bled as well for his daughter's dowry. Obviously, lords did not come cheap. That left mostly debts and an encumbered estate for Thomas on their father's death—with the exception of some stock in a shipbuilding business, but since no gentleman would engage in that, it was not considered. Yet, Thomas, not so high in the instep and with a desire to succeed at all he attempted, did so. He had foresight enough to transfer the shipbuilding operations to the Isle of Wight, and there also added a yachting line. So unique were those designs that Thomas Varrick won the friendship and patronage of Lord Bolton, the Governor of Wight. With Thomas's growing wealth and easy personality, Lady Bridingsley had been proud to invite

him to her own circle, even hoping for a connection that would
enhance her own standing. Instead he had disgraced her, turned
the *beau monde* upside down and left her to bear the shame, while
running back to that island with that scandalous woman. Was it
any wonder her ladyship refused to recognize him? Compounding
the indignity, he began making arrangements with merchants and
the East India Company to run cargoes with his ships, for quicker
profits. In short, he sunk to the level of *trade*. He was unforgiv-
able.

The years did not soften Lady Bridingsley, even when that
unmentionable woman, Varrick's wife, had died, leaving a young
child. She still could not bring herself to sink low enough to visit
the island. Although, after awhile, she gave her brother the
pleasure of receiving her letters filled with recommendations for
raising Charlette. In return for this advice, she was gracious
enough to accept a continuance of the yearly stipend her brother
had cut off. But now she needed more than that paltry sum. She
needed Charlette. To that end she roused her lethargic daughter to
pick up her quill, and stood over her for the composition of an
addendum.

"More feeling, my girl, else she shall not come! You must say
something in the vein of 'we are cousins, and cousins should never
be strangers.' "

"Yes, Mother," Francine said, then rousing herself added, "although I should rather hope we remain strangers. For Cicely, an
acquaintance of my most particular friend, Lady Marjory, informed
her and she me, that her sister knew Miss Varrick at school, and that
she was a perfect dowd and a bluestocking. If I were to be seen in her
company, it should mark me."

"You shall not have a Season without her, my girl. Consider
that!"

"Yes, Mother. But why must we plead for her to come? She
should be honored simply by our invitation."

"That is because she is not up to snuff, and does not realize
what is being offered. She prefers sailing about her island. You
must convince her the two of you shall be happy companions. Put
in a line about our love of the sea."

"Love of *what*!"

"Oh, very well. I shall have to handle this matter, as I do
everything, myself! I shall say, as a mother, I think of *her mother*
and feel that ignoring her child's future must seriously disturb the
spirit of that excellent lady! What think you of that?"

Francine went so far as to shrug, which had her ladyship continuing defensively, "Perhaps it is somewhat . . . sentimental, but island people, I expect, are, like country folk, more sentimental than we in the city. I shall definitely include it."

"Yes, mother."

And that line was the very one that convinced Charlette to journey to London. For it long had been the young girl's wish, growing up with only a painting of Mrs. Varrick, to somehow atone to her mother for her early death. Or at least do things to please her. But no one dared speak of what should please her mother, until Lady Bridingsley insisted that her mother's signal desire should be for Charlette to have a Season. Uncharacteristically, her father seemed of two minds about his daughter's departure for London; and as the months passed, he gave conflicting advice, leaving her rudderless and drifting into second thoughts. At last, she could delay her decision no longer.

Arising at four in the morning, Charlette went to a quiet cove, where she oft would take a dip in her white nightgown, then wrap herself in a hooded blue cloak and return home before anyone at Sea Castle was the wiser.

A full moon hovered like a helpful lantern, lighting her steps. Island lore had it, if you looked too directly at the moon, it would absorb all your God-given sense, becoming ready ground for the seafolk to sink their spirits into your soul, and lure you into the sea. Charlette had never believed such fustian; yet, sometimes, when staring directly into the sea, she had almost heard the sea sirens calling. Not a difficult life, she opined—spending one's time swimming and singing and combing one's hair while resting on the rocks.

Once, some time ago, Darrel had spotted her brushing her golden-red hair after swimming and accused her of being a sea siren. Promptly, she assured him that was so, and promised to use her powers only for the good of his ships, never luring them to their destruction. Not that such a promise was needed; she would scarcely sink her own father's ships. So certain then had they both been that this was their future—he captaining for the Varricks.

Sometimes Darrel would even volunteer to comb her hair, for it came past her knees, and its weight was too much for her small hands. While he was intently doing so, oft his hands would touch her back and neck, and she would feel prickles of pleasure throughout her entire body, never felt when her lady's maid briskly brushed her tresses. Once Darrel had taken out his knife

and cut off a lock; at which point Charlette had demanded one of
his dark locks as well. And they had solemnly traded, aware of
fulfilling a pledge, yet frightened to put it into words. And she had
looked deeply and seen what she called the stormers in his usually
calm grey eyes, and had moved away . . . frightened by it all.

The moon coming out from behind a cloud and thickly
spreading itself on the ocean top by the cove recalled her to
herself. She moved forward, till the bottom of her gown and cloak
were soaked with foam. Ahead, quite small, but there, behind the
moon's trail, she saw, sharply etched, a ship foundering, and a
man striding the poop deck directing his crew. A wave distracted
her, and she was soaked to her knees. Still, she walked farther in,
till her cloak spread behind her, afloat in the water, and she spread
her arms out on the sea's surface, as if holding onto it for balance,
staring ahead, till the picture returned.

A storm was striking. Sheets of rain. The man was waving his
arms, indicating directions and shouting orders that were lost in
the wind as he poked and prodded those about him. At last, having
ridden out the storm, he turned and grinned up at the moon, as if
to acknowledge his indebtedness to it for having chased the brief
squall away. And feeling they were staring at each other through
space, she, too, smiled and could then turn away and walk out of
the water.

Darrel had risked danger somewhere and conquered, she felt, as
she returned to Sea Castle. And he had enjoyed the danger—it had
made the triumph sweeter. Thus, she, too, would take on the
challenge of London and enjoy it. Her decision was made.

And as she traveled in the chaise through London itself,
Charlette eagerly sat up, rotating her head from window to
window. Of a sudden she informed Froth that they were come to
the fashionable section, where her aunt's house would surely be.
The cobbled stones beneath the horses' hooves gave an echo to
each movement, but that sound was drowned in the watchman's
calls. Rather early for this part of London. Probably would be
waking the household, she thought, and then grinned. Exactly so.
Why not start as she meant to go on? And fighting Froth for her
ruffled bonnet, she put it on. Then, brushing the cat's hair from
her spencer, straightening into her hard-earned, backboard-trained
posture, Charlette rose as the carriage stopped. With Froth in her
arms, she stepped down and faced her new home.

It was a grey stone two-story house with black wrought-iron
balconies. Actually, not overly imposing when compared to her

massive, deck-balconied Sea Castle, but it was a residence of substantial size for London. The postilions were quickly untying her trunks as she ascended the steps and pulled at the iron bell-pull.

She rang several times, and even made use of the doorknocker, till the door opened.

"Kindly inform Lady Bridingsley her niece has arrived as promised," Charlette said firmly.

"Your pardon, Miss," the butler began, "Nobody is at home. They have gone to the country."

"Can't be helped," Charlette said matter-of-factly. "I've made faster time than was expected, I gather."

After all her waiting and imagining whether her aunt should open up her arms to her, whether Francine would receive her with less formality, the last thing she had conjured was that *no one* would be there. She had clearly written the date of her coming. Any other young lady would be annoyed, frightened, suspicious, even not know what to do, but Charlette was none of those. She always found the unexpected a delight. And now, more amused then disturbed, she allowed herself a small laugh before waving in her luggage. Turning to the unwelcoming butler, she said, "I expect I shall have to make myself at home and greet them when *they* arrive, shall I not?"

Whereupon, causing the butler to totally lose his aplomb, she handed him Froth, and walked by him into the house that was to be her new home. Only the family was missing, but Charlette was accustomed to being without one, and could very well do on her own till they deigned to return.

Chapter Three

❧ ━━━━━━━━━━━━━━━━━━━━ ❧

THE next day, neither Lady Bridingsley nor her daughter had yet come home, but Lord Bridingsley was sitting down at a late morning breakfast, after having returned from an all-night carouse. He was savoring his time alone, knowing he did not have to brace himself for a sudden unpleasant reminder of the mistake he'd made in his salad days of marrying, and thus bringing strangers into his ancestral home. That one of the strangers was his own daughter in no way made her more palatable.

Actually, he did not care for either his wife or his daughter. Sometimes, he admired his wife for her determination and inadvertent drollery. Such as when she said: "Don't you care for me anymore, Cecil?" when she knew he had never cared for her from the beginning. But his daughter, Francine, was the merest commonplace. She never said anything but "good morning, Father." Sometimes she varied it with "good day, Father." But, basically, his pale progeny set up his hackles. She had inherited his paleness of eyes and hair and languid air, but none of his devotion to self-pleasure that lifted him above the ordinary. He was particularly adverse to his daughter at the present, because it was due to her having to be presented that he was so often called to account for his pleasure-seeking or gambling.

Thankfully, good old Prissy could be relied upon when the family was really in the suds. Recently her maneuvers had led to the coming of that disgraced girl from the island—with her rolls of the soft, that would, his wife assured him with glittering eyes and a self-satisfied set to her mouth, see them through. But when he heard that there would be no extra for him to settle some pressing gambling debts, he lost interest in the chit, except for a sigh at having yet another pair of female eyes disapproving his hours, his condition or his ribald reminiscences.

Just as he was taking a second helping of sausages, a strange lady seated herself at his table. Nearly choking, he exclaimed ungraciously, "Devil-a-bit, who are you?"

"Your guest. Lord Bridingsley, I presume?"

"Daresay I know who I am, but don't know who you are or what you're doing at me breakfast table," he said in his languid tones. His face was fixed in displeasure as he finished his sip of tea, and then leaned to the side for a better view of the lady at the other end. His eye was first caught by a blaze of golden-red hair piled up on the crown of her head, with ringlets falling in profusion on the sides and down the back. Looking at him with amusement in her large dark-blue eyes, Charlette was calmly accepting her tea from the servant, refusing the sausages (a point against her) but loading her plate with the Banbury and other cakes (a point for her). The dimples, as she frankly just grinned at him, decided the issue. He rose, signaled the servants to bring his plate along and set himself alongside her.

"Your wife invited me . . . and forgot, I presume," she said without anger, simply stating the facts.

"Heard something about going to visit Lady Marjory. Not due back till next week when that daughter of a tradesman is going to take us over. Forgot you, did they? Not likely any gentleman would do the same," he whispered, eyeing her unashamedly.

"Are you ogling?" she asked, curiously. "I've always been warned that a gentleman might do that, especially if I forgot myself enough to walk past certain clubs in London, but I've never actually seen it done."

He let out a bark of laughter. "You ain't seen my prime ogle, dear girl. I'm not at me best with a mouthful of food, what? But on the strut, and with me quizzing-glass—I can show you an ogle you'll talk about for weeks."

"Remind me to look out for it," she said placidly, and continued making a rather full meal.

He offered her more and was quite willing to put his reduced staff to the trouble of preparing anything she wished to eat, but Charlette was satisfied with the cakes. "Where do you get these? Never tasted anything like them."

"At Gunther's. They deliver all our pastries. Nothing but the best for our table. As long as we don't have to pay for it. Shortly, some is going to be paid, I expect."

"When the tradesman's daughter arrives? I hear, however, that she is close as wax with her money—wants everything accounted for."

"You don't say!" his lordship exclaimed, surprised, and then delighted. "I say, won't that put Prissy's nose out of joint. She's figuring on getting even the house redone under the cover of clothing expenses. Ha! Won't she look no how when she discovers our rescuer is going to keep us under a cat's paw."

"Speaking of a cat," the young beauty spoke up, pulling up from under her chair a rather disgraceful specimen of the feline species. "I'll take one of those sausages, after all. Froth has a liking for them." And keeping the black and white cat in her lap, she fed him a full sausage, cutting it up in little bits and placing them in the cat's mouth while she chatted.

"Froth is delighted to meet you. He has a fondness for other gentlemen who also make a hearty meal."

"Does he, by Jove," his lordship exclaimed, leaning over to add his contributions into the red, open mouth, and was rewarded with a lick on the hand.

"I say, me fingers ain't a sausage," he admonished, then laughed a bit. "Had hunting dogs, of course, but never accused meself of ever having fed an animal, let alone entertained one at the breakfast table!"

The animal reached up and pulled on one of Charlette's curls. It was something his lordship wished he could do as well; they appeared to be of unsurpassing softness and had a swing and a glow. E'gad, she was a great beauty. How could even Priscilla have forgotten inviting her?

"Friend of Francine's, are you?" he pressed.

"I hope to be," she said pleasantly.

"Ah! Then it would be me wife that invited you."

"Yes."

"Ah!"

"Yes."

"No, I don't see the connection," he finally admitted.

"Do not be dismayed," she whispered, "but you are sitting in close proximity to the infamous daughter of a tradesman! I am Charlette Varrick."

"The devil you are!"

"Well, I hope I am not that. Merely your niece by marriage, and your most humble servant," she said with an impish smile, as she inclined her head.

"Adorable," he said, frankly.

"Me . . . Froth . . . or the situation?"

"All three, but mostly yourself. Quite a diamond of the first water! Has me wife seen you? I mean recently?"

"No. I have never had the pleasure of meeting my aunt. Apparently, as an islander, I was not much in demand here at your social functions, but now I perceive I have some use, and so I was invited."

"Hmm. Not going to tell me wife what I told you?" he asked with some chagrin, yet ready to accept what would come, either way apparently not deeply concerned.

"Certainly not. Our conversations shall always be just between you and me. However, to tell the truth, I suspected I was not being invited for the pleasure of my company—as that pleasure has been so long ignored. I had hoped that Francine wished to know me," she added wistfully. "I have no brother or sister and have oft wondered what it would be like."

"If you've hopes to that end, I advise you to forget 'em. Francine can't warm up to anyone. She's a cold little fish of a girl, even if she's me own. Not that I've ever heard her speak. Don't, actually."

"Really! She is . . . dumb?"

"Might be. Oh, you mean . . . no, she's got a voice. Just so much of a lady, must consider before she says a word, and by then the word ain't needed."

"Possibly she fears you, and wishes to say only what would most interest, and thus hesitates. I expect she needs bringing out. I shall encourage her."

"No need. She ain't a poor little pussy cat your tender little heart would want to encourage. She don't care for anyone but herself. Cold, I told you."

Charlette shook her head, and allowed herself to be led into the morning room. Looking about, she noted a wealth of crimson silk and Axminster carpeting. Gilded sphinxes held up both tables and couches, while sterling chandeliers abounded.

"There seems not to be a lack of the ready here," she commented.

"Can't sell these. Part of the entailment. Pity. Would have seen my way clear with just that nest of Holland tables there. Or the Sèvres porcelain in the dining room. Pre-revolution that."

Charlotte knew instantly what was coming before he asked it, and replied civilly that she would be delighted to give whatever amount was required, but, unfortunately, her father, having thought of that possibility, had arranged that, aside from pin money, expenses were to be met by his accountants here in London, with strict orders on what could be included under his guidelines.

"Needle-witted. Would have bled him dry in a sennight else," his lordship admitted philosophically.

"Yes, he's a downy one, and so very, very dear."

"By Jove, you love him!"

Surprised at his surprise, Charlette stopped inspecting the room and turned to inspect him, face to face. "But of course I love him. He's my father."

"Don't necessarily follow."

"I'm sorry to hear that. What a lack in my life if I did not love my father. He has meant everything since I lost my dear mother when I was a halfling."

"You have the look of her. But she didn't have your sparkle. Nor your . . . charm. A diamond, like you. But her hair was paler blonde and she was smaller—all round. Let herself fall into that disgraceful marriage. Man old enough to be her grandfather. What a waste of a beauty, we was all whispering in the clubs. Must have agreed with us 'cause she took off. Some pluck, after all. Good breeding shows. On her mother's side, her family went back to the Normans."

"What are you saying!" Charlette exclaimed.

"Thunder and turf, don't say you ain't heard of Lydia's escape? The rattles still ain't stopped chattering! Mother's a proper scandal!"

"I . . . am at a loss. I knew something was amiss about my background. But no one has ever directly explained . . . I should be obliged to hear the particulars."

"No. If they ain't told you, I won't. Don't have the time, actually. Got to meet a few fellas. Get your aunt to explain. She'd be delighted to put you in your place, especially when she hears how the money's going to be arranged. Fact is, she's been moaning about your situation for years—not likely to miss the opportunity to make you aware of it all. But I ain't going to do it. Too pleasant a morning to have to put up with hysterics."

"I never have hysterics. They are not very helpful in any situation."

"By George! You are unique. Enjoy having you round. Do you ride?"

"Of course. And sail and swim and drive my own carriage."

"Not much use for the first two, but the young bucks'll take you up in their phaetons. Take you up meself. Today. Be back at five for a drive in Hyde Park. Beat Prissy to the mark and introduce you round! What say!"

"I should be delighted."

"That's the dandy," he said with a grin, and toddled off.

Charlette retired to her room and considered. It had been prodigiously difficult not to press him for the particulars, but she had taken his measure. Lord Bridingsley, it seemed, could never be pressed into anything requiring the least effort or placing himself in a disagreeable position. Her only recourse, while biding her time till her aunt's return, would be extracting smidgens of information in the course of subsequent conversations.

As for the other revelation of her aunt's reason for the invitation, she was philosophical. One always hoped, actually, to be wanted for oneself, but there was still the opportunity of making them like her despite their predispositions. What a lark if she foxed them by living *down* to their expectations and being as shockingly vulgar as they dreaded! She could put on the broad accent of the common folk on the island and even eat with her hands! But her laughter stopped mid-grin at the realization one could not maintain such an imposture for long, and, really, she did not wish them, even for an instant, to say, "You see, she is just as low as we thought."

Further, her every interest now was to uncover her mother's scandal. All told, his lordship had let fall some interesting facts. Her mother's family was noble. Heavens, she had always assumed that her mother was a commoner. Even a servant. And lately she'd begun to fear she'd been hatched by a reformed ladybird. Why else would she be so universally viewed as beneath everyone's touch. Now it was, however, even more of a puzzlement. Considering that her father, though a merchant, was the son of a gentleman, and her mother's background, it developed, was unexceptionable, what else could be the objection to her? His lordship mentioned a marriage with an older man. Had her mother broken an engagement? Had her father and mother run away to Gretna Green—marrying without Society's sanction?

Possibly. But, after all, this was 1817, not the Dark Ages. Could that simple transgression be the reason for all those whispers at school, and for her own aunt not wishing to invite her! Charlette shook her head and began to consider what maneuvers would be most effective for loosening his lordship's tongue—which had already proven through several slips to be thus inclined.

Yet, in the days that passed before her aunt arrived, his lordship's inclinations remained self-directed. He talked only about his interests, his past, his pleasures. He enjoyed showing her off to his friends, taking her in his *vis-à-vis*, a carriage made strictly for two, through Hyde Park at the hour of the Grand Parade when all of society was on the trot. To some of his least disreputable friends, he spread the word of her being an heiress, and quick as a tick that fact was all over the ton. Gazetted fortune hunters and several ladies with sons or nephews needing their fortunes replenished were soon leaving cards and making dashed nuisances of themselves, stopping for tea. His lordship refused to give them any and did not allow her to return their calls.

"Let Prissy handle all that. We'll just continue to have our little gaieties till she comes back and spoils it all. Going to take you to Vauxhall tonight. Spectacles and fireworks. Should you like it?"

"Oh prodigiously. And I should appreciate your helping me find a carriage and pair for myself to drive in the mornings. And a horse to ride. Shall we go to Tattersall's?"

"By George, won't I love to walk in with you on me arm. But it ain't done. E'gad, ain't we a pair? You ain't up to snuff. And I forgot what's done and what ain't. Not that I usually care. But you're . . . that is, you've been trusting. You're a good gal. You like to hear me stories of the Regent, without groaning or disapproving. I won't play you false."

"I think your stories delightful." And Charlette meant that wholeheartedly. She had learned more about Society from him in a few days than she probably ever would have living in it for years. Of course, she learned things her aunt would probably not have approved. All about the Regent's liaison with several respectably married ladies. Difficult to credit, considering His Highness was about to become a grandfather. She asked him to continue.

"I envy your father," he concluded. "Does he talk to you, and do you listen to him as you listen to me?"

"Yes. But he talks mostly about his shipping line. I've learned quite a lot about ships. Sailing I learned from others. But your stories, I admit," she said with a giggle, "have an education of their own."

"Faith, you're too good to be wasted on all these fortune hunters bussing round. Don't marry a man who just wants you for what he can get—they don't have hearts. I know. I'm one of 'em meself. And you're too sweet for us."

Charlette gave him a sustaining clasp with one hand, and his pale eyes saw concern in the dark, almost navy-blue eyes, and he was moved. By Jove, he felt a caring for this young fledgling. And he lifted that hand and kissed it with a flair.

"How dare you bring her into my home!"

At the screech of that voice, his lordship dropped Charlette's hand and calmly turned. "Hark, the dulcet tones of my dear wife," he began, spotting that outraged lady entering the drawing room, with a smaller, paler version peeping round her, seemingly in shock. "Ah, my love," he concluded, "and our proud offspring hiding behind. Come greet your beloved niece who has sailed from her Channel island just to take care of us all."

His lordship momentarily savored his wife's outraged face— which ran the gamut from affront to confusion to surprise. Then, leaving the situation he created for others to clean up, he kissed his hand to all three women, took up his cane from the waiting butler and went out to spread the story of his wife's mistaking her own niece for one of his ladybirds. His Highness himself would be prodigiously amused. Prinny always was delighted to hear of another fellow's wife returning—as long as he could continue to bless himself that his still remained permanently away.

Back in the drawing room, Charlette made a quick attempt to save her relationship.

"How kind of you to invite me, my dear Aunt. My father sends his love and other remembrances," she finished sweetly.

"Charlette?" her ladyship asked, wanting to be assured.

"Indeed. And this young lady is my cousin who so wished for my coming?"

Her cousin walked farther in, removing her gloves and bonnet, and nodded.

Then, while her ladyship was trying to overcome her surprise at the suddenness of her niece's appearance, and worse, the *beauty* of her appearance, Charlette further discombobulated both by running up and hugging them.

"I have been waiting here for several days and, it seems, for all my life before—for this moment. And you are both just as I imagined. I'm delighted to meet you at last."

Lady Bridingsley had recovered herself sufficiently both from the shock and the embrace to swallow the first and return the second. "My dear, dear girl. I am delighted also. As is your cousin. Aren't you, Francine?" she ordered.

"Yes."

"Then it is a universal delight. I expect we shall all get along famously," Charlette insisted, trying very hard not to laugh at their expressions.

"Without question," her aunt agreed tonelessly. "Do you not agree, Francine?"

"Yes."

"But you do not favor your father," her ladyship continued, accusingly, as if she'd caught Charlette in an impropriety. "He is dark. Both he and I are brunette; I had hoped, that is, assumed, you were as well. Francine is our only light-haired one. Was."

"Actually, I favor my mother, I believe. In all things."

"Good heavens!" That was the blow too many! All kinds of shocking possibilities followed that announcement in Lady Bridingsley's mind, but she was simply not up to coping with them. "I must rest after my journey," she said. "And then we shall both be better prepared to become acquainted. But presently I must lie down." And edging out of the door, her aunt made a last attempt at civility. "But I need hardly say that your appearance has cast me into transports of . . . delight. Both of us. Are we not, Francine?"

"Yes."

And the two ladies exited, leaving Charlette alone.

"Heavens," Charlette said aloud, "if they are so prodigiously delighted to meet me, wait till they have the pleasure of meeting Froth!" And smiling, she went back to the book she had been reading.

Chapter Four

HAVING, in essence, brought herself up for a good part of her life, Charlette rarely found herself at a loss at what to do in any situation. Further, she'd had nigh onto a week to anticipate Lady Bridingsley's and her daughter's reserve. Nevertheless, Charlette was quickly running out of overtures. There appeared naught she could do to warm her relations. They did not wish to exchange views or hear past doings. In fact, her aunt gave her the most unanswerable set-down: "Of what possible interest do you suppose we Londoners could have in your island memories. I suggest you confine them to your diary."

Lady Bridingsley was especially offended when Charlette wished to hear the particulars of her mother's story.

"That is *not* a topic I should wish to discuss. Though, I must say, I am astonished that your father did not acquaint you with the circumstances, in preparation for certain, shall I say, natural reactions to your presence."

"Perhaps, then, you would be so kind as to prepare me for those reactions?"

"I—No, indeed. If your father felt you could not be trusted to withstand the truth, I should certainly not go against his wishes."

"If my father was reluctant to divulge anything, it undoubtedly was because of his habitual concern for my feelings. That should hardly be a problem for you."

"There is no need for rudeness!" her ladyship snapped.

"I did not mean it so. Pray, believe me. I ought to have said: My father's excessive regard might have made him diffident, while you, not being burdened with that excess, would find divulging the story less severe a trial."

"However you dress it up, my girl, I cannot go against your

father's wishes. You must master your curiosity as you will. That trait is not very suitable for a lady. Only for a cat. Which reminds me: Your black feline has Francine in the fidgets; it is undoubtedly unlucky and should be promptly returned to your father."

Flushing, Charlette took a deep breath to keep her voice in control. "The cat, Froth, is not my father's. He is mine and shall not be given up. If Froth is not welcome, then naturally I must leave with him. We can depart by tomorrow."

Recollecting that she had already ordered Francine's presentation dress and new hangings for the drawing room, Lady Bridingsley replied with unusual civility. "If you wish to leave, no one shall prevent you, my dear girl, but I hoped you would be here for the Brontson Ball. It will be the social event of the year. The Countess is quite a lovely lady. High-spirited. An original. We are all looking forward to attending. New gowns are a necessity for that. We are to visit Madame Fanchot's establishment this afternoon. Should you care to accompany us, Francine and I should be most delighted."

Accepting that as a truce, Charlette remained. Actually, she was looking forward to purchasing some London outfits. Those she had had made for her by the Wight modiste were quite up to snuff, but not exactly of the level of Lady Bridingsley's wardrobe.

Madame Fanchot was patronized for her flair and fashion, but particularly for her susceptibility to "arrangements." A mention of her name at a tea party by milady assured a gown for Francine; raptures about Madame's styling at a well-attended ball assured the bill for her ladyship's gown would be permanently mislaid. After amenities, the two young girls were sent to look at materials while negotiations were in progress. Under an instant agreement, the bill for Charlette's dresses was to be inflated to cover the costs of Francine's and Lady Bridingsley's as well. All bills, actually, were to go to Miss Varrick's London accountant. "*Bien*," Madame Fanchot nodded, "*je comprends*. As we have said."

But her ladyship had an additional request that somewhat astonished. She was to tone down the young girl because she tended to "overdo," which put her ladyship to the blush. Another discreet nod, and the girls were called back.

Closer viewing of the spectacular girl gave Madame pause. It went against her artistic sense to alter her, but, as always, monetary sense prevailed. "You are *très jolie*, mademoiselle. It does not need so much color to bring you to notice. A little softening, *n'est-ce pas?*"

"*Oui. Je comprends*. I am to be watered down."

"*Un peu*. With your hair, no other color must be there."

"You see me all in white?" Charlette asked with some doubt, picking up a white lace shawl and draping it around her shoulders, throwing one edge back and standing there, looking like one's dream of a bride.

"*Charmante*," the dressmaker said, realizing of a sudden that this girl would look spectacular in anything, and thus defeat her arrangement. Further, when this heiress went into Society, her beauty and style would be noticed, and it must be said that that style had been given to her by none other than *Madame Fanchot*! Strictly in the interest of Madame's overall clientele, Lady Bridingsley's wishes were quickly discarded. Upon even closer observation of Miss Varrick, a shock of revelation went through the frail French lady. *Vraiment*, she had found the model for her wildest designs! This girl could carry off even the petal-pink rose ball gown no other lady had dared commission!

"You shall be my . . . inspiration," Madame whispered, swept away. You have so much *éclat*. I, and I alone must dress you! And I shall make you the talk of the ton!"

"I daresay that shall not be too difficult. They are already whispering about me."

"Then, you and I shall give them something to whisper about? *Oui*? We shall push you down their teeth! *Maintenant*, we begin!"

"That sounds distinctly uncomfortable. And I assure you, I do not need to be praised, just an occasional honest suggestion, in case I really do go beyond the line."

"You think I speak flattery! *Vraiment*, mostly that is so. But the ladies wish for that. You wish for the truth. I myself shall give it you. There is no way you can go beyond the line, for you shall create new lines for others to follow! You are an original! I must dress you!"

Charlette laughed. "Well, now you have completely twisted me round your fingers, and I am not certain whether this is the height of your usual flattery or if we have reached some wild understanding. Nevertheless, if your designs are as intelligent and original as you, I shall, doubtless, buy out your line."

However, some difficulties arose when Lady Bridingsley wished to make all the choices herself. Her first selection was a bright yellow gauze confection with rows of ruffles from bodice to hemline for Francine, and a simple, severe beige muslin for Charlette. Madame's experienced eye could see, as Francine held

the intensely toned gown to her, that the girl was overwhelmed
both by the color and design. All her hints were of no avail; both
Francine and her mother were enraptured by the gown. Indeed,
Lady Bridingsley ordered a similar one in mauve for herself but
with some necessary differences: a lower neckline and violets
blooming unblushingly from same. Pleased by her success, Lady
Bridingsley continued to point to fabrics and designs, choosing
the best for her family and throwing the leftovers to Charlette. Yet
Charlette simply left them. Flushed with the triumph of their purchases, Lady Bridingsley and her daughter concluded. Charlette
had accepted the first beige muslin, seeing a purity of line she
could not but approve.

As the ladies were departing, Madame Fanchot, in some
perturbation, signaled for another conference with her ladyship,
and then said what should have been obvious: Assigning all of
today's purchases for Francine and her ladyship unto one simple
muslin dress, all Miss Varrick had purchased, could not be done!

"How tiresome of the chit," her ladyship exclaimed. "And you,
Madame, I must fault you as well! Why were you not pushing
your designs with more . . . pluck! Oh, dash it—what's to be
done?"

The French modiste quickly replied that Miss Varrick must stay
behind for further showings, with the understanding that since the
girl would not be suppressed, her own style must be allowed. The
toning down of her niece had been planned in order to circumvent
gossip, and thus was for the girl's own good. It sprang out of the
goodness of Lady Bridingsley's heart, and thus was necessarily a
halfhearted desire rather than one her ladyship would hold to
buckle and thong in the face of losing all their purchases.
Therefore, Lady Bridingsley nodded. "As you think best, Madame. As long as she purchases a goodly amount."

"*Mais oui*, that is also my objective," Madame said sincerely.

Alone with her prize specimen, Madame Fanchot began. "Now
we adjourn to my private salon for the unveiling of my prized
designs. Mostly I wish to show my *Burst Of Lace*, which no other
lady has been able to, as they say, carry off!"

And taking the amused Charlette by the hand, she called all her
assistants and ordered the special chest to be opened and the
delicate lace material to be carefully removed. "And wear gloves.
It is so delicate, I would not wish even a thread caught."

"I was thinking of something in sea green," Charlette said
wistfully. "I do have a preference for colors that remind of my

beloved ocean. Although I am not adverse to white. Yet, in that *Burst Of Lace*, I fear I shall look like a fully rigged ship. Now, if the bottom were made in blue and the burst of lace around the décolletage were in white lace, I should chance it. As for that pink one, that is . . . I do not know . . . original certainly. I shall look unforgettable—either for ill or good. But, what ho! I'll risk them both . . . and that one . . . Oh, heavens, that blue gauze and green silk is lovely. Must have it. Very well, all of them!"

As the days passed, Lady Bridingsley found her efforts to subdue Charlette in Society were as about effective as her attempts to water her down at the dressmaker's.

First off, her ladyship, with only the experience of herself at her first Season and Francine as a daughter, could not countenance Charlette's exuberant enjoyment of all the entertainments. Just as the golden-red hair and deep-blue eyes made Francine seem more pallid than ever, Charlette's enthusiasm made both Francine and herself seem worn out. In truth, her wishing to see all London did wear them out! Where was the shy island girl, grateful for any introduction, Lady Bridingsley had imagined? The dowd that would walk behind the two London ladies—almost like a flunkey! Rather, often now, when entering into a saloon, it was Francine and herself in the role of attendants.

A good deal of Charlette's being so forward was caused by her father having raised her to never pull rein on her spirit of independence. Another gentleman was equally at fault. Lord Bridingsley. He had introduced her round before her ladyship had had the opportunity to advise her on the modest behavior expected of ladies, and especially of Miss Varrick. And thus, she had her own set of followers, resulting in Lady Bridingsley returning to a house filled with callers. Their cards overflowed the reception table, which made it impossible to squelch the girl! To her kindly meant suggestion that she attempt to be less noticeable, Charlette had responded with a twinkle, "But, Aunt, I have not come to London to hide!"

Charlette proceeded to bring even more attention to herself by her next outrage. Despite being warned that ladies did not ride high perch-phaetons nor drive such in the Park, she had, with Lord Bridingsley's aid, procured one with bright green velvet upholstery that matched her green velvet outfit. Her superb handling of her team, like a perfect whipster, caused an equal division of praise and censure.

There was no limit to her ramshackle behavior. Of course, Lord

Bridingsley was responsible for her knowing all the rakes and fortune hunters in society. He had even introduced her to the Prince himself, which brought on the discomfiture of Miss Varrick's receiving an invitation for a tête-à-tête at Carlton House. One could not advise cutting His Royal Highness! But Charlette did not bother to ask. She promptly accepted, inviting Lord Bridingsley to give the occasion respectability, if one could use that term in reference to him. His lordship was delighted to play chaperone, and was still laughing all the next morning at the Prince's surprise.

"Knows how to handle herself, does this gal. Proud to be related to the beauty."

He had never said as much about any other woman. Not any of his relatives, not his own daughter . . . not even his wife!

The only way her ladyship could discomfit this totally poised youngster was to comment about her mother. A ploy which was beneath her, Lady Bridingsley acknowledged. Yet, at certain moments she found herself making hints in that area. It was particularly apt, for instance, when explaining to the girl why she could not accompany them to the exclusive Assembly of Almack's.

"But there is no possibility that any of the patronesses shall give you a voucher! Not with your background! I should not even bother to ask Lady Jersey. She would say something very cutting, and I should not wish you to hear and be cast down."

Another time she resorted to such an allusion after a visit of Mr. Buckston, who was known to be as rich as Croesus. Previously, this gentleman had shown a decided preference for Francine, enough to have stood up with her for a waltz plus two country dances at Almack's, and indeed, he had even subsequently left his card. Yet, when he was invited to tea, Charlette had had the effrontery to monopolize the conversation. It was not known either to her ladyship or her daughter that Mr. Buckston was a connoisseur of tea, with a collection of tins. That fact, when acknowledged by Mr. Buckston drew a mere "Indeed?" from her ladyship and a nod from Francine. But Charlette responded with detailed questions, stemming from her knowledge of the teas her father's ships brought from China . . . Which led to her mentioning that the Sailing Race for the first tea cargo to port was shortly due. When the gentleman expressed an interest in witnessing the event, Charlette, not observing the twitching of her aunt's eyebrows, continued to extol the race as being above all great.

Gentleman and lady would have settled on a joint attendance at that moment if Lady Bridingsley had not thought to spill tea on his pantaloons.

Not all the gowns in London were worth this humiliation, Lady Bridingsley and her daughter subsequently decided. To flaunt her father's being in trade, rather than hiding it, and then acting as if the ships' race were Ascot! And then being within an ace of leading Francine's beau into an invitation of escort! Only Lady Bridingsley's quick reflexes had saved the situation. And while wiping the tea from the gentleman's pantaloons, she'd further thought to say that Charlette and she had already accepted an invitation to that race from Lady Marjory and her brother, the Duke of Wingshire, but Francine was free to accept Mr. Buckston's gracious escort and would appreciate the experience more if she could hear about the cargo, having so oft expressed a wish for variety in her morning cup. Instantly, the invitation was given to Francine, and both ladies could be comfortable!

When Mr. Buckston departed, her ladyship exclaimed with a shake of her head, "Next we shall be expected to watch the milk carts trudging into London, and cheer for the one that reaches one's kitchen quarters first!" Taking that gibe good-naturedly, Charlette merely allowed she was looking forward to attending the race with Lady Marjory and her brother, at which point both ladies did not know where to look. For that esteemed couple had been introduced into the conversation merely as an impeccable excuse (for one could never be expected to cry off from an engagement with a Duke). There was no intention of subjecting themselves or his grace to harbor doings. Not wishing to acknowledge the subterfuge, Lady Bridingsley was in some difficulty. Yet the engagement could not possibly occur, for Lady Marjory was one of the many who had even refused to be introduced to Charlette, and certainly they could not force her, as close a friend of Francine's as she was, into either being in Miss Varrick's company or attending a sea race! The solution was to accept another engagement for the time of the race and not mention it to Charlette till last minute. Her financial contributions —while providing the necessities, say even the elegancies of the Season—would be too costly if she were to lose them to Lady Marjory. Already several acquaintances of rank had given them the cut-direct, all because that girl was in their house.

For Charlette, the Duke of Wingshire's and Lady Marjory's visit had her in happy expectation. First, she had heard a great deal about them not only from her aunt and cousin, but all Society. But mostly Charlette was in high jig, for she felt this presentation to her by Lady Bridingsley and Francine signaled a new acceptance of her as family. Up to that point, she had not felt her welcome was always of the most wholehearted, especially when she was the subject of certain petty acts, such as the disappearance of her favorite seashell brought from Wight and kept on her dresser. When the world of London and her aunt became too much, Charlette would reach for that shell and be home again. And one morning the shell was missing. Its importance could not possibly be explained to Londoners. And then, after a few days, a maid, Lily, cleaning her fireplace, attempted, not too subtly, to catch her eye, and upon doing so, and being given a smiling nod, shyly approached. Several times previously, Lily and she had talked, and Charlette had once given her a shawl she admired. Now, Lily brought forth the shell from her basket, and with much looking about, whispered, "Letty did it, she did. Following orders, she were. I seen it and snatched it back." And the girl rushed off.

Thereupon, the shell and other mementos, including a lock of dark hair and a miniature of her mother, were locked in her trunk. Letty was Francine's private maid, but it did not bear thinking of, nor conjecturing, especially now that the conciliatory gesture had been made of the introduction to their exalted friends. On the day of their late afternoon arrival, Charlette informed Lady Bridingsley that she had accepted Sir Smithers Wilcox's invitation for a ride around the park, but should certainly be back in time for the introduction. Lady Bridingsley was quick to urge she not rush the outing, for Lady Marjory and his grace were making a good, long visit. And thus, at her escort's request for an additional turn around the park, Charlette complied. Sir Smithers secretly yearned to be a poet and considered that his efforts were minor merely because he lacked the muse. Having observed Charlette driving by in her high perch-phaeton, dressed in the green velvet with a froth of lace at the neck and sleeves, he felt he had found her at last. Charlette's love of poetry only escalated his attentions. He, it was, who first equated her with Botticelli's painting of Venus in the foam, and began the mode for each gentleman to create a poem in her honor.

Several times Charlette found herself alluding to the sailing race on the morrow, for it totally captured her thoughts. Sir Smithers was in some dudgeon at not having the privilege of escorting her, for he'd prepared several "ship-shape rhymes." She was civil in her regret, explaining Lady Bridingsley had made the commitment. Thus mollified, he was able to continue the afternoon with tolerable humor.

Upon returning home, Charlette inquired if the Duke and his sister had left, and was assured they were still having tea. Thus, she went up to change. Down in a trice, she entered, in great expectations. They were still there. A lady was speaking. Even if she had not expected to see her ladyship, the deference of both Lady Bridingsley and Francine would have proclaimed the visitor as Lady Marjory. Charlette stopped to view a rather large young woman, with light-brown hair worn in a tight topknot, and a generous mouth, half-open to receive food and half to continue her conversation. She spoke and ate, both at a prodigious pace, as if afraid of interruption—although never in her life had she had to suffer a denial of either of those pleasures. At her side, long having finished his sip of tea, and now lounging back on the Grecian sofa, was the Duke. Clearly a fashion dandy. His knitted beige pantaloons fit snugly on his folded legs. He was swinging his elevated foot back and forth, watching the shaking of the golden tassel on his gleaming Hessian. He had some difficulty looking over his huge neckcloth, another of his creations already being copied throughout society. Absorbed in swinging his quizzing-glass on a velvet string in concert with his boot's golden tassel, he ignored the conversation, concentrating rather on the feat of getting his glass and tassel to swing in synchronization.

Yet, it was he who first reacted to Charlette's entrance. Immediately, he stood and bowed. She gave a slight curtsy in reply. Lady Bridingsley, observing her niece, made the introductions, finishing with an ungracious, "We have finished our tea."

"Always ready for another," the Duke put in hopefully, smiling a wide, kind smile.

"Eh, certainly, your grace," Lady Bridingsley responded, casting another dark look at her niece.

"Red," the Duke said.

"Your pardon, your grace, we have merely Pekoe or Souchong," Lady Bridingsley explained nervously.

"Meant her," the Duke said, lifting his quizzing-glass. "Golden red. A sunset on your head, by gad!"

His eye was magnified to an awesome size, so that it appeared like a giant insect observing her. He let the glass drop, and looked her up and down, then at her moving hem, where he observed with surprise a paw sticking out. "You got a cat under your skirt, by gad."

"Yes, it's Froth," Charlette said matter-of-factly, and bent down to sweep up the cat, who frequently hid beneath her dress, especially when it had a nice bit of train. "Bow to his grace, Froth, or he shall think you have been badly brought up and are not aware of the honor of making his acquaintance."

The cat inclined its head, and the Duke exploded with laughter and picked up Froth. "Like animals meself. Have hounds mostly. You like dogs?"

"Of course. And dolphins."

"I say. Pity one can't have one about when one speaks. Encouraging blighters. They clap hands."

"That's seals. Dolphins dive with extreme grace."

Lady Marjory rose, finally having finished her repast, and feeling the discussion had gone on as far as need be. "I do not myself feel properly prepared to meet either of those sea animals. Regrettably, if you were planning to introduce us to them tomorrow, we must decline the acquaintance. I was just telling dear Lady Bridingsley that we shall be unable to watch the water sports, for the Duke and I are engaged for Countess Lieven's picnic."

"Most disappointing," Charlette said politely. "I had several requests of escorts which I declined since my aunt wished us to make a party of it. Excuse me, I must send out a note of acceptance, after all."

"Oh, I say!" the Duke cried out. "I'll be dashed if I'll go to a dull picnic when I could be attending a race with you! Not dashed likely! I'm your escort, Miss Varrick. You are not free to ask anyone else. We shall go alone, if Marj and her ladyship decline. I'll bring my footman, for propriety."

"That sounds most delightful," Charlette agreed, giving the Duke a view of her dimples, which had him overwhelmed, lifting up his quizzing-glass again.

The ladies moved aside and began talking at once, debating whether they wished to attend the picnic or the ships' race, and all its ramifications. Meanwhile, the Duke moved closer to Charlette and confided.

"Dash it, if you are not a prime beauty. Bet my affy davy, Marj ain't known that when she accepted being a party to the race. Don't like pretty things—neither she nor your cousin, I expect," he added, indicating the looks being directed her way.

"I'm rather wealthy, as well," Charlette whispered back.

"Are you, by Jove? No wonder they can't swallow you. Same reaction meself. Too young to be a Duke. Too rich by half. Not a particularly comely phiz, but I'm the height of fashion. No one handles a cravat like meself. Stab me, I can crease one in three seconds to a new dash. Do it with me chin." He demonstrated deftly. "This one's called *The Duke's Knack*. After me."

Charlette paid him the compliment of moving closer. He modeled the cravat.

Lady Marjory's voice made them guiltily spring apart.

"Percy! I say, I hope you're not ogling Miss Varrick. She is not quite up to snuff. Island girl, don't you know, and may not be aware you are merely . . . being civil."

"I'll be dashed if I'll take that, Marj! Never ogle a lady. Take me for a Bond Street stud on the strut! I say! I *say—say*!!"

"Your pardon, Percy," Lady Marjory countered in a softer tone. "I was merely funning. Actually," she came closer to Charlette, "Francine and I believe we should very much care to see this race, after all. Picnics one can attend anytime. One just eats, after all. Something one does everyday."

And Lady Bridingsley expressed a wish to come as well. Francine was off to send a note to Mr. Buckston changing back to the ships' race, after having sent a note canceling it and substituting the Countess's picnic.

Where a moment previously no one wished to attend the race, of a sudden everyone was highly insulted to imagine that they should be left behind. Two carriages at least would be needed. Perhaps a landaulet for the ladies' comfort.

The Duke had caused the change. It was not the first time Charlette saw the effect a titled man had on all about; but it was the quickest turnabout. She could not help but smile.

The Duke was enchanted with her. "Devil-a-bit," he thought, remembering Marj wished him to cut this lady because of something in her family, not that he recollected what or cared. Races were his passion—horse races, of course, but when assured there would be quite active betting, he would not dream of not going. In a few moments he further discovered this young lady had her own high perch-phaeton and a great desire to be driven in his, having heard so much about his bang-up greys. After a description of their points and perfections, he would have gladly escorted this lady even to a museum and suffered through it, but to a race— By Jove, he was in the devil of anticipation. The only rub cast his way was that Marj would be attending. She was very likely to cast a damper on the outing; she always did, but he was too kindhearted to cut her out.

That night Charlette was determined to think only of the Duke's interest in her, rather than allow her thoughts to wander to the possibility of seeing Darrel again. Actually, his ship would be in the competition. But it was not likely that, his first time out, he would be one of the finalists. After her father's ship *Sprinter*, the pride of the Varrick Line, won the prize, everyone would depart, and she should not be seeing the rest of the finishers. All for the best, it was, not meeting him again. For, as a man, Darrel had obviously altered drastically, and she could not bear to have her happy memories ruined.

Chapter Five

❦ ━━━━━━━━━━━━━━━━━━━━━━━━━━━━━ ❦

THE next day when the carriages arrived at the dock, somehow Mr. Buckston's landaulet with Lady Bridingsley and Francine had become separated from the carriage that contained Lady Marjory, the Duke, and Charlette. Most vexatious. They should have to meet subsequently and compare impressions, for by now they were locked in by others and unable to turn about. Yet, Mr. Gusson, of the Varrick London office, resorted to walking between the carriages to report the position of the Varrick ship, *Sprinter*. Several other Varrick agents were already on the pilot ship, as were both Bates brothers of the new Huntley-Bates line.

"Why are *they* there?" Charlette asked in alarm. "Has the *Lark* been spotted?"

Three ships were already making their way up the English Channel. Two had turned at Ramsgate. That was all the information Mr. Gusson could relay.

As yet, no continuous attention was being given to the Thames ahead, although occasionally spyglasses were lifted and lowered. No sail in sight.

Already Lady Marjory was becoming restless. "Why have not the ships lined up at the starting gate?" she exclaimed.

"Alas, you have misunderstood the kind of race this is, your ladyship," Charlette responded patiently. "The winner is the first ship arriving from the China Seas to bring its cargo to the waiting merchants. The contest is for the full sail. It becomes a true race to docking when the leading ships round Ramsgate and come up the Thames. That is why all these people are holding spyglasses. The first spotting of the sail shall tell us what kind of race it shall be—whether a two-, three-, or even four-ship race to the dock-gates. Or, as has most often been the case, simply a runaway victory by the Varricks—in this case our ship, *Sprinter*."

"Indeed," Lady Marjory responded, having long stopped listening. After a few moments she asked again, "But I do not see the ships lining up—how much longer before the race begins?"

Charlette threw up her hands and turned round toward the Thames, determined at least to enjoy it herself. She was having second thoughts about these escorts. They could not empathize with her need for a Varrick victory for her father. He cherished the consecutive plaques, and had often told her how imperative winning this race was for keeping Varricks established position. The winning prize, a mere hundred pounds was irrelevant, but the accolades from all, and the rush by merchants to be linked with the victor, was not to be denied. And the real financial inducement was the sizable side betting. Her father always proudly and deeply backed his ships. It had not taken the Duke long to gather the odds; eager to place his bet, he sprang with alacrity from the carriage. While looking around at the growing crowd, Charlette thought she recognized some of the Bates people going amongst the merchants' carriages and leaving their cards, not to mention partaking in lengthy conversations. Upstarts, she thought angrily. It was difficult to realize she included Darrel in that charge.

She looked back. Some of the merchants had obviously discarded the cards. For to many people after fifteen years of steady victory, Varricks *was* English shipping and English shipping was England. They would not dream of betting against him any more than they would not back their country. But others were considering the cards, even putting them in their pockets. "Insufferable cod's heads! Bunch of out-and-out flats!"

"I beg your pardon!" Lady Marjory responded.

"Your pardon," Charlette said quickly, not having realized she had spoken her opinion of the merchants aloud. "I was merely referring to the crowd."

"While I share your sentiments there, I cannot share your language."

Properly reprimanded, Charlette was quiet until the Duke returned. He was in an expansive mood. Nothing delighted him as much as putting a large bet on a sure thing. He had returned a true Varrick supporter—nothing binding one so tightly as spreading one's blunt. "The oddsmakers have your father a heavy favorite, Miss Varrick. Almost couldn't get me bet covered. But pushed through."

And after that, as the different segments of crowds began chants for different ships, his grace frowned at the opponents and yelled lustily for *Sprinter*. "Me ship," he nudged his sister, and she closed her eyes to it all. Charlette applauded and shouted with him, and they were beginning to feel themselves quite a team. The Duke was proud to point out that he was wearing his cravat in a new design he had created this very morning, in honor of the occasion. It was called, he bowed modestly, *The Splendid Sprinter*, and would, he was certain, start a trend.

That was not a very daring prediction, for, indeed, a great many of his cravat creations were trend-setters. And with this one, he had outdone himself. One edge of the cravat had been let loose to flap about like a sail. His valet was all humble admiration on seeing the finished effort. Even his sister, who was not very interested in fashionable attire, admitted she had never seen anything like. While the Duke was immodestly assuring her that *The Splendid Sprinter* would have impressed even Beau Brummell, and she was nodding, Charlette could not help but feel her lips quivering—for the cravat was flipping in his face as he spoke. And she felt called upon to comment that she hoped her father's *Sprinter* was made of sterner stuff.

Undaunted by her remark, the Duke nevertheless hoped he would bring the ship some of his easy luck, with which he had been possessed all his life. "Never lose, actually. Not at cards. Not horse races. Don't know about boats."

"Ships," Charlette corrected, but thanked him for the bestowing of his favor, admitting however that it was not really needed. "We Varricks never lose either." They nodded in satisfaction at each other, and affably Charlette pointed out, "Those over there are boats." She indicated a full regatta of boats in the harbor: river craft, skiffs, wheeries, all flagged and filled with happy watchers.

His grace was civil enough to pretend to glance that way, but Lady Marjory deliberately raised her eyes to the heavens, with an all-suffering air, doing all she could to take the edge off Charlette's enjoyment of the event. Upon their arrival, when their carriage had first been positioned quite close to the harbor wall, with a rather prime view, her ladyship had insisted on moving farther back, complaining of the odor from the harbor. Even now, from their more distant position, she kept her scented handkerchief held unwaveringly before her aristocratic nose.

Dash her, Charlette thought, this time careful not to mumble it, for, from here, due to the bonnets and plumes of the ladies in the curricle before them, she was forced to actually get on her knees on the seat to achieve sufficient height as she turned her spyglass toward the misted horizon. In a moment she was bobbing up and down in excitement as she cried out, "There! A sail! One ship is clearly coming ahead."

The Duke looked through his own spyglass. Lady Marjory did not shift her position.

"I say. Ain't there another behind? In the mists?"

"Yes. But too far back. It shall not even be a contest. Father's ship is far in advance. I'd hoped Darrel would be in contention."

"Good going, old sport. Did wish for a bit of a challenge. Something to have us on our feet, what? But I daresay victories are just as sweet for being easily won."

Charlette could not help but agree. And allowed the Duke to help her back down off her knees. She sat quietly for a moment, no longer anxiously scanning the horizon. Lady Marjory's predicament caught her eye. Her ladyship was breathing deeply through her handkerchief, but that frail bit of lace was of no benefit to camouflage the sights and sounds about her. There were the cries of the apple sellers, and other peddlers selling rattraps and cowbells. And again and again the packs of people coming close up jolted the carriage. The rattrap seller had leaned over and was earnestly addressing Lady Marjory, attempting to persuade her of the efficacy of his traps and how she could not run her home without. "Them big fellars, wot bite off toes, these'll snuff 'em out, right quick," he was assuring her, while she was attempting to wave him away.

"Be off with you, my man," the Duke cried out. "We don't need your traps."

"You gentry got bigger rats runnin' in them castles. Up and down them walls, they be, dropping leavin's."

"Percy!"

"Take a damper, Marj," the Duke cried out, turning back to the man. "Here, here's a shilling. Be off, and take your blasted traps with you."

Satisfied, the peddler slyly grinned through his exit. While watching that little skit, Charlette had missed something, for the crowd was now screaming altogether. Instantly, she stood up. No need for the spyglass now. Coming closer, in full view, was a tall ship of unsurpassed beauty. Nothing could ever equal the grace of a full-rigger coming toward one. Even Lady Marjory gasped and cried, "What a beauty."

Charlette was, as usual, moved almost to tears by the view. "Look at the height of her masts," she exclaimed, her voice as soft as a lover's when beholding her beloved. "Look at the length of her lines. She's built to sail full tilt."

The Duke looked. It was undoubtedly a pretty ship. Very good as ships went, but, dash it, just a ship, after all. And there was another very like it just behind. No possibility, he realized, of the two ever being neck and neck, as it was in horseracing. And where the devil was the finish line? Too tame for him, this sport. Nevertheless, he showed his interest to Miss Varrick by commenting, "Quite a bit of white sheets."

"Sails."

"Ah. Look like sheets on one's bed, rather." And at that indelicate expression, Lady Marjory was offended. Miss Varrick had not reacted; perhaps that meant she was totally shocked by his using such a ribald analogy. He was prepared to apologize profusely when Charlette, instead, began to name the sails, having concluded that his remark betokened interest in the different kinds.

"Upper and lower royals, gallants, topsails. Skysail. Jibs. Spanker . . ."

He obliged her by repeating them: "Gallant top and bottom sail, jibby sail . . ." She smiled momentarily, and then abruptly gasped. "Said them wrong, did I?" Then, as the look of horror on her face increased, the Duke realized she was reacting to more than his mispronunciation.

"Heavens! It's not possible! That's smaller than *Sprinter*!"

"What ho!" the Duke called, alarmed at the white face of the girl.

Clutching at her bonnet bow, she pulled it off, letting it fall on the seat, for the brim had interfered with her view. And suddenly the view was of greater import than anything to her. The lead full-rigger coming in was not a Varrick ship!

All her life she had been accustomed to her father's winning. It was as if someone had suddenly told her the sun was rising in the west and setting in the east. "It cannot be. Simply cannot!" she cried, and unconsciously accepted the Duke's proffered hand.

"What is it, my dear girl?" he asked solicitously.

She did not hear him, nor Lady Marjory's objecting to her brother's endearment. She could hear naught but the cheers all about—cheers for a new champion, and at the setting of the Varricks' glory. The ship ahead was Huntley-Bates' *Lark*. Had

Darrel, Darrel who had learned all about sailing on their ships, done this to them!

Yet, wait. A sudden hope. *Sprinter* was gaining, catching the right wind and coming on.

Even the Duke, who had ceased to watch the ships at all, but followed the entire race by keeping his eyes on Charlette's face, saw from her reaction that something hopeful was happening, for she had caught her beautiful bottom lip in her white teeth and was gasping out, "Oh, please! Please!"

"She's gaining, ain't she? *Sprinter*! We're going to have a bloody race!"

"Yes! Yes! Oh, but there's too much to make up. Yet, still a slim chance!"

The people all around were cheering louder for the coming ship, all wanting a race of it. Charlette's eyes did not deviate from the two ships and her voice was still hopeful as she cried, "There's no winner till the harbor gates are closed behind. Come on, *Sprinter*! Live up to your name! Sprint, blast it! Sprint!"

Lady Marjory's gasp at Charlette's language was somehow louder than the cries all around. And her ladyship protested even louder when Charlette plopped down and muttered: "Oh, the devil!" At that, Lady Marjory was not only put to a blush by her language but reached into her reticule for her vinaigrette. One reviving breath, and she was able to express her shock—something about Charlette's having tied her garter in public! But the Duke could not accept the white-faced silence of the young girl, now stiffening as if she'd had a flush hit: a leveller. Rather, he grabbed Lady Marjory's vinaigrette and held it under Charlette's nose.

There were instant objections from both ladies. Lady Marjory quickly retrieved her specially designed bottle of aromatic vinegars, while Charlette pushed it away—simultaneously.

"*Sprinter* is dead in the water," she said, attempting to brave it out.

"I say. Bad luck!"

As one gazes in horror at an accident, Charlette continued to watch the pilot ship, with the jubilant Bates brothers aboard, closing in on the *Lark*. Horns were being sounded from all the ships and boats round. Flags and pennants were being waved. King Varrick was dead. Long live the new King.

Here and there she heard the name: "Captain Huntley!" He was being cheered all round. The oldest watchers had confused him with his father; the younger members of the sailing world were seeing a new wind sweeping through. The *Lark* was squaring her yards—all her flags were flying. Her colors and numbers at the peak. A Lark Arising figurehead drew past the gate. The ship could no longer move, surrounded by boats crowding in. Tides of men were climbing up her side: pressmen, ship owners, merchants, men who had made the correct bet, and the jubilant Bates brothers, both waving their hats and shaking hands round.

Fire was applied to the signal cannon's breech, and it sounded the word to all. The old sea captain of the port made it official by doffing his white top hat and crying out: "Three cheers for the *Lark*—the winner of the China Tea Race."

Men were throwing up their caps; bells were rung; sailors beat their marlin spikes together. The dock gates locked behind the winner—locking out the Varrick ship. It was over.

Darrel had beaten them . . . beaten her. He had thrown a harpoon and it had hit her squarely in the heart.

There was now an opening round their carriage, enough for his grace to set his team about. Lady Marjory, understanding that they were leaving, finally began to smile. As the carriage turned, Charlette cast one last look at the victorious ship. On board, in the center of the jubilant crowd, stood a stranger. He was on the poop deck, where the captain would normally be. A tall, dark-haired man with a beard. Who was this stranger who had done this to her father and herself?

As the carriage moved on, several members of the sailing community recognized her and doffed their hats, as if at a funeral. She acknowledged them with a brave smile. One last look at the *Lark*. But the stranger was no longer visible, lost in the crowd of well-wishers.

Chapter Six

❦ ════════════════════════ ❦

CHARLETTE, if she wished, could have the pleasure of a closer view of Darrel at the London Prize Ball. The victorious captain as well as the ship's owner had always been invited to the award ceremonies. There Captain Huntley would receive the plaque as well as the one hundred pounds and other tokens of regard from various sporting groups, and even something from the Regent himself. After his first few victories, Mr. Varrick had stopped attending, but the elder Captain Huntley and Jem Barker always participated, returning to describe the ball as the most prodigiously elegant affair ever. The description of the ballroom had to be repeated several times for young Darrel and Charle to see it clearly. All about were table models of all the past winning ships, not to mention other nautical insignias, such as anchors and nets. The winning ship had a gilt rooster placed on its wind vane and several of those were also displayed. But the most memorable decoration rested on the elevated platform where the official ceremony took place. It was a life-size wooden mermaid that had for years been a favorite with Jem Barker. But the moment everyone enjoyed most was when the entire room erupted into a wild rendering of the Sailor's Jig. The two children being told of that would immediately demonstrate their own version, with Jem obligingly playing on his mouth organ while Captain Huntley laughed and clapped. On Darrel and Charle would whirl, all vigor and abandon, till they collapsed on the ground in total exhaustion.

That recollection was painful, indeed, especially as Charlette must presently visualize Darrel as the winner at the ball, dancing the Sailor's Jig with a stranger. But then, *he* had become a stranger, after all!

Early on the morning of the ball, while Lady Bridingsley and

Francine still slept, Charlette was welcoming, as she was wont to do, Lord Bridingsley back from his nightly play at White's. They both made a good meal, while his lordship gave his opinion of the people she had met. This morning he was gracious enough to commiserate on her ship's loss, urging adoption of his philosophy of loss—at which, he owned, he was a master. "Never admit one loss had done you in. Carry on, I say, as if it be a mere first toss and the game is continuing. Erstwhile, all assume you have been beaten all hollow. Not bloody likely to write you off, if you don't write yourself off, what? Keep on with the game, dear gel, keep on!"

Nodding and accepting his advice, Charlette left the old roué not only feeling satisfied with her but with himself for having done a good day's work, despite his earlier having fallen another several thousand pounds in debt.

Later, Charlette was in the morning room attempting to plan exactly how to "keep on with the game," when the butler ushered in a Mr. Hitchens, a Varrick London agent. She wished she had denied herself, not up to hearing commiserations, but her innate courtesy forced her to greet him with a pleasant expression while he did commiserate. But then her face froze into open dismay as he implored her to attend the London Prize Ball. Not giving her the opportunity to refuse, he began bemoaning that the Huntley-Bates forces were spreading rumors of the Varricks' day being over, not only because of its out-of-date association with the ancient East India Company, but because of the preponderance of retired navy captains in Mr. Varrick's stable, not to forget the war surplus ships to be refurbished. "It is imperative, Miss Varrick, that a Varrick representation be there to blunt these rumors."

"One does not honor such rumors by replying to them, Mr. Hitchens. Certainly, my father's reputation does not rest on such shaky ground that this scuttlebutt can overset him. Both the Bates brothers and whoever else has joined with them to use such tactics are beneath contempt."

"Naturally, Miss Varrick, no one assumes you should be put to the discourtesy of replying to such blatant falsehoods, although there has been some problem with the old ships . . . I merely meant that if you could see your way clear to attending the ball, your very presence there would give evidence that the Varricks are far from in a decline. By Jove, one look at yourself and everyone would know how blooming and glowing the future of the Varricks is, indeed."

Charlette dimpled and curtsied at this civility. "But my appearance at an affair whose very purpose 'tis to honor Captain Huntley would, rather, give rise to the belief that we are capitulating to him, would it not? For, indeed, the very celebration is to be of *their victory*—with presentation of several awards to him . . . eh, them."

"There is that," Mr. Hitchens admitted, humphing and hesitating. "Yet, if you would but come," he added wistfully, "we should give a much stronger appearance."

The old man was perspiring. Charlette would have pleased him if she could, but she could not bear to do anything that would hurt her father's dignity; nor, indeed, could she bear being put in the position of seeming to honor a traitor. But there was the advice of Lord Bridingsley. She wished to minimize the Huntley-Bates win, and the Varrick loss—and that could only occur by carrying on with the game, as he advised.

"If there could be a reason for my attending . . ." she began, giving the old man hope, but he could not devise any saving excuse. He merely looked confused, and then hopefully her way. She was forced to make the suggestion herself. "There have been previous balls which my father did not attend. The awards, I recollect, were sent to our house on the island. But there had never been *an official presentation* at any of them. Could not some kind of proclamation be read to that effect, and given me, representing my father? That should certainly give me the excuse to attend, and at the same time remind all—the merchants and investors—of my father's history of winning. A timely reaffirmation that one victory does not make a shipping line, as one swallow does not make a summer."

Overjoyed at the suggestion, Mr. Hitchens was prepared to see what could be devised. Quickly, she reminded him of the need for speed, since she wished time for her own preparation. And then, grasping that some added incentive would not be amiss, she gave it him. "If I attend, I should be escorted by my escort at the race, the Duke of Wingshire. Rather interested in a shipping investment, actually, I collect."

"I *say*! If *His Grace* shall be attending, there can be no question . . . that is . . . it shall be of all things . . . to be devoutly desired."

Eventually, after many more comments in that vein and expressions of gratitude, he departed, sending back, almost in an hour's time, a personal message filled with so many comments of

obligation it took two full pages before Charlette came to the gist,
namely, that there would, indeed, be an honoring of the Varricks:
not a mere plaque but a silver bowl, as the award for the most
victories by any one line—a Grand Prize! Thus, if she would be
so gracious as to attend, and receive it from the hands of the
Director of Lloyds of London, it should be sufficiently outstanding to detract attention from the Huntley-Bates victory of a mere
one year.

Charlette, although that had been her objective, wished the man
had had discretion enough not to have to put their stratagem in
writing. But, by now, obvious from his self-flattery, he had
claimed the idea as his own and was expanding on it, by running
around half-cocked, encouraging more and more gifts from
organizations. Actually, all who heard of her willingness to
attend, and with his grace, were falling all over themselves to be
represented by contributions to the Grand Prize for Miss Varrick,
as evidence of their appreciation for her condescension.

A sharp groan was Charlette's response to this flagrancy! For
what had sounded, from her own lips, as plausible, now enlarged
and tossed back at her by Mr. Hitchens began to seem the grossest
impropriety! All his additions! One simple plaque would have
been sufficient to blunt the tactics of the Bates' team, without
bringing undue attention to herself and making it seem as if she
were shockingly maneuvering for a showy gift. Too late now, the
deed was done. Thankfully, no lady of her set would be present to
be disgusted at her want of conduct. Her promise of being
accompanied by the Duke should just have to be broken. There
was no time, nor could she, in all decorum, extend a last minute
request for his attendance. They did not stand on such terms.

Although, he was a jolly sort who just might be cajoled into it.

Heavens, she flushed, her thoughts were shameless, and she
should rightly be judged by others as having gone her limit. On the
other hand, had not she often been viewed as improper, and for
some minor infraction, such as galloping in the park? Why, then,
should she not risk more censure for so important an occasion?
Fiddle, let Society think her dead to all shame, she must have his
grace's escort! But how!

Generally, it was known that the Duke of Wingshire did not
favor ladies with second invitations—certainly not hard upon his
first escorting. This skittishness explained why, approaching his
mid-thirties, and after having so many caps set for him, he was
still unwed. Lord Bridingsley had warned her as well about the

Duke's undependability. Lady Marjory was too strong a guard dog, his lordship continued, and as long as Lady Marjory was unwed, her brother should probably remain so, using her services as his hostess, while she kept him as her escort.

Nevertheless, these reflections did not daunt Charlette when she was going full tilt. Her policy in life had invariably been: all sails unfurled! At the very least, Charlette concluded, she should send his grace a note. Moreover, could she not phrase it in such a way as to make him believe he had *already* offered his escort to the ball? Amused by that possibility, Charlette ran quickly for quill and paper.

The note announced her agreement with his grace's belief that, having both lost, they should show themselves good sports. She was therefore prepared to accompany him to the ball tonight in their opponent's honor. Although she was loath to do so, she must just conclude that as a noted sportsman, he knew best what was done on these occasions. And, at least, she should have the pleasure of affirming for herself the universal report of his having a very pretty way of tripping the light fantastic.

What a disgraceful concoction of toad-eating gammon! Charlette exclaimed, and went into whoops when she reread the whole. Yet, she made no correction, rather closed the note with a blue wafer, and sent it off with her footman.

Despite her amusement, the audacity of her act had her in the fidgets. Froth nearly tripped her as he solicitously accompanied her pacing. "Go to the window and let me know if the footman is returning," she ordered Froth, who eyed her with disbelief, and went instead to stretch out on her bed.

Giggling at his response, Charlette shook her head. "Well, you are of no use whatsoever. But, what ho!, I have probably disgraced myself for naught. The footman shall not have a reply, so I might as well stop waiting!" And sitting next to Froth on her bed, she continued to rationalize. "And in the unlikely event that he believes he asked me, and agrees to escort me, how can I be responsible for his grace being at such a lowly ball, one that no person of the slightest consequence would honor with his presence, let along a Duke! It would be preferable, she assured Froth, if the Duke did not respond at all. "Ragamuffin ways," Charlette announced, shaking her head at herself.

By the by, the young girl concluded that, very properly, the Duke was snubbing her note, and therefore she must go on her own. Her entrance would not have the same éclat, but, after all of

Mr. Hitchens's effort, she had to appear. Besides, a Varrick always delighted in a challenging occasion.

Thereupon, she turned her attention to her wardrobe. The milieu being so inappropriate, she sought to rectify that by wearing a most appropriate gown. Madame Fanchot had delivered several of her creations and had outdone herself. The most outstanding was, of course, to be held in reserve for the Brontson Ball. Her present choice had to come from the rest. Green would be the correct note, as nature had so often established. There was one of Madame Fanchot's green masterpieces: a combination silk and gauze in dark and light shades of the sea. Obviously, it was meant to be chosen for this occasion. Charlette was holding it up when there was a discreet knock.

Hope that it might be the footman with a reply after all was dashed; and then a larger hope aroused when the butler announced a visitor in the drawing room. She rushed out, shoving Froth back into the room when he also wished to see who called.

It was the Duke himself.

Anxiously, Charlette curtsied to his bow, prepared for the worst, and as the usually amiable expression on his face was missing, she braced herself for his excuses.

"Dashed sorry," he began.

"You are unable to accompany me, your grace?" Charlette asked in a low tone.

"Oh, no! My pleasure and all that! But devil-a-bit, we're in the suds!"

"Indeed? How are we so saponaceously situated?"

"Marj saw your note."

"It was mistakenly delivered to her? I did not think I had so seriously misdirected my missive."

"Peeks."

"Ah, does she? Most regrettable. Over your shoulder or inside the wafer?"

"Both."

"I see. And she told you no lady would ever dream of sending such an invitation to a gentleman, especially upon such short acquaintance."

"Righto," the Duke acknowledged, absently accepting her indication that he take a seat. "Said all that . . . but . . ."

"But she also added that both of you had had enough of being acquainted with denizens of the sea?"

" 'The vulgar rodents of the harbor world,' " he repeated absently, nodding his head. "But . . ."

"Heavens, there was more!"

"Oh, rather. We are in a devil of a hobble . . . veritably bum squabbled."

"She will not let you escort me?"

"Not able to do that. Older than her, don't you know. Been on the town for years. Do what I like. But fond of her. So it ain't a question of my living under a cat's paw. But when Marj wants something, she holds to it buckle and thong."

"And she wants . . ."

"To come along."

Charlette let out a sigh of relief. "Is that it! Well, I certainly fear the affair shall be beneath her touch. But if she wishes to attend, that is perfectly acceptable to me. Lady Marjory cannot but add to the consequence of any affair she deigns to grace."

The Duke rose and sat closer to the astonished Charlette. He held up his quizzing-glass. "Must examine. Dashed it! How's possible a young girl's manners can be as exquisite as her face!"

"We have no time for compliments, your grace," Charlette said, blushing at his rapt attention, and rising. "If we are to be dressed in time for the ball, we must bustle!"

"Oh, I daresay. Must dash to create a cravat for the occasion."

"I shall be looking forward to seeing it . . . and you."

After many a bow, Charlette was finally alone. She had done it! The Varricks would shine tonight—the Duke *and* Lady Marjory! Heavens, that alone should sufficiently take the shine out of Huntley-Bates' moment, not to mention the Varricks receiving the Grand Prize.

And, actually, Charlette's assessment was on the mark. For right from the entrance of the Varrick party, the entire ballroom was captivated.

First, there was the appearance of the Duke. Upon his removal of his many-caped cloak, he proudly revealed an outfit so complete to the shade that only a Pink of the Ton could have carried off. The cognac pantaloons were silk knit and fit like skin. As for his satin waistcoat, it was intricately embroidered with explosions of golden suns, covered by a light-blue satin coat with extra buckram wadding in the shoulders. But his proudest moment was bringing Charlette's attention to his newest cravat creation. Not that one needed to point it out, for it just short of exploded before all. Rows and rows of it seemed to downright billow!

"Call the dashed thing *Storm-Tossed*," he said seriously.
"Rather fancy it like a dip in the sea. Not that I should actually
subject my person to that element. Ain't my element. Not above
half. But one likes to give the sensation of . . . that sensation.
What?"

While Charlette was prodigiously admiring it, the Duke was
beginning to look her over, but Lady Marjory was agile enough to
come between them, showing off her favorite heavy crepe grey
gown, always worn with her five rows deep of matched prized
pearls, costing a fortune and making her look like the Duchess she
felt in her heart she was.

At the parade of merchants and their wives dressed to the teeth,
the Duke's quizzing-glass and Lady Marjory's eyes were constantly raised. A heaviness of colors, yellows, browns, purples
and oranges abounded, in substantial fabrics of satins, bomba-
zines and taffetas. Even more ample was the display of jewels.
The ladies were determined to wear every bauble owned. A
tea-merchant's wife, with ten diamond necklaces across her purple
bosom, standing next to Lady Marjory, fair outdid her in glitter.

His grace having now noticed everyone else's appearance,
Charlette felt it was properly her turn for his attention. She was all
in shades of sea green, forming panels of gauze and silk that
blended together when she stood, and yet when she walked rippled
like a storm at sea. For the occasion, she had allowed the back part
of her long red-golden hair to float like a spinnaker sail, while the
top was in its usual bunch of curls at her crown. Then, scattered
here and there in her coiffeur, were dewdrop emerald chips, giving
the illusion of being baptized by a sea spray. Those and the
emerald earrings surprisingly found green glints in her eyes. Last
minute, she had added a sheer green stole to cover the rather
daring décolletage, concluding the design more suitable for
Mayfair affairs than here in the center of middle-class morality.
And her instincts had not betrayed her. Most of the ladies wore
high-necked gowns with an abundance of sleeve.

But Charlette's primary interest, after years of descriptions, was
in spotting, one after another, the sea decorations, including ship
models of past victors, giant anchors and actual figureheads. But
she could not be content until she had sighted the main attraction
of every year. Yes, there on the raised platform, where the awards
were to be given, stood the life-size mermaid that had so endeared
herself to Jem. The old sailor had drunk many a toast to her in his
life. A closer viewing revealed she had not worn well. Her green

fishtail was chipping, and her prominent bosom, wrapped demurely in seaweed, needed washing. Long blonde hair fell in musty clumps, and, heavens, there was a spider on her outstretched hand. Deucedly disappointing.

Could they have not afforded a new mermaid? Or was it tradition to have the same old sea siren? But there was no skimping on the chandeliers. One blinked at the veritable parade of crystal and silver fixtures, all ablaze. And the refreshments were the kind to satisfy a sailor's hearty appetite. But one definite stroke of gaucherie was the orchestra's tuning up while the crowd talked. The cacophony of sound had Lady Marjory raising her permanently astonished eyebrows even farther. Her ladyship, having learned from her dockside experience, brought along two handkerchiefs well-drenched with scent and was relieved to discover they were not needed. Yet, everyone else around her was taking several steps back. Not that anyone would criticize her ladyship; indeed, several ladies returned home to announce the style amongst the ton was to carry two lace handkerchiefs, and no stinting on the cassia. The resulting subsequent liberal usage of scent would have much astonished the gentry.

Mr. Hitchens was in his element, for what he had promised had more than come about, exceeding even his most exalted hopes. He and his wife were one of the lucky couples to be introduced to the noble visitors. Lady Marjory was gracious enough to incline her head, and they received two fingers and an elegant bow from the Duke of Wingshire himself. One of those fingers bore his signet ring, and Mr. Hitchens had almost felt the desire to kiss it. He refrained, but with difficulty. Most of the men present were in awe at the glow of his grace's boots, that had the added gleam of golden rings around the top that clinked when he walked. So many ball guests approached him with heads so low to glimpse his boots that even Lady Marjory felt the bowing was of sufficient humbleness. His grace, being a known exquisite whose apparel had often impressed even the First Gentlemen of England, or the Regent himself, was not the slightest bit discommoded by the commotion he created.

At the other end of the ballroom, Charlette spotted another commotion: a fluttering of people surrounding a tall man. She first saw only the back of his head, yet recognized him. Albeit the dark hair was worn longer than she remembered and longer than most men in Society. His figure rose like a mast—half of which was crowded in by shorter sycophants: retired seamen and their

friends, men who wished they had gone to sea, and women of all
ages who thought captains were romantic by their very title.
Actually, Charlette begrudgingly acknowledged, there were several sea captains in attendance. Many she recognized. And some
were as tall as he. And some as young as he. And a few as
adventurously handsome. But only one had all of those qualities,
and only one had the dark grey eyes she recollected—now sighting
round.

Across the ballroom, as if looking across the years that
separated them, they spotted each other. And connected.

Charlette turned her eyes away first. Yes, it was obviously
Darrel, now that he had shaved off the beard sported aboard ship.
But this new Darrel was an enlarged version of the boy she
knew; magnified, as if the years were a lens that had done that to
him. Every detail that she remembered was filled in with new
dimensions. Her attempt to continue assessing him from the
corner of her eyes while carrying on a conversation with the Duke
was a failure. For her words were faltering as she sensed Darrel's
glance, like an invisible tentacle, reaching across and touching her
gently, experimenting with his power of reaching her, probing
deeper, then swiftly demanding her attention—and she looked
back at him.

Charlette had previously discussed with Froth the possibility of
meeting Darrel, and both had decided that she should simply not
recognize him. Certainly, he did not deserve acknowledgment
after what he had done to her father . . . and after, as Jem
Barker had claimed, he had shown himself a traitor to England—
and now a traitor to the Varricks. And the rumors he and his Bates
friends were spreading had been the final straw. No, she would not
meet him, she would not talk to him and she would definitely stop
looking back at him.

She looked back at him. He was making gestures—little signals
with his eyes and finally even his hands that she could not help but
understand. It came back in a rush. How they could communicate
at the island even while standing silent before her father and other
members of the gentry who would have frowned at her speaking
openly to him; and yet, yet, they had known how to make their
feelings clear to each other. Had laughed at the unseeing,
unknowing adults. In a determined pull, she turned completely
around so that he could only see the back of her head.

And then, impossibly, Lady Marjory became his surrogate.

She, who rarely observed any gentlemen, even at the most exclusive balls, suddenly found her attention drawn to a tall man with staring, intense eyes. She blushed and leaning forward asked if anyone knew his identity.

"A sea captain, I expect," Charlette answered stiffly.

At that point one of the many directors of the affair, a Mr. Yanks, who was to later give the awards, having hung around the fringes of their group, hoping to catch a stray crumb of the nobility's conversation or be of some use, moved a step closer and had the honor of supplying the captain's name to her ladyship and mentioning the award to be given Captain Darrel Huntley that very night.

"Ah, *he* is the captain of that first boat we saw at the harbor—the one that dashed Miss Varrick's hopes?"

Uncertain how to answer that with Miss Varrick standing so close, Mr. Yanks spoke several sentences that meandered to a stop until he drew breath and began anew with the diplomatic announcement that while Captain Huntley was this year's winner, Miss Varrick and her father were the perennial winners.

Miss Varrick was gracious enough to incline her head at that civility and give him a dimpled smile. Tenacious of desire, her ladyship asked if the gentleman knew the Captain, and was assured that he did. Would her ladyship care to be introduced? Before Charlette could intervene, Lady Marjory had inclined her head, and Mr. Yanks was off running in the Captain's direction. Never had Charlette felt less in charity with Lady Marjory—this request was all the attention needed by a captain who apparently was having a surfeit of it tonight. Instantly, Miss Varrick opined that she and the Duke walk away and discuss the inspiration for his cravat. Nothing loath, the Duke was quick to promote that into their taking the air on the balcony. At that point Lady Marjory discovered that she, too, wished for a refreshing draught of air. As Mr. Yanks was thankfully waylaid by the other directors, in preparations for the award ceremony, Charlette suggested the Duke take his sister for an airing, while she met her obligation of speaking to several Varrick representatives.

Relieved of his quandary, the Duke bowed his gratitude to one lady and his attendance to the other.

Eventually, Charlette, unable to keep her vow of disregarding him, sent a brief glance the Captain's way. He had been patiently, confidently, waiting for her to do so. At once, he made the well-remembered gesture of tossing seashells, signaling their meeting, and indicated the other balcony.

The effrontery! Not only did he intend to speak to her, but he presumed to remind her of their past without first being given leave to do so. And he further wished for her to act as if she were a child again, leaving a party to sneak away for a private meeting with him. Then he was blatantly walking to the other balcony, on the starboard side of the ballroom, opposite the one where Lady Marjory was probably giving the Duke some of her invaluable opinions on the ball and how the entire room smelled distinctly of *shop* as well as of the sea! Charlette had heard her whisper that remark upon entering the ballroom, and as her brother had been too preoccupied to respond, and Charlette too much of a lady to acknowledge it, she would have a fresh audience for its repetition.

Without realizing it, Charlette had walked toward the starboard balcony. She kept hoping someone would come and cut across her path. Or that the Duke would reenter the ballroom in time to head her off. Or that Lady Marjory would find the balcony breezes too pressing and demand to be taken home. But none of those interruptions occurred, and in a few more steps she was directly at the balcony door. There, she hesitated. And, then, unable to go farther, had stepped back, instead of forward, when the door suddenly opened and a hand pulled her through the doorway.

They were alone on the balcony—a few feet apart, attempting in the shadows to assess each other.

The breeze was blowing her hair about, and he was staring at it, as if in painful remembrance, while she was eagerly looking at him for signs of the boy she had once loved. They were in a whirl of peaking emotions until he spoke—and all shattered.

Not only was his voice different, pointing out his strangeness, but he said words that set up her back, and had them ready to come to cuffs.

"I've had honor after honor tonight as the winner of the London Prize, but the one I claim for myself is a salute from you."

And before she could call him to account for his effrontery, he had pulled her into his arms and kissed her heartily. As if she were a doxy on the wharf that a sailor could embrace with impunity without fear of repulsion or reprisal.

Neither pulling away, nor responding, Charlette stood stiffly, imperiously, in his arms, until he himself stepped away, confused.

"Charle?" he whispered.

She walked to the balcony's edge and leaned against it. "You were not always so . . . common. Or were you? And I, as a child, simply could not see it?" She asked softly, almost as if speaking to herself.

The astonishment on his face was not clearly seen in the darkness, but she heard his indrawn breath.

"Mayhap you've merely learned pirates' ways—seizing what does not belong to you?"

"I never take what does not belong to me. Only what was sworn mine," he said huskily.

She let her hand run over the stone balustrade. In the distance she could see the harbor. The wind was coming from there. It was freshening, she nearly said. Let's go for a sail, Darrel, she nearly said.

"You were at the harbor today?" he asked proudly. "I showed your father my tail. *Sprinter* was awash in my backwater! You've come here to honor me—isn't that why you've attended? The Varricks never attend these affairs. And when I saw you here, I knew it was to fulfill our oath that we would be here together. I, winning the Prize, and us, dancing the Sailor's Jig in celebration—together."

"That was to be if you were sailing for the Varricks!"

"Aye, and is that the kind of sport you are? Hardly sporting not to accept defeat graciously and honor the victor."

She shrugged. "You might have won one race. What is one race? In the scheme of things, one wave in the sea. And how can one honor the dishonorable? There is such a want of honor in the Huntley-Bates rumor tactics as must put all to the blush. Hardly surprising you took advantage of a distant friendship to take liberties."

And all of that Charlette said softly and without anger—as if merely stating facts. And while he was digesting it all, she walked back to the ballroom door, but he stepped before ·her. In close proximity now, with the candlelight from the open door throwing flickering lights on their faces, he leaned close and whispered, "You've lost all the sweetness you once had, Charle, my gal. No wonder you brought a Duke to this affair! To put us all in our places, eh?"

"I need not do anything to achieve that. You are all . . . in your proper places." And with that and a set smile, Charlette glided past him into the ballroom, where the Duke was on the hunt for her.

"Thought you'd been captured by pirates," he said with a laugh.

"I nearly was," she said.

As he escorted her back to the waiting Lady Marjory, Charlette could not shake her disappointment. Darrell had turned out, indeed, to be a stranger. An ego-seeking, lowly, grasping stranger. Well, henceforth she should treat him like a stranger—casting him back into the sea of his own world. Yet, there was a loss. Somehow she had imagined he would be the same. Perhaps he was. Before, as a child, she had not seen that pride, that self-serving ruthless way of reaching out and taking what he wished—and undervaluing everything else. The Duke's graciousness shone brightly in contrast. She wished the ceremonies were concluded so that she might be able to leave. After that, she need not stay for anything else.

And then, unfortunately, Mr. Yanks recalled his mission and was whispering something to Captain Huntley. In a few seconds Darrel was being introduced to Lady Marjory, as she had requested. She simpered at him.

Good gracious, Charlette thought, having assumed she could at least count on Lady Marjory's hauteur. But directly before her there transmogrified a new Marjory who was—could it be believed?—fluttering her eyelashes! Lady Marjory, who only became tolerably enthused at the points of a hunter! Possibly she saw more of the real Darrel—a magnificent animal that one could take on for a race but must be left, after all, behind in the stables.

Determinedly, Charlette refused to take part in the conversation. The Duke, always affable, stepped in to relieve the situation, as one lady was too forward and one too backward.

"Good show, my good man. Jolly good. Enjoyed the race. Did we not, Miss Varrick?"

Feeling his grace's eye on her, she rose to the occasion and emulated his ease of manner. "We did, indeed," Charlette said, finding her voice.

"Even the finish?" Darrel challenged.

"The finish was not what one expected. But we Varricks cannot be selfish. We are quite willing to allow an occasional intruder into the winner's ranks, as long as they do not make a habit of it."

His grace let out a loud laugh at that, and the Director, still hanging by, was quick to assure her that they were highly honored by her presence and by her affability and graciousness, not to mention her condescension. It was toadyism at its highest.

Ordinarily, Charlette would have been revolted by it, but at this moment felt it welcome.

Captain Huntley was looking at her and the Director with equal contempt—the same look she recollected he had given the upper classes on the island, swearing to her that someday he should make them eat their words and snubs.

She could not allow him to think she had totally lost all her understanding, and in keeping with the graciousness that marked a lady, she said civilly, "*Lark* was not up to *Sprinter*—either in design or strength. I must only attribute its winning to your seamanship, Captain."

Captain Huntley bowed at the tribute.

"It is so fortunate that you were brought up in the Varrick Lines, having learned all your sea ways there. I cannot help but feel, in some small way, even Captain Huntley's victory is still a victory for the Varricks. My father taught him all he knows."

"My father taught me all he knew," Captain Huntley said coldly.

"He did not teach you his main virtue: the value of loyalty," she said coldly as well, but with a surface smile.

"I am loyal to those who earn my loyalty—to the sea, to my ship and . . . to old memories."

That was what one received for attempting to be gracious, Charlette thought, and had turned away as if in dismissal, whereupon Lady Marjory pushed her aside and took her place in the conversation.

"Loyalty is always to be admired, I daresay. But we women should prefer a man give it us, rather than to such a paltry thing as a ship."

"Hear, hear," Mr. Yanks cheered, receiving a small smile from Lady Marjory.

"A sailor's first loyalty must always be to his ship," Charlette could not resist inserting.

But Lady Marjory was already talking over her statement, asking question after question of the Captain. He had learned, Charlette noticed, not to stumble when talking to quality. He was smooth and bowed just the correct amount, quite pleased to answer her ladyship's questions, now centering on the difficulty of living aboard a ship.

"The cabins are not of a size to please a lady. Even the Captain's quarters are rather on the close side—all space must be reserved for the cargo."

The Duke's attention was attracted to the Captain's cravat; it was a mere ribbon of a thing. Paltry, the Duke felt, and sought to bring attention to his invention. Charlette understood what he was about to do, and whether because she felt Darrel would not understand the importance of a dandy's designs, or because she could not bear to have him looking down at her friends, she drew the Duke aside. His grace could not help but ask for her opinion on the Captain's cravat; she agreed it was insignificant, and then he could be easy.

They were interrupted by the sound of a ship's horn. Mr. Yanks bowed hastily, making so many profuse apologies for his departure they all feared he would never make good on his promise of that departure. At last he stepped away and rushed toward the raised platform where he would announce the awarding of the London Prize.

At that, Captain Huntley, after a mere bow in their general direction, left as well. His face was excited, as it was when they were going to climb the Freshwater Cliffs. He knew this was going to be his moment, and he could not contain the smile glowing fully. The Bates brothers came close, escorting him to the center, and then, reluctantly standing back, allowing him his moment alone. Proudly, he held up the plaque for all to see. And there was general cheering. Also given him were a variety of other awards. The Regent sent him a snuffbox. Liverpool gave him a promised dinner and the freedom of the city. The sailors of Great Britain gave him a walking stick made of a shark's backbone. The schoolchildren of England gave him a traveling bag.

To all he was gracious in his acceptance, giving a short speech about the children looking forward to completing their dreams, as he had his. He looked at her at that moment, and she remembered that this was his dream of dreams, and she almost smiled in friendship at him. But he had looked quickly away.

After the applause, most of the people thought the ceremonies were over and began to talk, when, of a sudden, the horn called them to attention again.

"And now," Mr. Yanks proudly announced, "for the moment we have all been waiting for tonight—the presentation to the Varrick Line for *consistency* of winning. The Grand Trophy, a new prize this year of a silver bowl, designed by Paul Storr, goes to a lady representing her esteemed father—Miss Charlette Varrick."

Darrel turned and shot a look of such surprise and shock in her direction that she almost stumbled on her way forward.

Again, she understood. And again, the understanding came against her wishes. Here, he had been waiting all his life to receive the main award, and somehow, his had been made secondary, and the Varricks had won a grander prize—even while having lost! It was not to be believed! The Bates brothers made no secret of their displeasure, complaining aloud. Huntley-Bates had not been informed of this additional award! It was demeaning to their man. Yet, as Charlette walked forward, they were crossly hushed, as everyone wished an undisturbed and unobstructed view of her.

The panels of her silk and gauze dress showed various shades of green as she walked, turning actually into moving ripples of the sea. Rather as if a Sea Nymph herself had deigned to come to land to show them all why they loved the sea. And in that moment of votive regard and voluble ahhhs!, the whole ballroom, with the bitter exception of one or two, loved her.

The Duke did her the honor of leading her to the platform, and then bowing, as if she were a Queen, left her alone to accept the homage. That act elicited a gasp of appreciation from the royalty-loving crowd. And when Charlette merely inclined her head and curtsied to them all, not saying a word, it seemed the most fitting and queenly gesture of all. Especially her slight wave to all sides, as she allowed the Duke to escort her back to her table—followed by a footman holding the massive silver Grand Trophy.

"Well done, Charle," Darrel whispered. "You've outplayed me again."

But while he was grinning, his eyes as she flashed past him were not smiling. Storm clouds ahead, she thought with a grin, and then turned, staring at him, as she had as a child, now clearly transmitting "*I win! I win!*", as when they had raced across a beach, or in search of gulls' eggs up a cliff, or when competing, perched on the crow's nest of her father's ships, for the first sighting of a dolphin's dive. "I win! I win!"

He lifted his hands over his head in a victor's salute to her, and bowed to her in defeat. But when she looked again at him, flushed with her triumph, she felt a warning flash that froze the smile on her face. And she knew instantly, as she had always known about him, that another's victory only made him try even harder to upset them. To even the score. Or totally leave them foundering. He would not give nor ask quarter. And neither would she.

Chapter Seven

THE dancing had begun, and Lady Marjory was concerned that she might be forced to dance with the commoners who had been eyeing her with unmasked anticipation. She wished her brother would make it known to whichever gentleman had the audacity to approach that she was not dancing this evening.

"No need to fret yourself into ribbons, Marj. Me quizzing-glass will put any such hedge bird in his place."

But Lady Marjory was not content with that as a mere protection, having been previously promised it as a defense while her brother, too occupied ogling a pretty lady through it, failed his obligation to her. Thus she often, at less ramshackle affairs than this, had found herself having to resort to her own way of curbing pretension, or simply walking away from the gentleman before he'd finished asking her to be his partner.

Turning to Charlette, she suggested it was surely time for them to depart; they had seen all this assemblage could possibly offer. Miss Varrick herself was not reluctant, and the ladies being in agreement, it needed merely to discover the location of the suddenly mysteriously missing Duke, who had disappeared in the blink of an eye. Lady Marjory signaled the hovering Director, and he was quick to attend her. He had no idea where his grace had gone, but would, without fail, discover his whereabouts if he had to put every spare man on the assignment.

"That shall scarcely be necessary, Mr. Yanks," Charlette said, with a slight edge of irritation in her voice. "I have discovered him, waltzing with that lady in scarlet."

Mr. Yanks was delighted to have the mystery solved, and since the Duke had set the pattern, he felt emboldened enough to ask Lady Marjory for a twirl. With an all-suffering air, and a flash of her eyes in Charlette's direction, as if to communicate, did I not say I should reach this outrage, she allowed herself to be led to the dance floor. Next was the gavotte, and the Duke had returned to claim her for it. Expressing her surprise that they were staying for the dancing, since his sister had so strongly been against it, the Duke responded he could not permit Marj to let him be discourteous. "I shall twirl off with one or two of these anxious ladies, and you and Marj with several of the directors. Then we can be off, feeling we've done our all, don't you know? Give 'em something to remember, what?"

"You're a very gallant man, your grace," Charlette said sincerely. "That is, of course, what must be done. You always know what is or is not the thing."

Pleased at her panegyric, he admitted that he had been around the town enough to know the correct ways, and that he had no wish for them to appear top-lofty. "No need to dashed-well rub their noses in our position. One is, or is not what one is."

"Exactly so. How well you express yourself." And Charlette was not doing it too brown. She meant everything she said to him, and, in fact, could only fault herself for not having realized that it would have been shockingly rude to have left before some dancing. It would have seemed that she was merely interested in getting the award and running with it. Yet, when Lady Marjory had said as much, it so accorded with her desire to leave quickly that she went along without thinking out her decision. And mainly, she acknowledged to herself ruefully, she had been anxious to leave for fear of coming across Darrel again. Any lingering, and she should lose the advantage she had. Any delay was giving him the opportunity to retaliate. Yet, she could hardly say that to the Duke.

The Director, Mr. Yanks, had the felicity of not only dancing with Lady Marjory but with the focal point of all eyes, Miss Varrick herself, while the latter was smilingly ignoring his reaching just about to her shoulders.

Leaning against one of the pillars, decorated with variously colored shells and fins, Captain Huntley observed Miss Varrick. Like a moving light in a dark room, he found himself unable to focus on anything else. A retired captain from her own Varrick Line, Captain Miles Wilton, known to keep as lax discipline on his ship as on his own imbibing, was, Darrel observed grimly, close to being three-sheets-to-the-wind; yet he had the sheer gall to bow to Miss Varrick. Darrel hoped she would refuse, but she did not, recollecting him from when she was a child, and he, not remembering her, seeing only a bosomy ladybird, was whirling her about in such an abandoned manner that even Charlette's graciousness was wearing thin. At this exhibition, Darrel was torn between thinking it would be a salutary lesson for her pride and feeling shame that this captain should so disgrace their profession.

A hint from Captain Huntley and Mr. Yanks rushed to Charlette's defense. But Captain Wilton apparently had drunk a great deal more than was first assumed, for he would not give up his "booty," he shouted. Mr. Yanks was only making matters worse by his ineffectual remonstrating. The Duke, dancing with Mrs. Yanks, smoothly maneuvered her before her husband, bowed his appreciation for the honor she had done him, and tapped the by now cursing and weaving Captain Wilton on the shoulder. When the inebriated man turned, he saw a huge magnified eye staring directly above him, coming closer.

"Giant squid," the Captain called out in alarm, and abandoned his booty, allowing the Duke to take her by the waist and whirl her away, while the frightened Captain weaved his way back to the refreshment table.

Captain Huntley was delighted that he had not had to intervene; he had no wish to come to that blasted girl's defense, not after her having ruined his night and somehow made all he had accomplished up to now seem lowly. She had put him in his place, indeed! A place he had thought he had risen from by becoming equal with her father, in that he, as well, was now a ship owner, and rather plump in the pocket, even having bought the late Sir Richard's manor house at Cowes for himself and his widowed mother. Yet, as high as he'd risen, a pair of sea-blue eyes told him, it was not high enough. Never high enough. And even the ease with which the Duke had handled the situation had deflated him, for secretly he'd been hoping for a scene from which he alone could rescue her.

The only balm to his pride was that Charlotte had not looked offended; she had, instead, as he remembered so well, found the whole incident quite amusing. Dancing away with the Duke, he heard her clear laughter over the rumbles of the crowd. Ah, Charle, my girl, he thought with a deep pang. And then, then—are you still there, inside that starched up, dressed-up lady? And then, blow-me-down, he thought he'd find out, and proceeded toward the orchestra.

Charlette was finding herself becoming repetitive. "I shall bore you excessively, your grace, by once more finding myself having to be indebted to you for your good sense. I actually never thought a mere lifting of your glass could be so efficacious."

"Never fails me," he said contentedly. "The man had shot the cat—anything could have terrified him. But dash it all, never had me eye called a squid!"

The memory of that had Charlette in the whoops, and the Duke looked at her with affection. "Good gal. You don't make a fuss. Got a good head on your shoulders. E'gad, not to say the rest of you ain't prime."

"Much obliged," Charlette smiled back. "Do you feel after this dance that we have stayed as long as we must. Lady Marjory, I perceive, is tapping her foot."

"Is she, by gad? Trouble that. Means she's going to say something I'll wish she hadn't. Must head her off."

And they rushed quickly back to her ladyship, who was telling a merchant that she found the entire event too excruciating to be endured.

"Too excruciatingly, dashed fine," the Duke put in, to the confused man. "Lots o' fine fish all around. And mermaids."

The man was delighted to have his grace notice their famed mermaid; she'd graced this hall for over ten years.

"Looks a bit long in the tooth," his grace said commiseratingly, and, bowing, took the ladies to a table.

"We simply must leave this minute," Lady Marjory protested.

"It should break the hearts of all the sailors at this ball, your ladyship," a deep voice intervened.

Her ladyship smiled as she recognized the magnetic winner of the race. "Captain Huntley," she addressed him. "I feared you had forgotten us."

"Hardly possible anyone in the ballroom could forget your ladyship after you've been gracious enough to grace our small affair."

She laughed loudly at that, pinking at the edges of her already ruddy complexion.

Precisely at that moment the orchestra struck up the Sailor's Jig. There was a cry from the crowd of both pleasure and surprise, for that was usually danced later in the evening—when people were in more of an abandoned state. Miss Varrick paled and shot a wary look at Captain Huntley. He grinned back at her.

"Shall Miss Varrick do a lowly Captain the honor of joining me in this dance?" he asked smoothly, yet louder than usual, so that a great many people who were crowding round would hear her reply.

Charlette was in a quandary. Recollecting what the Duke had said about not deliberately humiliating others, and seeing the baited attention all around, she knew it would be shockingly uncivil to refuse. Yet, she feared his motives. And more, she feared herself—they had too often danced that on the beach together. Was he trying to show her titled friends that she was more of this lowly group herself than of theirs? Or was he trying to remind her of that?

Captain Huntley continued to press. "It should be most appropriate, do you not think, for the *two* winners of this night to celebrate the occasion and show all how we do it . . . back on our island."

Charlette was, she realized, not going to be allowed to demur.

"Unless," Darrel said with a deliberate taunt, "Miss Varrick is ashamed of the island's ways . . . and the island itself . . . before her august friends?"

There was a murmur through the whole room, and Charlette became aware that the orchestra had stopped playing and was waiting for the signal from the Captain, thus making their words audible to a great many in the hall. And all were waiting in happy expectation of seeing the two victors of the evening in the wild Sailor's Jig. Nothing could be more entrancing. It would be the high point of the entire affair.

"I would be delighted to accept, Captain. However, I fear I have forgotten the steps and should not do justice to the dance. It should certainly be more of an honor if you chose one of the lovely ladies here who, more adept, would do the dance proud."

He and she stared at each other. Had she succeeded in checkmating his ploy? He was shaking his head at her, letting her know he would not allow her the escape of that pretense. "I do not fear your . . ." he'd begun, when Lady Marjory interrupted their duel.

"I am known to sport a fancy toe," she said, in her trumpet-like tones. "I flatter myself, Captain, that if you direct me, I shall give you a dashed good whirl."

Charlette turned with delight, seeing herself being given a perfect escape. Darrel had a momentary flash of annoyance, but he quickly masked it and was all compliance. "That would be an honor I did not think I should merit," he said. Lady Marjory, grinning unceasingly, gave him her hand, and signaling the conductor, Captain Huntley led her to the center of the floor.

Slightly disappointed that the dance was not to be done by their two favorites, the crowd still was anxious to observe this moment. For a Lady Marjory doing the Sailor's Jig was clearly something worth watching!

She caught the basic steps and was able to perform the jarring, jumping dance for a few moments, the Captain being gracious

enough to limit it to the essentials, without the wild circling and
the turns. But it was too sedate a version for the watchers, and
several couples came onto the floor to do the authentic dance.
Soon the whole room was whirling. The music was infectious.
Charlette was almost unable to withstand its call. At last, she
could no longer remain like stock on the sidelines, and taking the
astonished Duke by the arm, jumped them in. The Duke was
gallantly attempting to keep pace, but as they passed the faltering
Lady Marjory and her sea captain, the Duke stumbled.

Captain Huntley moved in a flash, and the two couples had
exchanged partners. He had Charlette in his arms and was dancing
off with her, while Lady Marjory and the Duke sedately danced
back to their table.

The two were exhibiting the Sailor's Jig exactly as it was meant
to be done, and even with their own innovations. The crowd
sensing something extraordinary occurring, thinned out around
them. A few moments more, and they were alone on the ballroom
floor—the King and Queen of the shipping world, the Captain and
the Sea Goddess, performing the dance as if born to it.

Ducking here and whirling there, the two were moving at a
speed even the other exponents of the dance had never seen. The
golden-red hair of the Goddess was a bright spinnaker sail,
fluttering in the breeze they themselves created. And the Captain
was sailing his craft, smoothly, determinedly, through all the
shoals and eddies, bobbing, diving and sailing smoothly on. The
breaths were held in awe. Little murmurs of pleasure came from
each group as the couple spun past them, and several sailors
shouted out "Aye, aye, aye!" as tables and chairs were being
beaten to carry the rhythm on, and to show the delight of all.

And abandoning herself to the rhythm and the music, Charlette
forgot all that had occurred between them since, and gave herself
to the wild challenge of the moment. It was Darrel and she, just
the two of them on the beach, with Jem Barker playing the tunes,
and they kicking up sand and holding onto each other—and now
keeping eye contact throughout, they similarly merged into the
music and into each other, reveling in the motion and the joy of
each other's presence . . . together again.

And Darrel whispered, "Welcome back, Charle."

And Charlette said nothing, a small smile of pleasure was all
she allowed, but it was enough for him . . . and them.

The dance ended, and they both came gradually back to
themselves. "Charle," Darrel said, holding onto her hand for a

moment. But she shook her head and ran off. The room was shaking with applause and cheers, but she merely gave her hand to the waiting Duke, who deemed this the correct moment for departure. He bowed to the still shouting crowd and led his two ladies out of the ballroom.

Charlette did not look back, but her heart was still beating to the rhythm of the dance and the sea. It was not till she was in the carriage that she realized Darrel had won his round, after all.

Chapter Eight

❦ =================================== ❦

THE next few days after the London Prize Ball, Charlette found herself the object of much disapproval. And the surprise was that the worst of the censure came from the two men she thought would always approve of her actions. Lord Bridingsley, during their morning chat, expressed himself thusly: "Trafficking with London cits, not done, my dear child. You'll be stamped as having a taint of the shop, and with your father dealing with tea-merchants and the like, you're too near to encourage that connection."

Feeling that his easy, forgiving manners only applied to himself, she decided, henceforth, to be occupied when invited for a morning ride. Instead, she accepted the company of Sir Smithers, who found her a pattern card of virtue and perfection, shown in his sonnets on her hair, eyes, eyebrows and toes. Slightly longer was a poem to her fan, depicting his being transformed into that said object and thus able to spend his days in close proximity to her breast, cheeks and lips. She wished she had some lady to laugh with over its absurd lines, Francine having repulsed all such overtures for sharing. That left Froth, who though making no objections to hearing the poem, yawned throughout, dismissing both poet and subject.

The second censure for her actions at the London Ball arrived a few days later in a short note from her father. He would not countenance her associating herself with the very people he had sent her away from the island to avoid. Nor did he need a silver bowl to remind his investors of his past record. What he would have preferred was his daughter acting like a lady by remaining in the very Society for which entry he was paying his sister exorbitant sums.

"I'm really in the suds," Charlette whispered, shaken by her father's unexpected coldness.

But what really had Charlette taken aback was her aunt's reaction. She not only refused to accept either her brother's or Lord Bridingsley's censure, but dismissed both them and their opinions. After all, the ball, though low, indeed, and stuffed with mushrooms, had been sanctioned by the presence and escort of the Duke himself. Therefore, what right had anyone else to pronounce judgment! Actually, Charlette was conducting herself properly, and might even exceed all their hopes. When Charlette did not grasp what was being suggested, Lady Bridingsley merely winked and walked away, humming!

The next day her ladyship's unexpected felicity of manner continued unabated. "It appears I am basking in the sunshine of her approval," Charlette concluded hopefully. And upon a note arriving from the Duke of Wingshire requesting the pleasure of Miss Varrick's company at a picnic in Green Park with his sister, her escort and himself, Lady Bridingsley was all abeam, until, with a sudden frown, she urged a discussion on a serious matter that could no longer be ignored.

Adjourning to Charlette's room, Lady Bridingsley was not backward in broaching the topic—Charlette's outfit for the outing. It was immediately presented: a green spencer of figured Levantine silk over a matching green muslin dress. The latter was of deceptive simplicity, yet so form-conforming as to cause quite a sensation. All her Fanchot gowns were thus shaped, resulting in the good modiste having many ladies coming to her with requests for a "Varrick style."

"Unexceptional," Lady Bridingsley approved, and then revealed her real object of concern; her niece's bonnets. The young girl often wore her island ones, or, more seriously, omitted them altogether. And her aunt felt for this occasion something rather decidedly smashing was required.

At a signal, a maid brought forth the smashing candidate. Lady Bridingsley's own straw chip bonnet with a hanging feather. Presenting it with pride, she said softly, "I have known a lady's entire future to be decided by the choice of the correct bonnet for the opportune moment."

"Indeed?" Charlette responded, restraining her giggles. "What a heavy weight for one's head . . . and one's milliner!"

Nevertheless, Charlette modeled her aunt's candidate. The

ostrich plume curled intriguingly round the brim and finished by stroking the wearer's cheek.

Francine, following the maid into the room, was astonished by both her mother's offer and her exclamation upon viewing both profiles, "Capital. Capital. Could scarcely be improved upon. It gives the suggestion that your cheek is for touching—and putting *that idea* into a gentleman's head is all one can expect from a bonnet. The rest is up to the lady."

Charlette laughed aloud at that, and Francine's eyes fluttered to see her mother laughing as well, and actually winking.

"I beg pardon, Mama. What did you say this bonnet did?"

"It promotes tactile thoughts."

"Oh."

Turning to Charlette, her aunt said with deep concern, "His grace is rather an elusive gentleman; one must use every means possible to direct his thinking, even if one must tickle his imagination with a feather."

"In other words, I am to allow my bonnet to tickle his grace into wanting to tickle me! Heavens!"

Although Charlette believed her gowns were talkative enough without further discussion from her bonnets, she felt to refuse Lady Bridingsley's gesture would be in essence refusing the lady; so she donned it.

While walking down the stairs to the waiting carriage on the appointed day, with the ostrich plume bobbing and stroking her cheek with each movement, Charlette began to imagine the plume as an octopodian tentacle. Indeed, she could not feel its touch without being shamefully aware of its ulterior motives.

Lady Marjory's escort was not present. It was only the Duke, Lady Marjory and herself. At Green Park they all three went on a stroll, before sitting on the stone benches and partaking of the baskets from Gunther's. Each one of Charlette's actions elicited a reproof from Lady Marjory. Her stopping to smell the flowers was lowering her position ("literally so," Charlette had responded, getting down on her knees), her picking a daisy was a cruelty she had not thought a lady would sink to ("I can sink no lower, indeed," Charlette acknowledged) and, lastly, playing the "he-loves-me, he-loves-me-not" game with the bunches of daisies eagerly provided by the Duke for that purpose, "injurious to the health and well-being of all botanical specimens and those with botanical concerns."

At that, a deep voice from behind Charlette contributed, "Miss Varrick never thinks of injuries when she is at play!"

Without turning, Charlette recognized the speaker. Lady Marjory's delighted face assured her. "Captain Huntley, I was beginning to fear you had forgot our outing," her ladyship pouted.

"Hardly. I was merely detained. I always keep my appointments."

At last, Charlette turned her head. The blasted feather turned with her and obstructed her view of him. He was standing with the sun at his back, and it sent a blaze around him. Undaunted, she continued her game with his grace until both had received a satisfactory answer from the last flower. Then she scattered the corpses to the ground and allowed the Duke to help her to her feet.

Captain Huntley was dressed in obviously new apparel: snug-knit blue pantaloons and shining Hessians, and a lighter blue waistcoat and navy coat. Yet, though fashionable, he continued his open-throated shirt style, with a mere slip of a dark cravat. There was a casualness about the way he wore his clothes as there was in the way he walked and moved, even now, in his languid mounting of an abandoned tree trunk. Leaning over and picking up the denuded daisies Charlette had rejected, he whispered, "Cruel fate."

At last the two past friends were able without obstruction to look at each other fully in the daylight, and both unabashedly took that opportunity. The wind moved the feather across Charlette's cheek, to the tip of her lips and back to her eyes. He watched it hypnotically, as a child watches all who approach him—rapt and unswerving.

Conscious of where his eyes were lingering, Charlette was feeling ambivalent. First and foremost, she was annoyed that her aunt's tactics were working with the Captain. By contrast, they had not done so with the Duke, who had merely pointed out helpfully, "Feather's a bit long, I say. Needs pruning." Secondly, she was in dismay that she could not object to his indecently following the feather, when she had agreed to wear it for that very reaction!

Her annoyance won out, she pushed the feather back and went to seat herself alongside the Duke, leaving Lady Marjory and the Captain in a cozy chat. It was discombobulating, his being familiar and yet unfamiliar. Yet, familiarity seemed to be his strong suit as he closed in on Lady Marjory. His actions were observed by the Duke, who whispered that the Captain was making a dashed nuisance of himself. "Marj has been out with the chap twice already. Rode in the park. Went to Mrs. Friendton's rout. Ain't he just a sailor?"

"A Captain, and the head of his own line," Charlette, in justice, had to reply. She added, "Do you believe his attentions to Lady Marjory are sincere? I fear he is merely funning . . . even trifling."

"Can't trifle with Marj. She won't allow it. Always gets what she wants. Makes life too difficult if she don't. Better leave it all to her. She won't thank me for interfering, I daresay."

"I daresay not," Charlette agreed. Yet, whatever Lady Marjory's objectives—a light flirtation, or a strategic diversion—Charlette could not help but be concerned over Captain Huntley's motives. Why was he pushing himself forward into her milieu? Mayhap he felt himself grown so grand he must needs now establish *himself* in Society?

When the picnic boxes were being opened, an unwary footman brought another special case and began to open that. *"No!"* Charlette cried, but too late. Out popped Froth, running about in the grass like a newly released prisoner.

"I meant to open it carefully and allow him a few moments frolic," Charlette bemoaned, "but now he has lost himself, and, gracious, what if I do not find him!"

"Better leave him, then," Lady Marjory said, dismissing Charlette's concern. "Animals belong with other animals in the areas provided for them. Such as a park. Would you not agree, Captain. Surely, you would not bring a shark onto your ship?"

"Not a shark, for it should not wish to join our voyage. Petrels, at times. And, actually, I have a cat of similar coloring," he answered politely, but his attention was fixed on looking about.

Charlette was off searching.

"I daresay she herself is more at home here in the wild," Lady Marjory reproved.

"A wild thing, is she?" the Captain said with such interest Lady Marjory felt she had erred, and corrected herself.

"Rather unruly, I should say. A bit of a hoyden, actually. She has had groups of gentlemen writing poetry and calling her a Sea Nymph. A lady would never allow herself to be the prize of any contest!"

"And *she* was the prize?" the Captain inquired, lounging back on his log, and keeping his eye on Charlette's fruitless searches. Her hat was in her way, and she removed it, feather and all, throwing it on the ground, while she ran around calling after her pet. His grace had long since joined her in her search.

"A day spent in her company was the prize," Lady Marjory whispered. "The entire ton was appalled; not that it was unexpected. She comes from disgraced lineage."

"Because her father owns a shipping line?" Darrel's face was somewhat coldly set as he waited for that answer.

"Nay, the problem does not lie with her father. After all, he is Lady Bridingsley's brother. Rather, her *mother*."

"I remember the lady. She was quite a beauty, and gentle and kind."

"Fortunately, I never met the . . . if you would say . . . lady. Her only concession to propriety was to remove herself from Society—first to that island, and, then, by dying. But the disgrace was such, it has marked her daughter forever. Yet, Miss Varrick seems not to be the slightest bit aware that she, above all other ladies, should be more circumspect, lest it be assumed she has inherited her mother's wayward tendencies!"

"I say, I wonder you risk being in her presence?" Captain Huntley responded.

"I! With my lineage, I can afford to do anything and never be whispered about. One accepts any action from, say, the Regent. Who would dare question him? Or myself? No, it is more Francine, Lady Bridingsley's daughter, who suffers from her relation, not to mention association, with the islander."

The Captain had heard all he wished on the subject, bowed his excuse and went lazily to join the search. Whistling through his teeth, he heard an answering meowing, took two steps and whisked the errant cat from behind a bush; then he brushed him off and presented him to the harried Charlette who was running forward. "Your cat, Miss Varrick," he said softly as she grabbed the wandering Froth. "And if you do not take better care of him, I shall be forced to take him back," he warned, with a wink.

"Froth, you darling, how could you have made me worry so!" Charlette exclaimed, while Froth, putting his dirty paws all over her dress, settled down in her arms for a nap, having had an exciting morning of exploring.

"You should punish him," the Captain said, "for straying. Else, he shall never learn, and will be constantly frightening you. Froth the Second has perfect discipline, or he should have long since have found himself a watery grave. He knows enough to come when I call, never to get tangled in the gear and stay off the rail."

"Is he happy? Your mother's Froth was . . . met with an accident, I fear."

"He ran away with a tabby and was never heard from again. I expect he is the happiest of the three," he grinned.

"He was stomped on by a bull in his wanderings. We did not tell your mother. I made up that tabby story, so she could feel happier about him."

"I see. And you gave her the Persian that has her combing its hair all day long, I expect."

"Yes, your mother is quite attached to Penelope."

"What a blasted name! I knew Mother could not have so named her. Calls her 'Bad Penny,' but yes, she loves her. As did I, upon first sighting."

For a moment they were back to being children, and Darrel continued this good feeling between them. "Do you remember when I gave Froth to you? I had him under my shirt the morning I went away, and we climbed down to the beach to say our good-byes, and you wanted to come with me." His voice was low and she was mesmerized by it and the memory.

"You abandoned me," she whispered. "You went off and became a pirate."

"And you went off and became a lady!" he teased. "Which is worse?"

Another lady interrupted their remembrances. "I hope the cat has no other plans for interrupting our repast? The flies are making themselves quite a meal."

Both Charlotte and the Captain turned in surprise, having forgotten where they were, and returned dutifully to their place. Later, while entering the barouche to return to the city, Lady Marjory explained to Miss Varrick that the Captain had agreed to escort her to the Brontson Ball tomorrow night.

"I must say, old thing," the Duke put in, "for the Brontson Ball, we'll have to do something about getting you a decent cravat, or we shall all look no how."

"I always wear my own style, your grace. That is my truth . . . and my pride."

As for Lady Bridingsley's pride, Charlette returned the feathered hat, with the sad report that the feather had not tickled the Duke's fancy. He'd even threatened to cut it off, for fear it should put out her eye.

"It served its purpose in getting him thinking of your welfare," her ladyship countered and handed the bonnet over to the waiting

Francine. "Wear it at your tea with Mr. Buckston; we'll see what it can do for you, my dear."

"Better study the lists of teas I gave you," Charlette said. "He rarely talks about anything else."

Francine, accepting every help, had memorized the teas and wore the hat. She returned with a satisfied smile. Mr. Buckston was taking her to the Brontson Ball. "And I understand," she added, her smile broadening, "that the Duke is accompanying his sister and her current flirt, that captain. You, I expect, are coming with my parents. Pity." And she walked off, triumphant.

Indeed, the ball itself, that had once loomed as a high point to Charlette, now was secondary to her seeing Society's reaction to Darrel. If they found her outside the pale, for having a father who owned ships, what would they do with an actual sea captain?

Two islanders setting sail onto the good ship *Society*—dead ahead.

"Let's claim her in the name of the Isle of Wight," she whispered with a grin to Darrel somewhere in London.

And then, abruptly, her smile faded as she wondered if that was not already his objective—only not a joint one, after all. The challenge continuing.

Chapter Nine

BEFORE it even took place, the Brontson Ball was already the talk of the ton. For, Erica, or the new Countess Brontson, known as somewhat of an individualist, had scheduled something out of the ordinary. It was conjectured that there would be a surprise guest. Some were guessing the Regent. Others, the return of Lord Byron from exile. Or even Beau Brummell back from Calais. The possibilities were only limited by their imaginations.

As for gowns, all the ladies were attempting to outdo each other. Lady Bridingsley and Francine chose their favorite Madame Fanchot ruffly confections in mauve and yellow, respectively, as well as two pearl necklaces and diadems. Both were quite satisfied by their regal appearances. Francine was further contented by the gift Mr. Buckston brought her—a specially blended tea in a tin, which, she felt, proved he was on the point of making a declaration—of some sort.

When Charlette descended the stairs, she was covered from hood to toe in an ermine wrap that had both the waiting lord and ladyship salivating as to the cost.

Entering the Brontson mansion, with Charlette on his arm, Lord Bridingsley felt himself reliving a moment from his rakish youth. The picture, he owned, was somewhat diluted by having, on his other arm, his wife. But with one eye on the wink, he could at last see himself as he devoutly wished.

The ball had already begun, and the Earl and Countess Brontson were at the top of the marble stairs receiving, while behind them came the sounds from the ballroom, indicating it was already quite a squeeze. The ladies went to the right and the gentlemen to their left, to leave off their cloaks before ascending the stairs. Thus it was that Lady Bridingsley had the privilege of being the first to see Madame Fanchot's outré *Burst of Lace* creation. She stood rooted, uncertain whether to applaud or whisk Charlette home.

Clinging closer than if it had been wetted (a practice much frowned upon by ladies of decency and much resorted to by ladies of daring) was a deep-blue slip; the gauze overhang was similarly snug. But the surprise was at the bodice, where the blue ceased and there burst out an abundance of white lace that barely covered her bosom and, further, left arms and shoulders shockingly, scandalously bare. Not even a puff of sleeve for convention's sake! Her topknot of golden-red hair had similar explosions of lace tendrils, flowing into her own hair, hanging down in the sides and back.

Lady Bridingsley's silence did nothing to reassure Charlette, who wondered if perhaps she had given Madame Fanchot too much license, but she squared her shoulders and walked to the foot of the stairs. Lord Bridingsley was awaiting his ladies, both arms out. He dropped them at the vision approaching him.

"E'gad," he ejaculated. *"E'gad!"*

As Charlette took his arm, and the three were going up the stairs, she had not as yet had an assurance that her outfit was outstanding rather than outrageous. His lordship's response was equally enigmatic.

As she approached the bored Earl of Brontson and his vivacious wife, who was dressed in one of her well-known brilliant red gowns, she received her assurance at last from them.

"Charming," the Earl said, eyeing her as she curtsied before him.

"Ah, I knew someone would take the shine out of me tonight," the Countess said with a kind smile. "I am delighted it was not one of my friends. You are a vision, Miss . . . eh, Varrick."

"You are most gracious," Charlette responded with another curtsey. "I am most obliged to you for your kind invitation."

"Not at all," the young Countess exclaimed, and then, with a slight grin, whispered, "I hope you shall not take it amiss if I ask a favor of you, Miss Varrick. Do not accept if my husband asks you for a waltz." The last was said loudly, and directly to her husband, who responded with his usual tolerant affection. "I have all my waltzes spoken for by a madcap in a red gown, but I shall certainly ask this lady for a gavotte." Kissing his wife's hand, they laughed over that.

Charlette could only reply, "I shall be most honored, my lord.

We are all looking forward to the surprise that is so much being spoken of."

"Oh," Erica exclaimed, her eyes twinkling, "but *that* is going to be the surprise: There is *not* going to be a surprise!"

"Erica, my dear one, behave yourself," a blonde young matron in a simple white Grecian gown whispered as she came by, and introduced Charlette to her husband, Mr. Astaire. Before Lord Bridingsley, approaching, could bespeak the next dance with her, instead of his waiting wife, Charlette instinctively stepped aside, accepting Mr. Astaire.

The ballroom was a fantasy of flowers, and potted plants as tall as trees, and vines crawling up to the overhanging balconies—one holding the orchestra and the other a curtained stage. There were bowls of fruit everywhere. And on the various plants, wax apples and other fruits had been carefully connected.

"Are we in the Garden of Eden?" Charlette asked her partner.

"Right. I told Erica she had enough fruits about to transmit that idea, but she always tends to come on too strong. Wait till you see what's behind the curtain."

While waiting, Miss Varrick danced with several other gentlemen and lords, at last giving one to Lord Bridingsley, who was looking peeved. The Duke of Wingshire approached and was promised a carefully reserved waltz. He remained at her side, and upon her asking if his sister and Captain Huntley had arrived, nodded and muttered a bit.

"What's amiss?" Charlette began, and then realized several misses were, as following the direction of the Duke's pointing, she saw the raised head of a surrounded Captain Huntley. "It appears the young ladies of Society are just as vulnerable to his sea-going swagger as their lesser sisters at the Prize Ball."

"We ain't had a moment's peace. Even Lady Jersey came to call on the chap. Met us in the park. Flirted with the fellow. Invited him to her house. Marj put her foot down. Fellow's staying with us. Ladies making calls all day. Feel like a blasted guard, fending them off. Marj is in a snit."

The gentleman under discussion was just then waltzing off with their hostess. And watching, Charlette felt in a bit of a snit herself. But then she had the good fortune of seeing Lady Marjory's affronted face, and that mirror-image had her quickly rearranging her expression into a smile. Turning to the Duke, she attempted to restore his amiability and was so successful that when claimed by her next partner, his grace regretted listening to Marj's pleas that he accompany her, lest she be alone with the sailor. Pure fustian, he saw now; she had no need of protection from him, rather the reverse. And as a result of his not being Miss Varrick's escort, he had to be satisfied with one measly dance. And in view of the demand for her hand, that really rankled!

Captain Huntley was receiving assurances of his own social success by the patroness of Almack's herself, Lady Jersey. Dancing with the Captain, she informed him that not since Lord Byron had walked into a ballroom had one man caused so much commotion amongst the ladies as he! Actually, the Captain rather reminded her of that "bad, mad and dangerous-to-know" gentleman, for whom Lady Caroline Lamb had once slashed her wrists to get the poet's attention at Lady Heathcote's ball!

The Captain replied he was not conversant with gossip, either current or passé. They spoke then of *his* adventures; and he was obliging enough to exaggerate.

When supper was served, Charlette was placed at the same table as Darrel, Lady Marjory, the Duke and Lord and Lady Jersey. Lady Jersey was calling for more of Darrel's exploits, and Darrel, with a twinkle in his eye, was more than ready to exploit her—launching into a tale of his ship docking at Port of Madagascar, when an Arab sheik rowed up calling for assistance! At his side was a lady totally covered in veils. "I peered over the taffrail and saw this enveloped lady, the sheik's daughter, who was promised to me in marriage, if I would only save them from their pursuing enemies! Neither my crew nor ship was in a state for me to be able to put about. We sore needed a refurbishing of our stores, not to mention the scuttlebutt needing fresh water! All of which I mentioned, but he merely shouted that his life was at stake, accompanied by moans of the most affecting nature from the veiled lady. What could a gentleman do?"

"Before I committed myself, Captain," Charlette could not help but interpose, "I should certainly have insisted on the lady's dropping one of her veils. You might have very well have found yourself leg-shackled to a positive antidote."

Darrel laughed. "Your advice would have been invaluable to me on that occasion, Miss Varrick. Pity we were not sailing together." As usual, his words brought back memories which effectively silenced her.

"But what did you do, my dear Captain?" Lady Jersey cried out, annoyed by the interruption which had caused the Captain to look over her head to that young chit in the most shocking blue and lace dress. Miss Varrick, it was, who was shamelessly flaunting herself all over London. Thankfully, she had not been asked for a voucher, because with the stigma on her name and now the shocking demonstration of her forward ways, Lady Jersey decided she should definitely not have obliged!

"I could not commit my crew," the Captain was answering, "nor could I leave a lady in distress. Not the British way, by Jove." Again, he flashed a look at Charlette, and she tried not to smile, aware he was hoaxing the older lady shamelessly, and merely shook her head.

"Miss Varrick objects?" he addressed her again. "Miss Varrick should know, a captain's word is never questioned—not aboard my full-riggers! You have the look of a full-rigger, rising out of the blue sea, with all sails flying. Ahoy there!" he ordered, of a sudden approaching her and whispering, "Keep all fast for boarding."

Calmly, Charlette counter-ordered, "Coming on thick. Shove off all hands!" and had him laughing.

"Miss Varrick should allow us to hear the end of the tale before she turns the discussion to her doubtful apparel," Lady Jersey cut in, and, turning to the Captain, urged, "What did you do with the veiled lady!"

"Rescued her, naturally, your ladyship. Rowed both her and her father out to a friend's ship that was departing. With my own hands I had the honor of carrying that veiled lady up the side of the ship and placing her safely into her own cabin. As a reward, one of her childlike hands crept out of all those veils, permitting me to place a kiss on its quivering . . . palm."

"Ah . . ." Lady Jersey cried out, satisfied. "Then you never saw the lady."

"Never. Though she oft appears in my dreams and warns me of destruction. For apparently, although I saw them safely away, the sheik had a spy in his entourage, and both he and his daughter were poisoned before the sail was over. But the pouch, clutched to his chest when we met, he left with me. I opened it and found a message claiming if he should meet his death, I should take the jewels in the pouch and his daughter, and keep both under my protection. Apparently she had formed a good opinion of me. That one look we had exchanged . . . burned into our souls."

"I thought you only saw her veiled," Charlette risked pointing out.

"It was the veil I was in love with," Darrel confirmed, and she and he again were overcome with laughter.

Lady Jersey was turning red. "If Miss Varrick could restrain herself, I wish to hear the end of this tale! Tell me, Captain, what occurred with the jewels, if the lady herself had met her fate? Which I presume she had."

"Rather. Both she and her father were thrown overboard. The lady in all her veils went floating down into Poseidon's arms—who alone was privileged to remove her veils and see at last her lovely face . . ." He paused there dramatically, with all eyes fastened on him. His grey eyes were dancing, and he could not resist exchanging yet another look with Charle. She turned away, respectful of Lady Jersey's wishes. But he was not so reticent. "Before I am asked by Miss Varrick how I knew the lady was beautiful, I say all young brides of Poseidon are washed into loveliness by the sea's caresses. And she is remembered with particular affection, since her father had thoughtfully added in his note that if his daughter were assassinated as well, I was to keep the fortune for myself. Which I did. Actually, I had many fortunes thrown my way in my travels, and most often by mysterious ladies."

"But, my dear Captain," Lady Jersey exclaimed. "You should put it all down in book form. A great many ladies should be most interested to hear the full particulars."

The Captain merely bowed and was off on another tale. By that time the supper was over, and the other young girls were thickly surrounding him, eager to be told the veiled lady story themselves, which he obligingly repeated with added embellishments.

"Demmed fellow, can't keep his mouth closed," the Duke exclaimed.

But the Captain's tales were aborted by the sound of trumpets, announcing the unveiling. All eyes obediently turned toward the balcony. The curtains parted and out stepped Adam and Eve *en tableau*. Both were attired in close-fitting, flesh-toned cloth, and covered in apples. A moment of shock before a few helpful viewers pointed out the pair was fully clothed, and thus the ladies, on the point of swooning, regained their senses. Still, the daring of the tableau hung fire, until the gentleman playing Adam came to the edge of the balcony rail, removed his long wig and obligingly waved to his people. It was the Royal Duke of York himself, a friend of the Earl's who had good-naturedly agreed to the tableau. Immediately, the reaction swung to approval, with wild applause. The Duke's tall form bowed in response. And then, casually, he plucked an apple decorating his attire and tossed it to the Countess below, who laughingly kissed her hand to him.

Smiling throughout, the Duke began to denude himself, throwing apples to several ladies of his acquaintance, and then to several that had caught his eye. Charlette felt one fall directly on her bosom and settle in the lace. While everyone applauded the hit, Charlette discreetly fished the apple out and bestowed it, ceremoniously, on the Duke of Wingshire, at her side. He held it as a relic, while Darrel, eyes flashing, said, "If the Royals can so presume on their privileges to sport with a lady's person, I'll be blown if I won't cut them out," and he swept her away from an astonished lord arriving for his promised dance.

So pleased was he by his maneuvers that he continued, "I'm reserving your first waltz at Almack's tomorrow night." And then, unable to keep the satisfaction out of his voice, added, "Would you believe *I've* been given a *voucher* by Lady Jersey. It seems all of Society has opened its arms to a lowly sea captain!"

"That is more than it has done for me," Charlette confessed frankly. "I have not been admitted to that sacred hall. And after the looks Lady Jersey gave me tonight, I never shall. But perhaps if I had had a few of my own sea tales, I might have wormed my way into her good graces."

A languid touch on his shoulder prevented the Captain from replying. It was the Duke of York himself, now more suitably cloaked, having made his appearance on the ballroom floor to more applause, and headed straight for Charlette.

"I claim Paris's reward for choosing the fairest Eves at the ball," he announced loudly, and was applauded again by all about.

As the two danced, his royal grace commented, "You're a dashed beauty, you know." At his request, she gave her name. "Ah, the lady with the ships and the stigma."

Charlette nearly missed a step. "What stigma, Your Highness?"

"Knew your mother, by Jove. She was a beauty, too, not quite in your style. More conventional, but her actions were dashed daring. Left the Earl to whistle for her. Played nip-shot . . . tipped him the double. Right thing, too. Fellow was a cold fish and close as wax. Not the way to treat a lady, I told him, when he came to me, kicking up rare dust. But the fellow had the right. She was his wife, after all."

So shocked was Charlette that she did not even hear the Duke's compliments as he turned her back to the waiting Duke of Wingshire hovering at her elbow.

When she and Percy were alone, she attempted, "The Duke spoke of my mother."

"These Royals! Ramshackle ways! Ain't a proper topic for a ball . . . or a young lady! Not the thing, I say, devil-a-bit."

And he was further shocked by her attempts to carry on the discussion.

"But, your grace, is everyone to know—but me!"

"Not to be thought of, Miss Varrick," the Duke advised kindly. "Jolly well a thing of the past. No need to dig it up. Bad ton— shockingly bad ton to do so."

"Your pardon," she said, crushed.

And that night Charlette, rather than reflecting on the flattering attentions from both Dukes, could only concentrate on Lady Jersey's disdain and the obvious cutting of her by several older ladies. The only true triumph of the evening had been Darrel's! Score another win for him!

Even those who were gracious, such as the Duke of York, were dropping such obvious hints that she could no longer close her eyes to her situation. She must be told a round story, with no expurgations to protect either her or her teller's modesty. She must know the reason for her ostracism!

When Society opened its doors to Darrel and not to her, things had reached a pretty pass!

It was then she recollected a meeting with Lady Austen at one of the very first Assemblies she had attended. That lady had been gracious enough to claim she was a friend of her mother's, and not seem horrified to own it. But at that time Charlette had not realized how special that attitude would be, and merely made a civil reply. All along she expected those closest to her to finally reveal the truth! But they had not. And Lady Austen now rose in Charlette's expectancy like a new moon. Tomorrow she should pay that lady a visit and speak to her with words that had no bark on them. If that lady had the slightest bit of kindness left for her mother, she should not allow her daughter to continue in this state of flux and confusion!

And if that lady as well failed her, by heavens, Charlette knew someone who had never had any scruples about speaking the truth to her. He had always done so. She had no wish to have to humble herself before Darrel, but without question, having been on the town, he would by now have discovered the full story. And he, at least, would not be deterred by thoughts of her swooning on the spot. He knew her better than that. Yes, by heavens, through fair means or foul, through Lady Austen or Captain Huntley, she should discover the truth about herself before the next ball!

Chapter Ten

❦ ━━━━━━━━━━━━━━━━━━━━━━━━━━ ❦

A note of some urgency sent to Lady Austen produced news of the most unsatisfactory nature. The Lady was visiting her relatives for a sennight at least, delaying the discovery of the secret of her mother's scandal.

With Lady Austen unavailable, that left Captain Huntley. Yet, Charlette hesitated. Considering his facile and universal success, she could not put herself in the humiliating position of requesting why *she* was deemed so inferior. In their continuing war of challenges, this would be an admission of surrender she could not countenance!

At that moment a sound erupted through her closed door that signaled a cacophonous reprieve. It was her cousin playing the piano. Francine! She was just the sort who would have wormed the full story out of someone! Or at least she might have some details that, added together with her own, would produce a round story. Thus, rather than covering her ears, Charlette rushed to the music room and seated herself. Never had anyone played with less expression and more volume. After awhile Charlette realized that Francine was playing the same piece over and over again, without pause. Indeed, she now realized, she'd always played that one particular piece. The third time the finish came round, Charlette was quick to nip in with applause before another beginning. It had some effect.

"I do not wish an audience," Francine interrupted herself long enough to quietly announce. And when Charlette did not instantly leave, too surprised by the pallid girl showing such decided feelings on anything, Francine was even more emphatic, "I detest being listened to. People sitting there hoping for my hitting a wrong note are always disappointed. I never miss. You need no longer remain for that."

"But, my dear cousin, you mistake me. I sat here merely to admire."

The young girl crashed a chord loudly and turned from her bench to glare at the islander. "Do not attempt to gull me. There is as little truth in that as there is in you. Possibly you have taken in my impressionable father and mother, but I never allow myself to be so overtaken by one of your sort. Not all your money or fashionable clothes can quite conceal your dreadful . . . commonness."

"I am not common. In any sense," Charlette said softly, still attempting to recover from the shock of not only hearing Francine speak, but doing so with such distaste.

"You are! You are!" Francine spoke up, like a hiccup of hatred. "You are dreadfully low. A sea wharf rat who has snuck its way into an aristocrat's home, and spread your commonness to us all. Lady Marjory, as my closest friend, has revealed her feelings to me about you—which verify my own. She has appealed to me to arrange for your return to your island. But what can one do if you are so shockingly unaware? It is a sleeveless effort. A true lady, sensing her lack of welcome, would instantly depart."

In great perplexity Charlette responded, "What have I actually done to you? I am your cousin. We have the tie of blood."

"That is my shame . . . I wish no tie with you!" Francine cried out, and her pale face had such a flush of color she never looked more alive.

"Because of my mother? I understand, rather than being a commoner, she was of higher social level than your mother."

"That is not so! Your mother must have been a common jade. A Cyprian ladybird—why else would you be so whispered about! Even my own mother would not speak to me about her, unable to soil her lips!"

"Lady Austen has told me that she was my mother's bosom friend, and I do not believe anyone can be of more unquestionable lineage than that lady!"

"I don't care! It shall probably turn out that your mother was a Princess, for you have such a fantastic way of making things turn your way! I hope she was a ladybird, but even if she were not, you are *somehow* in disgrace, and have spread that disgrace to us. And I wish you to leave, if not from my home, at least from my music room!"

"You are, I collect, rather indifferent to my charms. I regret it prodigiously. We might have been friends. But your only accepting friends exactly like yourself leads to a commonness, indeed, in your thinking and in your music selection."

And with that, Charlette rose, made a half-curtsey and left the room.

That evening when Francine and Lady Bridingsley were leaving for Almack's, the look of pure joy on Francine's face could not be denied. Lady Bridingsley did not improve matters by commiserating on Charlette's being left behind. And then, next day, Lady Bridingsley had further cause to commiserate. Lady Jersey had openly pronounced Miss Varrick as *unacceptable*, and other hostesses were following her lead. This was further demonstrated in the next few days by an immediate diminution in Charlette's invitations. Never had Almack's loomed as so important in her mind. And when Lady Marjory and Francine began discussing it before her, Charlette had too much pride to quit the room. And then, she had too much interest in their next topic. It was Captain Huntley's eyes. Apparently the ladies felt his hypnotic grey eyes had a way of fixing themselves on a lady, as if he could see through her outer apparel and glimpse the outlines of her chemise!

To that, Charlette was simply unable not to reply. "Captain Huntley has not the slightest interest in your apparel, whether of the outer or inner variety, so neither of you need fall into such dissolute fantasies!"

" 'Tis not a fantasy if the gentleman is enamored of me," Lady Marjory said confidently. "I have more proof of his feelings than a look. He has kissed me several times, and quite, quite passionately."

"On the hand, I expect," Charlette said with a grin.

"On the hand . . . as well."

"And where else?"

"On my lips. Last night on the terrace of our home, when I asked him to bring my wrap, he wrapped it and his arms around me, and kissed me good-night. I felt it down to the toes of my slippers. I need hardly say what that means . . . but I am expecting an offer before he returns to his ships."

Fully routed, Charlette merely nodded and departed. Obviously, her ladyship had become closer to the Captain than she.

It then became clear to Charlette that she was definitely in the suds. Just before the London Prize Ball, she had been a sufficient success to have high hopes. And now all had cartwheeled. The Duke of Wingshire had noticeably cooled. He continued to attend

Almack's with his sister and the Captain; and those three visited the zoo yesterday, while she had received no request to accompany them. The few invitations arriving were not worthy of reply. One was for a rout being given by a lady not quite in fashion, and would consequently not be widely attended. The other was from Mr. Plowton, a gazetted fortune hunter, and not worthy of even a reply.

What had made this astonishing reversal, she suddenly grasped, was the arrival and influence of Captain Huntley. Her non-admittance to Almack's had not been of prime concern to others before Lady Jersey made it her duty to alert society of her polluting presence, and who had influenced Lady Jersey, if not Captain Huntley? Even more vexing, who also had not been gracious enough to call on his old friend or even leave his card? If he had a card!

At that point Charlette picked up Sir Smithers Wilcox's card; it was always there. He did not falter in his devotion. In reward, on the morrow Charlette accepted his invitation to a poetry reading just outside London. After she had the pleasure of giving the young poet her most heartfelt praises, they fell into a discussion of her island. She remarked that at Wight there was a glory of flowers even in the winter months, and he was all eagerness to see it—with her. She described her feelings about London and its tameness. Even the birds made neat little sounds, not the ragged wild squaw of the gulls as they swung their way over the sea. And the feelings here in town were confined and corseted—little gestures with snuffboxes in hand. A quizzing-glass to sight a stranger, instead of a spyglass to scan a horizon, while she longed for full, open views from cliff heights.

And he stared at her with wild, wild eyes, and told her that there were birds here and people who had emotions that would wipe out an ocean with their scope, that if she had never heard a nightingale here singing in the dark, calling out its full heart to its mate, she had not heard true passion! And she wished she could walk with him in his garden at night, and he wished he could walk with her on her island.

Considerably refreshed by the encounter, she was in high jig upon returning to Lady Bridingsley's house. At the entrance she paused, for Mr. Buckston and Lady Bridingsley were at the doorway of the drawing room. Her ladyship was thanking him for the honor of stopping for tea and apologizing once more for Francine's absence. Apparently she had been apologizing throughout the repast and continued to do so—long enough for Charlette to duck into the conservatory, and thus not have to greet either one. Within the indoor green world, she was just making friends with a philodendron when she observed Mr. Buckston ducking in after her. It was fortunate, he claimed, his eyes had caught a glimpse of her, lest she miss the opportunity of testing his new tea; happily he had a sprig on his person and would appreciate if she would sniff it. As he was blocking her exit, Charlette could do no less than incline her head toward the offered leaf, while he leaned his own close as well. In this compromising position did Francine come upon them. Having returned in speed from her visit to Lady Marjory's, upon receiving a hurried note from her mother, she had been reassured by the butler that her visitor had not departed but was refreshing himself in the conservatory. The sight in there of Charlette and Mr. Buckston head-to-head was the last straw for Francine, and she burst out: "How dare you! He came to see me! You low, common *jade!*"

Lady Bridingsley, hearing the commotion, was quick to appear and smooth the situation. Explanations of the innocence of the moment were made, and accepted, but believed only by the participants.

While Charlette was quickly changing to take Froth for his constitutional, Lady Bridingsley stopped in her room for further smoothing. Francine's insult was inadvertent, due to surprise of the sighting, and, indeed, Charlette herself was somewhat to blame for allowing their being private in such a private place.

Charlette's explanation of being followed Lady Bridingsley was willing to allow, attributing Mr. Buckston's actions to his disappointment in not seeing Francine, and Charlette's own natural attractions. "You should not waste that beauty, the only benefit you derived from your mother," she warned with some concern. "For the Season is fast coming to a close and back on that island you shall be forced to settle for a sailor."

At her ladyship's departure, Miss Varrick took stock. Here she was, a girl who loved a challenge; therefore, she would not sink into a decline simply because her incursions into Society had struck a reef. If one person, Lady Jersey, could have such a noticeable effect on her position, perhaps another person could reverse her dictum. Charlette ran through the lords and ladies of her acquaintance and found none that answered. Lady Sefton, another patroness, was known to be kind, and Charlette rounded on herself for not having attempted friendship with her while she

was still being received. Only Lady Bridingsley and the Duke of
Wingshire remained. Somehow she must persuade the former to
give a party to reestablish her, and the latter must be her escort.
Else she would be returning to Wight a failure, while Captain
Huntley, her old competitor, had breezed through the London test,
leaving her sputtering ashore!

Those were her thoughts while leaving the house to take Froth
for his usual late afternoon romp, accompanied by a footman at
her aunt's orders. As she came down the stairs, Captain Huntley
was coming up, and she almost expected him to cut her as well,
so topsy-turvy had her world become. He did worse.

"I was about to call on you," he said seriously. "I have
something to tell you before you hear it from others."

Charlette wished not to hear it, but she was a game girl, full of
pluck, who had climbed with him the highest chalk cliffs and
never faltered, nor would she now.

"I shall be delighted to hear whatever you have to say," she said
grimly, and paused to listen.

Chapter Eleven

ERE Captain Huntley would communicate more, he allowed, it would be more private if they waited to reach Regent's Park. Indeed, Lady Bridingsley always felt the overlook from her town house onto the park was one of its principal attractions. The park had the additional benefit, for gentlemen callers, of private walks. And Captain Huntley was quick to find one and direct the flunkey to frolic with Froth while the two islanders sat upon a stone bench farther apace.

"You have something of significance to impart to me?" Charlette asked politely, as if it could not possibly be a major matter to her.

With the benefit of the setting sun, she could not cease subjecting him to a lengthy perusal. He had significantly altered. Although his dark hair remained long and in a bit of disorder from the wind, which indicated he had not succumbed to the practice of applying Russian oil to pomade his locks, yet the rest of him had definitely taken on a touch of town bronze. The driving coat, with its fashionable sixteen shoulder-capes over his own broad shoulders, gave him a dash that could not but attract several ladies with abigails in attendance. Still, Darrel had not succumbed to the enormous cravat nor the high points on his shirt collar. The almost open-throated shirt look, tied casually with a bit of black ribbon, had become his signature; and little did he realize that some of the younger men were already rebelling against the tiresome and time-consuming practice of arranging foot-high cravats and beginning to wear what they called *The Captain's Ropes*.

Merely planning for an unnoticed walk, Charlette had not done her best in outfitting herself, and she appeared with her hair simply arranged and in an ordinary sprig muslin dress. Indeed, she seemed closer to the young girl Darrel recollected, which added an ease to their communication. Unconsciously, he fell back into his old sharing of their exploits, certain the other would be pleased.

"I have become quite the vogue," he said laughing, expecting her to laugh with him.

But she did not. She merely said, "Have you?" with a matter-of-fact indifference that was not the slightest in Charle's style. It rankled more that she could look so much like his Charle and sound so unlike her.

"Raaaaather," he said, imitating the bored swells of her Society. "Actually, one does not know where to turn to avoid them, what? Stab me, there's always a lady about, enthralled by my wicked sea tales." Throwing his head back and laughing at himself, he continued in his own voice, "It's true enough. Last night at Almack's I was followed by droves of them. I know Miss Varrick shall not credit it, but my tale of the draped Arab girl has become quite a favorite. There have been some significant additions since you heard it—notably a description of the booty discovered in the Arab's tent. Nothing makes Society salivate, I've found, as does a full description of booty. And what I found in that tent, my girl, was sacks and sacks of gold, and sacks and sacks of silver, and spices, and chests of Indian muslin, and Persian shawls and armlets and anklets and turtles and . . ."

"Turtles!"

"A delicacy," he inserted.

"Were they running away from you?" she pressed, falling into his enjoyment.

"One does not use the word 'running' when referring to the tortoise class—rather they were circling aimlessly at a moderate trot."

"And you . . . circled aimlessly with them, and captured them, holding turtles and Persian shawls and armlets and spices in all. Quite a remarkable arm span."

"I have been known to be able to hold several women in my arms at once," he inserted helpfully. "The latter is mentioned not to puff myself off, but in a purely explanatory sense."

"Gammon," Charle huffed. "You're saying that to arouse a romantic image of yourself, as you continually do to your coteries of young girls. These ton ladies see sailors as romantic because of their travels about, while the little widgeons live restricted lives of enclosed rooms with an occasional outing in a park!"

Laughing fully at that, Darrel remarked, "I protest. Am I the only traveler they have had the opportunity of meeting? From my many nights with the Duke, I have become quite familiar with every aspect of his grace's several Grand Tours. And I expect other gentlemen have similar escapades to relate to these ninnies. Which puts rather a sizable hole in your theory, my girl."

Charlette resented his brushing aside her arguments, having become accustomed to the polite manners and rapt attention of her escorts; she twirled her white parasol, and opened it to shade her face from the sudden heat that was not actually due to the sun but to his effrontery.

"I expect you wish me to account for your effect on the ladies by making simpering little comments on your appearance."

"That would be delightful, although, I own, unexpected. I hold my breath in anticipation."

"You shall have to keep holding it then until you turn quite, quite blue."

"You recollect I could hold my breath quite a long time when we dove under the waves. You had to keep bobbing up, like a gull on the surface, for gulps of air, but I could stay down till I found every shell we were looking for."

"It's really amazing how you remember only the events where you shone and I faltered!"

"That is how it usually was, actually," he said, attempting to restrain himself from laughing aloud at her chagrin.

"Indeed!" she exclaimed, rising and snapping shut her umbrella. "And when you were struck by that jellyfish on your arm, and you made such a fuss, who was it who sucked the poison out *with my own lips*, and made you a cool mudpack?" She faced him in fury, her lips that had sucked the pain out of his bite closer to him than ever, backing him up with her old determination not to be seen as less of an adventurer than he.

"I had forgot that . . . delightful encounter," he whispered, and touched her lips gently. "Were you to do it again, I should not so lightly now ignore your sacrifice."

She stepped back, remembering herself, and that a lady always kept her distance. In fact, she quickly returned to her seat and placed both her reticule and parasol between them. "I believe it most incumbent upon me, Captain, to explain why you are having a *temporary* success with the ladies, lest you allow it to go to your head, which I perceive has already swelled to quite a significant size. For several years there has been a decided fashion sweeping the ton for reading the works of Lord Byron, whose heroes are all adventurers. However, his wife's unmasking him in her suit for separation as a person of the most shocking morals shall in all probability reduce that influence. Nevertheless, you are benefiting from seeming to fit somewhat in that mold of a world-weary Childe Harold, and, of course, your own tales of pure gammon have assisted you in that presentation of the heroic as well. You need only add an occasional moment of falling into a brown study, suggesting you are recollecting the darkest of deeds, and, faith, you shall be totally irresistible!"

"By Jove, it is most considerate of you to be so helpful in my conquests. A 'brown study,' did you say? Like this?" And placing his elbow on his knee and resting his chin on his hand, he looked intently at her.

She choked back a laugh and objected, "But you are not supposed to be looking *at* someone. Look into the distance, so that one may imagine you are recollecting moments of . . . well, shocking depravity!"

He did as she recommended. And she, becoming Charle again, applauded. "That is it! Perhaps a small groan?"

Throwing back his head and laughing with her, he exclaimed, "Would not they then assume I suffer from some more physical sailor's complaint—that would not be romantic in the slightest. Like Jem's lumbago?"

"I shall not reveal your secret lumbago," she promised.

"I shall keep your secrets as well," he swore, taking her by the hand.

She remembered herself again, and stood away from him. "I have no secrets."

He stared at her a moment, considering. Then he plunged in, as was his want. "It is about *your* secrets that I wish to speak to you."

Charlette turned, understanding immediately, and she colored. "You have learned about my mother?"

"I knew a bit from home and my own father, but here it is told everywhere!"

"*Except to me*! No one shall tell me! Not my father, not my aunt, not Lord Bridingsley. They all just hint and hint and cut me dead! I'll be slap-dashed if I can continue being so much in the dark. Good God, what could my poor dead mother have done that makes *me* such a threat?"

He was eyeing her with compassion. "Blast 'em, I thought they were letting you twist in the breeze. Lady Marjory implied it was rather loose of you to even wish to know. I said I thought it was rather natural. We nearly came to cuffs over that, till his grace came down on his sister's side, saying no lady would wish to hear the details of anything of *that* nature. But, since I know you're not quite the lady you pretend, not one through and through, I thought . . ."

"What do you mean by that! How have I not been a lady!" Charlette gasped, becoming sidetracked.

"You are too much a person . . . you tend to laugh when something is amusing rather than when the person who says it is exalted . . . and you still have natural feelings rather than prim posturings!"

"Oh." She paused and then with a twinkle agreed that if that was his criteria she would not be overly offended by failing to live up to it. And then, they fully exchanged smiles, almost holding out their hands to each other. In this new confiding sensation, Charlette recollected what he was going to tell her, and she looked unswervingly at him, her deep-blue eyes wide with hope and suspense as she whispered, "Tell me."

"The devil. If anyone has to tell you I'd rather it be me. 'Cause I know you can take it. You never shirked from anything. You're a game girl—pluck to the backbone."

"You are alarming me. Without the encomiums, just tell me."

"Your mother was a lady, Charle," he began. "She was the daughter of the Viscount Belton, born to the Viscount and his lady when both were at an advanced age. At sixteen, she was rushed to have her Season. Ignoring the many requests for her hand, the Viscount married her to the Earl of Hawton—an old friend, and I use the word "old" in both meanings. She became the Countess of Hawton for five difficult years, during which the Earl, because of her beauty and his jealousy, kept her away from all society. Almost confined."

Coming to the more difficult part, he paused and took her hand in his. "Everyone knew he was a harsh man, of uncertain temper and nip-cheese ways, and he lived up to his reputation. No visitors and no visits were allowed her. Not surprisingly, her health failed. The Isle of Wight was chosen for her recovery. There, she met your father, and they fell in love. That restored her health. The Earl wisked his Countess back to the mainland, but your father followed and returned her to Wight. And they lived together as man and wife. Yet the Earl retaliated by choosing the most humiliating grounds possible to sue her for separation. His victory assured your mother was disgraced, yet not free to marry. To the ton, she was living in sin. Not till the Earl's death, which occurred shortly after you were born, were your parents wed. And even then, the Earl's family would not relent; they continued to hound your mother, spreading false rumors about her death, claiming she was unbalanced and had taken her life by jumping into the sea! Talk about pure gammon! That last, I can and *have* denied, for the truth is known on the island."

Having said it all, he was hoping for some sign from Charle, but she was so still, almost not breathing. He continued to hold both her hands now in a sustaining grip, squeezing harder, realizing she needed more time to compose herself, and proceeded. "The good news about the Earl's death was that he died beating an insolent stable hand, and thus was punished for his own cruelty. Yet, even that revelation did not mitigate your mother's affront to society, for she had deserted a nobleman, and there is no acceptable excuse for insulting *one of them*! Blast their sanctimonious, self-serving souls! I know what it's like to be beaten. I was flogged till my backbone was laid bare at the orders of an English gentleman who did not know anything about the sea and sought to use violence to save his face and his inexperience. I left His Majesty's navy and was happy for it. And I've lived to be highly gratified by my escape, as she must have been for hers."

Charlette continued clasping his hands with all her might, still keeping her head lowered as it had been throughout his speaking. And when she lifted it in a few moments, her face was soaked with her tears, as if a salt sea spray had hit her fully.

And he held her then, tightly in his arms, attempting to hug away her pain. To give her a sense of safety and comfort that would last only for a moment but might be remembered as being offered with all his heart.

Roberts, the footman, who had been with Lady Bridingsley's establishment for a good many years, felt it incumbent upon him to interrupt at this point. A tête-à-tête alone in the park he could close his peepers at, but this cuddling in full view was doing it too brown; any more and he'd have to report back to her ladyship, unless he were able to stop it. An inspiration popped out of his idea-pot, and instantly he began to yell, "Get off me, you crazy cat!"

Thus addressed, and in so loud a tone, Froth immediately took exception and went in a dash for his mistress.

The Captain and Miss Varrick broke apart, both moving to pick him up. Darrel had him in his arms first, and in his Captain's voice was demanding to know what the devil the footman meant by attacking this cat. The footman explained the cat had nipped him, upon which he had merely expressed his human resentment. Charlette was outraged, taking Froth from the Captain and petting him until he ceased quivering.

"Froth is a perfect gentleman," she insisted in her lady's voice. "I have never known him to forget himself and bite without *cause*."

Roberts cowered, and both gentleman and lady began walking out of the park, while the footman, following respectfully in the rear, smiled at the success of his ploy.

"I need some time to adjust to this tale," Charlette said at last, coming back to their conversation when interrupted.

"You need only sail it out," Darrel urged. "Like a storm, you must come at it, and its challenge. Lay your ship before the wind and you shall laugh all away."

She grinned. "Aye, Captain, I have been attempting to do so since my first sail into Society. Heavens! Now I recollect, you shall think me all about in my head, but speaking of laughing in the face of a storm, I saw you do so just before coming to London. I went down to our cove one night and walked into the water, and saw you laughing in the face of the storm . . . and you did not lose your ship."

She had whispered the last, but he had his head bent down so low, and was so accustomed to hearing her every word, that he not only heard but shuddered. "And you were wearing a blue cloak with a hood."

They stopped walking and looked at each other. "I saw you."

"I saw you."

They had been speaking in unison, and then both shook their heads, unable to explain it either to themselves or each other. But it was accepted.

They walked a ways in a haze of emotion, and then Charlette, recollecting, said, "But is *that* what you wished to communicate to me today? To tell me of my mother?"

"That was one of the things. Since all else were allowing you to sail blindfolded . . . that is, I was there at Almack's and you were ruled as unacceptable. And all the talk! It was beastly. I felt so blasted sorry for you!"

"Sorry for *me*!" Charlette echoed, in some dudgeon. She was vexed to the point of almost being incapable of retorting. Better if he had laughed at her, snubbed her, but to pity her! Recovering her composure, she continued, "You need not concern yourself about my position in Society, Captain. My inadmissibility to Almack's is purely temporary. With so many gentlemen making offers to me, I shall be well established in a trice. It needs merely my choosing one to accept, and all Society shall be at my feet!"

"Delighted to hear that. I made the mistake of thinking you needed my assistance, as of old. Obviously, I was mistaken!"

They both walked on in a huff. At last, the Captain spoke again. "As an old friend, I hope you shall be equally as delighted to hear that I, too, am considering being a tenant for life . . . eh, matrimony."

"That is your news!"

"That . . . is it," he snapped, and both of them were fiercely angry, when a moment before they were closely caring. A sudden squall had overtaken them, and they both headed for home. Charlette walked at a fast clip, and he strode easily beside her. The footman was running to keep apace.

"Lady Marjory has finally sent out the proper lure, I expect. Shall we be hearing the announcement?"

"I am much in demand. I need not settle for Lady Marjory. She is in the running, of course," Captain Huntley allowed. "But, of late, I have become the object of Viscountess Frances's attentions, as well. She writes me perfumed notes of great length . . . and passion. Then there is that wealthy daughter of Lord Broxdale. She has already assured me I need only make a formal offer for her hand and it shall be given me, along with anything else I could possibly wish for!"

"Indeed! Pity there are not several of you. You need only put yourself up at auction and the kingdom would be yours!"

The Captain smiled lazily. "I expect it would—if we had a Queen."

"You are insufferable," Charlette exclaimed, and without responding to his bow, she walked up the stairs and into her aunt's house.

Not wishing to be impolite and not say good-bye, Froth meowed at the Captain causing Charlette, for the first time in her life, to speak harshly to him. "You idiotic, indiscriminating creature. Don't you know when to cut line!"

And as the door closed behind her, she heard the Captain's hearty laugh.

Chapter Twelve

LADY Bridingsley, when pressed, refused to host a party to assist her niece, but went so far as inviting the Duke for a private tea. Her eyes, if not her actual words, warned that Charlette was running out of opportunities.

Fully alive to the possibilities of a tête-à-tête tea, Charlette chose her most fetching afternoon outfit: a peach muslin with transparent long sleeves descending from short puff sleeves, with a similar intriguing gauze insert above the bodice advancing up to her throat. She placed peach flowers in her hair and felt she had gone her length; if the Duke was not pleased with her appearance, she could do no more. But her aunt, falling into the spirit of the event, furthered Charlette's cause by developing a discomfort in her templer region—the excuse for allowing the two to be alone.

Not aware of Charlette's hopes and Lady Bridingsley's objective, the Duke brought along his sister, who immediately requested the presence of Francine as well. Thus, the duet tea threatened to turn into a quarreling quartet.

In keeping with the motif, a two-tiered cake dominated Lady Bridingsley's ordered spread of cucumber sandwiches, bread and butter, muffins, as well as strawberries and clotted cream as the removes. The Duke was too occupied with eating to engage in conversation, not that Francine and Lady Marjory needed anyone else to take the lead. The topic was their prodigious delight at a special Almack's event: a Costume Ball to be hosted by Lady Jersey herself. Nothing could be more select—only the very choice people would be in attendance. Thus, there would be no fear of *close* proximity with *lowly* connections.

Charlette moved her chair away a pace, as if she, too, feared their proximity, and grinning, picked up a cucumber sandwich and munched on it.

The ladies parried by discussing their costumes for the ball. That caught the Duke's attention, and he, unaware of what was going on between the ladies, merely put in, "Lancelot."

"Your grace?" Charlette asked.

"Me costume. If Miss Varrick shall be my Guinevere."

The ladies could not believe their fortune. His grace had given them the very opportunity they had been seeking, making it unnecessary to continue with indirect comments. They could say what they wished openly. Both spoke at once, informing the Duke that Miss Varrick would *not* be attending the Costume Ball, since it was an *Almack's* affair to which she had not been given a voucher. Attempting to save the moment, the Duke made it worse by indicating that Miss Varrick should scarcely be missing anything, for Almack dances were shockingly dull affairs.

Instantly, Lady Marjory objected to that description—she had enjoyed herself excessively, especially listening to the Captain's sea tales. "No one could find a space around us," her ladyship continued placidly. "We were quite the cynosure."

That set up his grace's bristles. "Dashed fellow had the ladies all thrown into quakes. Talked about sailing. Sea captain—what did they expect? Daresay his stories will wear thin. How many times can the blighter rescue the same dashed lady in veils?"

"I wrote it all down in my diary," Francine exclaimed. "The moment I entered my sitting room, I rushed to my diary and wrote above ten pages on his adventure, and an additional five on his particular remarks to myself."

"Five pages!" Lady Marjory exclaimed. "How is that possible? I am certain he did not exchange above a few commonplaces with you! His attentions, when not fully occupied with myself, were general in nature."

Of a sudden Lady Marjory and Francine were eyeing each other with distaste.

"If you care to see a verification of his remarks, I need only summon the footman to bring my diary."

Despite her ladyship not seeing the least necessity for that, Francine did so. With the two ladies coming to cuffs, Charlette finally began to enjoy her tea, picking up a muffin. The Duke took a fourth piece of cake, topped with marmalade.

The moment the footman returned with said diary, Francine quickly found the correct entry and read aloud, with this preamble. "These are the remarks either addressed to me or of me. He said, and I quote, 'The lady was about the diminutive height of Miss Farweather. Most of the dear ladies of the east have that delicacy of form. And are similarly soft-spoken.' Unquote. That occurred upon the occasion of his being asked to describe the veiled lady. Subsequently, he looked me most deliberately in the eye and said, 'Miss Farweather seems to have fallen into a doze—I regret if my stories have had that effect. Remind me to include my more eye-opening tales should we find ourselves in closer proximity.' I replied that I found his tales quite unexceptionable—and he replied, 'As are you.' Must I repeat that? He implied that I was myself 'quite unexceptionable.' "

"Those seem to me to be of the most tepid compliments," Lady Marjory judged, unimpressed. "One might conclude that when he said 'Pardon me, my dear lady' to Mrs. Brakleton, that he was using endearments to that ancient! I hesitate to curb your pretensions, Francine, but you have refined too much on mere civilities."

"And I dislike excessively to disturb your rationale, Marjory, but I have but read you the preamble—there are *five more pages* which describe his actions when he and I were alone in the conservatory of this very domicile. And I blush to admit that if Mama were to read those fiery pages, she should have something to say about protecting my honor." Francine had panted while disclosing the latter, and Lady Marjory eyed her with such disbelief and disfavor that both Charlette and the Duke forgot to swallow for a brief moment, and then did so, almost in unison.

"You are falsifying my Captain's behavior. Dare you imply he has made advances to *you!* To my certain knowledge he ne'er goes beyond the line of propriety with any lady of worth. Unless she communicated a willingness to be so . . . . mishandled."

"I shall leave my diary about, and whoever doubts me has my permission to peruse it—at length."

And with a smugness that was positively unendurable, she rose and opened the diary to a further page, perused it raptly for a brief moment, colored in a maiden's blush, sighed and then pointedly left the volume open at that particular page—whereupon, humming a bit, she resumed her place at the tea table.

The Duke did not stir to avail himself of that reading. Invited to do so by the young lady, he lifted his quizzing-glass to observe her, and then responded that it was none of his business what the fellow said, that he had heard enough from him without having to read more and finally, that there was nothing one disliked more than encores of opinions one wished one had not heard the first time!

Next, Francine looked pointedly at Charlette, but she too declined.

It was Lady Marjory's turn, but the Duke, to deflect the offer, addressed Charlette. "Ain't got a diary, I hope, Miss Varrick?"

"I remember what is said to me without having to preserve it for posterity."

"By Jove, but what if I oped my mouth and out popped 'your glowing eyes could light a ballroom.'"

"That should make a most delightful entry, your grace," Charlette laughed. "And would almost make me regret not keeping a diary, after all."

"By Jove, would it? And it just come to me. Ain't spread it around to every young lady in my way."

"Then it is, therefore, doubly appreciated."

While this exchange was occurring, Lady Marjory decided she needed a constitutional, and rose to walk about the room, stopping by chance, directly before the diary. The displayed page tempted, and she succumbed.

"No! Shocking! Sham! Total prevarication! The grossest Banbury story," she exclaimed, returning to the table where she fanned herself with such deadly accuracy it cooled the entire assemblage. Nor could she stay seated. "We are leaving, Percival."

"Righto, old thing. We'll be toddling off. Ladies." He made his most elaborate bow to Charlette and a slight one to Francine.

At the door's closing, Charlette was retiring when Francine called after her, "You may take the diary along. It also contains my full opinion on your visit, and the remarks of several ladies and gentlemen spoken about you, as you passed out of earshot."

"Most obliging. Somehow I'll force myself to resist that treat. Best peruse the volume yourself to keep your stories in order. If you have difficulty, I shall send Froth to you, he is an expert in *whiskers*."

Refusing to believe her cousin could totally resist peeking, Francine left the diary open on the table in the hopes Charlette would return.

An hour hence, a scream of great magnitude filled the house and had both Francine and Charlette rushing to the source. Lord

Bridingsley, just entering and giving his stick and top hat to the butler, immediately took them back and turned to leave.

The source of the outcry, Lady Bridingsley, now called out, "Cecil!" sensing that her husband had not yet closed the door. He paused in ambivalent consideration on the doorstep. "I know you are there, and you might as well face this now, or I shall be forced to send a footman with a very explicit message to your club."

"Oh, certainly, my dear," he mumbled, and entered to find his wife pointing to the open diary. She had come down to catch her husband before he changed and left for his all-night gambling at his club, and spotting the open diary, had read enough to give her serious palpitations.

"I shall have your father call on this . . . sailor before the week is out." And she handed him the diary.

"Blast it. Don't care to read that drivel. I've had the girl on my hands for over twenty years without troubling to discover what she thinks. See no reason to do so now, when we're getting her off our hands!"

But Lady Bridingsley refused to allow him to fob off—she forced the offending passages under his nose. He groaned. "Put his hand where!" he ejaculated.

"You must call on him and ask his intentions."

"I believe I am not needed here," Charlette said, and attempted to leave.

"Where are you going, Charlette?" Lady Bridingsley exclaimed. "It is through your connection that we have this bounder in our midst. You surely have the responsibility of telling us his circumstance, and whether we are to believe his intentions are honorable."

"I can scarcely discuss the honor of his intentions, since I do not believe he has any intentions at all as regards to Francine. Nor do I suggest that Lord Bridingsley embarrass himself by visiting the Captain, who has higher aspirations than Miss Farweather. Lady Marjory has also described his attentions most particularly. Then there is Viscountess Frances. In any case, the Captain's attentions or intentions are irrelevant, since Francine's diary is false. Indeed, I wonder how either of you can swallow such plumpers."

"Why plumpers?" Lord Bridingsley asked, amused. "If you tell us that this cad has been amusing himself at the well of all of our young ladies' innocence? I would have wished for someone of more substance, but what ho! And if, while not in earnest, he has given her an intolerable affront, I should dash well call him out!"

At that serious conclusion, Charlette ceased being amused, understanding, of a sudden, that a code might have been breached with which she and Darrel were not conversant and that might lead to some disaster. Francine was demurely keeping her eyes down, but occasionally her blue eyes lifted, showing a flash of satisfaction.

"I declare," Charlette exclaimed, "Francine has revealed a surprising tendency to make herself the main attention, perhaps because she has been so often overlooked. And most particularly overlooked by Captain Huntley."

"My daughter is a lady," his lordship responded with his full dignity. The friendliness that had for so long existed between Charlette and himself was no longer taken into account where the question of his name, and an affront to it, was concerned.

"Yes," Lady Bridingsley agreed. "And that man is naught but a sailor. If one were to take anyone's word, it should certainly be that of a lady."

"But when did this advance on her person occur? Is that too much to ask?"

Lady Bridingsley consulted the diary, as if it were the Magna Carta. "It occurred . . . on the fifteenth—the day Mr. Buckston surprised us by stopping in for tea, if I recollect correctly. Shortly after Mr. Buckston departed, the Captain arrived and was received in the conservatory. Gracious, my own home!"

"Most amazing. The Captain was escorting Froth and me on a walk in Regent's Park at the same time. Naturally, I was accompanied by your own footman, Roberts, who can testify, if needs be."

"Possibly I mistook the date," Lady Bridingsley said, and referred again to the hallowed pages. "No, it says here clearly—on the day Mr. Buckston visited. You must be mistaken as to your outing with the Captain."

"I am not. However, you need hardly take just my word against such an irrefutable written document as your daughter's fantasies. Have Roberts brought here. And you shall know the truth right enough."

At that, his lordship made a sweeping gesture and spoke up in a, for him, raised tone: "I certainly do not intend to make such a cake of myself . . . nor allow my daughter's name to be so publicly bandied about. I suggest we drop this matter right where it is, and see to it that Francine is not allowed in that man's company, since he does not seem to be able to withstand the . . . temptation of her."

At that conclusion, Francine's eyes glowed. Lord Bridingsley bowed to his ladies and left the house for his club. Francine, picking up her diary with great tenderness, and casting a look of triumph at Charlette, left the room.

"I expect it shall be rather difficult for you to continue remaining here," Lady Bridingsley said somberly, "after doubting my daughter's word. And, indeed, after bringing with you such questionable associates. You are not invited to Almack's, despite all I have done in that respect. To all other balls and assemblies, I have presented you. It is no longer necessary for you to remain."

Not having been brought up in Society, Charlette did not recognize the closing of the elite whenever seriously threatened. The drawbridge went up, and all outsiders were no longer received. Still attempting to make a connection through logic, Charlette exclaimed, "You know she is lying. She resented that Mr. Buckston followed me into the conservatory, and attempted to retaliate with this . . . this fustian. Even making the interlude occur in the conservatory, as well. Heavens, do you seriously believe that Darrel, a man of some scope, could be interested in such a mealymouthed ninny!"

"He is a man of ambition, as well. I saw him maneuvering amongst the young ladies last night. He shall, I believe, marry only to oblige himself, and set himself up in Society. He has Lady Marjory, but yet he dallies and looks for both beauty as well as position. Francine has both. Ah, you were not there—he was shamelessly flirting with her, possibly because he sensed her prodigious attraction to him. Not many women could be immune to his casting out his lures. Very possibly I myself, in my youth, should have been overset, although I should have realized he was an opportunist, and protected myself. Francine is too much of an innocent to do so."

"Innocent! But, but, you have not been attending! She is lying. He could not have possibly made an assault on her person that afternoon. He was with me!"

"I am aware of that. Roberts had reported your outing with the Captain."

Aghast, Charlette cried, "Then you knew Francine's diary was a lie upon first reading it!"

"The facts were not accurate. But if she felt that she wished the man to do what she describes he did, it proves to me how much he has disorganized her senses. He is a danger. Like that dissolute poet, Byron, that had Caroline Lamb running after him dressed as his page, and slashing herself in the most indecorous scenes because of his disregard. Francine is like Caroline—a girl who remains submissive and quiet, and then, of a sudden, breaks loose into a wildness that disgraces her entire family. And we have had enough of *disgrace*," she added pointedly. Silencing Charlette's protests by continuing in a louder voice, "Your presence here has been disturbing to her. It has been disturbing to me, as well. I, for awhile, forgot myself and my duty to my own daughter and enjoyed your frolics, especially when it seemed as if you were going to make a noticeable triumph in capturing the Duke from his sister. But now I can no longer while my time away with you, my dear child—my own daughter's needs come first. You must make it your business to arrange for your return to your father's house as soon as possible."

And not allowing Charlette to respond, she walked out of the room.

If Charlette ever needed to live up to her concept of herself as a young woman of pluck, it was then. And determinedly she did so, even laughing at the realization that Francine had fulfilled her promise of getting rid of her, after all! There was more strength to this girl than anyone had assumed.

Her first essential duty was to write to her father and inform him of her having fallen shockingly low of his expectations. But she could not do so! The ink dried on the quill several times before she could do more than conclude the salutation. "Dearest Father" seemed such a moving thought, she could not quite move on. Roberts appeared with a note, and she welcomed the distraction, and then upon opening it welcomed the contents! A towline to a lady-at-sea, indeed.

It was from Lady Austen, her mother's onetime friend. She had returned from her visit to find Charlette's letter, and after some investigation on her own was appalled at the treatment being accorded to her own dear Lydia's daughter. Her immediate actions more than made up for her previous tardiness. Not only had she cajoled Princess Esterhazy, who also knew her mother, and who was a patroness of Almack's, to secure the voucher for Charlette's entrance, but she even discussed the problem with Lady Jersey. Actually, Lady Austen knew exactly how to manipulate that rather vain lady, using a few judicious recollections of Lady Jersey's having at one time almost been ostracized herself as the Regent's mistress, proving, Lady Austen claimed, that Lady Jersey well knew what it meant to throw all to the winds for love! Had dear Lydia done anything less? And with Countess Lieven as well as the Princess on her side, and Lady Sefton always easily appealed to, Lady Jersey began to weaken. Most helpful was not having the young girl before her to rouse her ire; and so, at last, she succumbed, especially when it was pointed out that she alone could cause such a reversal in Society's opinion! A master stroke! For Lady Jersey, above all, most enjoyed showing off her power. The voucher was obtained, and Miss Varrick was even invited to Lady Jersey's Costume Ball! Lady Austen herself would be sending her carriage to bring Charlette to her for a discussion of costume choice, which must be of the first stare!

"What a timely turnabout!" Charlette exclaimed, in prodigious relief. Amazing how oft when one was on the point of foundering, positively adrift, there would appear someone to scoop one up, and, next instant, one was safe, and bobbish adeck a new ship.

Lady Austen in person was quite as overwhelming as her letter. She not only acted as a fairy godmother, but looked the part as well. Upon being ushered into her private saloon, Charlette gazed in awe. And her heartfelt comment that she could not believe this lady was the same age as her mother would be won immediate approval.

On the return to the Regent Street town house, Charlette concluded with a gleam of mischief that she need not inform her aunt of her appearance at the Costume Ball. Let it be a delightful surprise. Lady Bridingsley should see her there, as should they all who did not expect her and had made no effort to help her— starting with Lord and Lady Bridingsley, to Francine and Lady Marjory, and even the Duke, and lastly, that sea captain of Society. In happy anticipation, she thought of naught but her moment of showing them all that she *and her mother* belonged back in Society. Yes, with her head held high, she should make her entrance for both of them—and put a silence to the whispers of the ton at last.

Chapter Thirteen

THE obstacle, the major wall to her acceptance into Society, or Almack's, was to fall before her assault that very night, Charlette thought blissfully.

It had not necessitated Miss Varrick's equivocating on her plans for the evening, since no one had inquired about them. Francine and her mother were concentrating the past fortnight on their costumes for Lady Jersey's Costume Ball, the two keeping heads together and then ostentatiously silencing upon Charlette's entrances. She made as few of those as possible, having communicated to her aunt that she was making arrangements for her departure from their home within the fortnight.

Merely a nod, followed directly by her rushing about to meet her appointments, was all the reaction Lady Bridingsley afforded that announcement. Any second thoughts her ladyship might have about her niece's departure were squashed by the arrival of a letter from Mr. Varrick's accountant. He regretted to inform her ladyship that Mr. Varrick was refusing to allow her redoing of her bedroom under the qualification of making the house suitable for Charlette's receiving guests, for he could not believe Charlette would be so indecorous as to do that! He also quibbled as to the payment of past bills. The latter totally unlike her brother, who had never inquired as to the purposes for the monies he had provided the Bridingsleys for so many years. And the first few months of Charlette's Season, he had underwrit all. But, lately, he was becoming quite boring with requests for specifics, and even going so far as to wish for estimates before the charges were incurred. If he were going to make that kind of difficulty, she might as well deal with the tradesmen on her own—at least they did not have the effrontery to ask why she had made certain expenditures. Obviously, for all about, Charlette had outlived her usefulness.

Her main absorption now was how to add the cost of her daughter's and her own costume to the last bill sent to Varrick's accountant. Fortunately, Madame Fanchot was willing to continue not specifying for whom the costumes were made.

The one problem that persisted—indeed, had enlarged itself to shocking proportions—was Francine's diary. It was now grown into several volumes. All of which were openly placed at key points around the house. The thought that one of the staff might be privy to more of her daughter's affairs than she herself had Lady Bridingsley running around and picking up the diaries. Francine was filling volumes enough to comprise a library. It was rather surprising that this quiet, subdued young miss should have erupted with this full-blown passion for scribbling. As if something, or apparently someone, had sparked her into feeling, and now she was boiling over and splattering all about.

Among the prime places for these extra diaries were everywhere Miss Varrick was known to pass—her chair at the table, her favorite Grecian sofa in the library, her stone bench in the garden and always, always, the doorsill leading into her room. Tenacious of will, Francine still intended to lure her cousin into reading her thoughts. So far, Charlette had not succumbed to even a glance, pushing the volumes aside. It reached the point where Charlette tripped over a diary on her doorsill, but she merely walked on, muttering an indignant "Stow your gear."

So rarely was Charlette at Regent Street that if Lady Bridingsley had not concluded on her own that her niece was taking last visits to the historical sights of London, there might have been some curiosity roused. Actually, the sights Charlette was daily observing were Lord and Lady Austen.

The first tea between Lady Millicent Austen and Charlette had been most satisfactory. Her ladyship was relieved to hear that Charlette had learned the particulars of her mother's story, and adjusted to it sufficiently not to need the aid of Lady Austen's collection of vinaigrettes. Only Lady Austen herself had recourse to her favorite aromatic composer, keeping it close to her nostrils when describing the moment dear Lydia had asked her whether she dared run away from the Earl.

"I can remember her beautiful, large blue eyes anxiously staring at me, and cognizant of the significant effect on her future, I could not but advise her to 'follow her heart.' And so she did."

She paused for Charlette's reaction, which was most gratifying, for Charlette not only applauded the advice, but saw her mother's entire story as a wonderful romance, with Lady Austen in the role of fairy godmother. Which could not help but please.

"And father and mother lived happily, and had me," Charlette contributed.

"Why is it that one's main concern in stories is always at the point of one's own entrance?" Lady Austen said with a grin, and Charlette laughingly apologized for intruding herself. Lady Austen generously continued, "Now that you mention your entrance, little minx, I *do* recollect that Lydia was delighted to be having what she called 'the culmination of our love.' I expect that was you."

"It is not a title my father has ever addressed me by, but I appreciate the sentiment," Charlette countered, with a small giggle. Again and again, Charlette wished to hear her mother's story, in particular her mother's own first Season—what she wore, what she enjoyed doing, what her accomplishments. And Lady Austen was nothing loath, for that had been her own first Season as well. These delightful tales of Lady Austen (née Millicent Worthing) and her friend, the beautiful blonde Lydia Delacourte, had an unending fascination for both. The recollections took several luncheons and teas, and still they were not exhausted. "Do tell about the time you and Mother found yourselves lost in Green Park and were rescued by Lord Austen and Major Rockham!" Charlette exclaimed, and Lord Austen, overhearing, was pleased to add, "Jolly good time, that!" taking Lady Austen by the hand and both exchanging a warm and loving smile that had Charlette tearing. It did not take long for Lady Austen to wish that she herself were bringing out Charlette, especially since, with two sons as her offsprings, now at Harrow, such an opportunity would not be coming her way.

Lord Austen provided the solution, recommending that Charlette come to them for the finish of the Season, which should save the horses the trouble of being put to, a prime consideration. Lady Austen, instantly, joyously, took that up. And Charlette, after the necessary polite demurring, agreed. The invitation had, indeed, come at a most fortuitous moment, she decided with prodigious relief.

In their present mood of felicity, the unhappy part of Lydia's life was glossed over, although Lady Austen did mention the Earl's anger at Lydia's "wifely shrinking" brought on by his gross temperament. The latter was also the reason for the constantly changing staff, for only the heartiest were able to withstand his rages. Nor was there much incentive for remaining with him, for he was a known miser, positively close as wax, grudging every mouthful a servant, wife or guest took. Lady Austen could attest to that during her own infrequent visits. "It was scarcely any wonder dear Lydia had sunk to a mere shadow of her former hearty self."

To quickly lift their sinking spirits, Lady Austen introduced the hero of the tale, or Mr. Varrick. Lydia had felt an instant attraction to the young man sailing by in his own yacht. The romance was fully described, and Charlette, though rapt, could not quite picture her father in the role.

On another visit Lady Austen put to rights any suspicions about Lydia's demise, assuring it had occurred in childbirth—that being well known to the Earl's relatives. And the Earl's death while beating his stablehand made clear to all which party was unstable.

Other discussions were of Lady Austen's anger with Lady Bridingsley for her halfhearted efforts to procure a voucher and scarcely giving Society the lead in backing her niece. If she had kept her head high, others would have followed! Thus would Charlotte and she behave at the Costume Ball, and the entire reaction of the ton should be visibly different!

There was one pressing topic Charlette had not yet broached with Lady Austen, and that was Froth, who was slipped in during a discussion of Lady Austen's bonnet collection, for which she was justifiably known, as well as for her passions for fans of every kind. Lady Austen only wished that she could have an extra hand to display her selections, and with Charlette in tow she was delighted to have two extra such, not to mention an extra head for her chapeaux.

"As well as my hands and head, I have," Charlette began hopefully, "a rather charming gentleman—named Froth. He is a black cat, splashed all over with white."

"Ah, I gather he is visiting us as well?" Lady Austen asked with a twinkle.

"He should be so delighted to meet you. He has borne my dear aunt's dislike with remarkable fortitude and constant hiding under my chair when she approaches."

Laughing at that, Lady Austen cried out, "He certainly shall have no cause to hide at my approach. I flatter myself I have never had that effect on any gentleman, whatever his species."

Charlette hugged her in relief, and when subsequently Charlette recalled a Romney portrait of Lady Hamilton at a gallery and suggested her ladyship's costume duplicate that, Lady Austen was so pleased she claimed the young girl could bring an army of cats with her! Both recollected that the recently deceased Lady Hamilton had been an extraordinary beauty. A further similarity, Charlette inserted, was that Lady Hamilton in that portrait also wore a rather prime, wide-brimmed and ostrick-plumed hat.

"I knew we should be of inestimable help to each other. Why, we're like young girls together, are we not? I shall visit the gallery immediately, and bring my milliner with me. It shall be a broadening experience for her."

With Lord Austen promising to dress as Lord Nelson, and Madame Fanchot coming to Charlette's aid, all was in happy progression for the Costume Ball.

Most of Charlette's belongings had already been called for by Lady Austen's two footmen and a newly hired personal maid, Rose, who should be serving Charlette's every need. Froth had been transferred and found life at his new abode a constant delight. The attraction was the hundreds of plumed bonnets he could stalk and capture. Thankfully, Lady Austen lost interest in most of her bonnets after several outings and saw no reason why Froth should not have the wearing of them.

On the afternoon of the ball, Charlette was on the point of biding her aunt adieu when that lady was beforehand, assuming that Charlette's luggage had been sent to Wight. Claiming they should not be up early tomorrow, she sent her remembrances to her brother.

"I should perhaps tell you I am not immediately leaving London, after all."

"If you are determined to visit all of the city's museums and so forth, there is no need to move to a hotel. Certainly, Francine can contain her emotions toward you for a few more days. Happily, she has stopped that habit of leaving her diary at your doorstep."

"Yes. Froth cured her of that. I believe he forgot himself on what she claimed was her most 'memorable passage.' But he is not to be criticized, for he has come to expect that any piece of paper left on the floor has but one purpose. In any case, Francine, from the cries of outrage I heard outside my door, was not disposed to be forgiving, and since Froth has a delicate constitution and cannot stand being harangued, I feel I must depart tonight. We almost became friends. I regret we were not quite able to make that an actuality. I have often longed for a lady to take my mother's place. I had hoped it would be you."

"If you expect that to be the last thing you say to me, I should request an immediate apology. To be like your *mother*, indeed!"

Charlette's face remained composed. "I have heard the entire story. And I can only say she was more sinned against than sinning. Apparently, she was a child wed to a brute who hid his temperament under his title. My father was her rescuer. I never knew till my visit here how admirable both of them are. Anyone who ever again speaks slightingly of either of my parents shall not ever be recognized by me again!"

"Are you serious! The whole of London has done so."

"Not in my presence! Nor shall I ever allow anyone else to do so!"

"You are mistaken in that attitude. Strive instead for humility and an apologetic air. Perhaps then some of your suitors should be willing to continue their pursuit. And if Francine is wed, I might be willing next year to allow you another attempt at a Season—if you've learned enough decorum not to put your relatives to the blush."

"I understand the model you are holding before me. I am to rarely speak, until one day when I break out into wild fantasies and queer starts of leaving volumes all over the house and reading them aloud when others refuse to read them on their own! I think not. I shall continue to be myself and proud of everything I am . . . including all of my heritage."

"That ends all hope of your being received by anyone of any standing. You are set to spend your life hiding in that island—as did your disgraced and *abandoned* mother."

Staring Lady Bridingsley in the eye, with barely restrained fury, Charlette spoke, "I told you I would not countenance a remark like that . . . from anyone. I shall leave immediately. This moment."

But at that moment Francine came running into the drawing room to display her costume, exclaiming with glee: "Who am I? Cannot you tell! Never mind, I shall tell. I am a sea captain's lady! Because," she eyed Charlette with a glowing defiance, "because I am. You refuse to read it, dear cousin, or hear it. But I am now shouting it to the rafters. *I am Captain Huntley's love* . . . I have been to his rooms at the Duke's town house, and I have received promises that no gentleman could deny."

Her gown was a replica of a naval uniform: a full jacket with golden epaulettes, and a gown below, and on her head she had a captain's hat.

"Your selection proves how little you know him. He has very little love for the navy. I suggest you dress yourself as a tin of tea, and concentrate on one who has the possibility of returning your affections."

Francine smiled smugly. "I have a letter from him which shall prove you wrong. If you'd care to see it. I expect you know his hand, for he tells me that he wrote to you when he first went to sea."

Charlette was stopped by that truthful revelation, but refusing to partake any further in that discussion, returned to her room.

Undeterred, Francine rushed to collect her letter and shouted its contents through Charlette's closed door. That confrontation did not offer her the pleasure of seeing her cousin's face, but she gained some satisfaction from the continued silence within. Lady Bridingsley's voice was the next sound heard, and Francine, giving up her cornered quarry, followed her mother to the waiting carriage.

"Fiddle!" Charlette said to the closed door. But when she heard the two ladies leaving, she opened it and went to the head of the stairs. Gone. And she herself, after changing for the ball, would depart and never return to this house, or have to listen to those two ladies ever again.

But they left her with the added concern that she must advise Darrel tonight to act with more circumspection. Obviously he was not up to snuff about Society ladies, not aware they were not like her—still able to see the humor in his remarks and the challenge in his actions, and not take either seriously. Yes, despite having a full plate of objectives tonight, such as at long last demonstrating her own social worthiness and the reclamation of her mother's lost pride, now as well she had to concern herself about Darrel's unwise and unbecoming conduct. Really, she would have so preferred it if he had never come amongst Society and disturbed it . . . and disturbed her.

But she would not give him the honor of thinking of him any longer. Her every attention must be on her costume. With Rose as her assistant, Charlette went about preparing for her transformation. All the ladies at the ball should probably be dressed as Queens and Princesses. Yet, her costume, instead, was to depict the greatest Queen of all, and the very reason her mother had thrown away her position. And that was *love*. She should be

Aphrodite! And further, as well as explaining and proudly proclaiming her mother's actions, her costume similarly brought to mind one of the very acts for which she had been so criticized: allowing herself to be the prize for the contest of sonnets, equating her to Venus. Actually, that Venus, arising newborn from the sea on a shell, was not fully clothed; and somewhat the same illusion was captured in the Fanchot costume, while in actuality it was the height of respectability.

Madame's staff had been working on the creation up to the very last moment. Finally complete, it had just been delivered, moments before. Even Lady Austen had not seen it, although she had enthusiastically approved of the character to be depicted.

A full satin cloak with a wide hood covered Charlette totally to allow of her entering into the coach without shocking the liveried footmen. Her escort, Sir Smithers, was prepared for her appearance as Aphrodite by Charlette's saying, with only half-truth and much courtesy, "I expect you are responsible for my choice, Sir Smithers." He was delighted at the compliment, and was only distressed he had not been earlier informed to have dressed as Neptune rather than Romeo.

At the entrance of Almack's, Charlette recollected with a glow of satisfaction that this was the moment she had been awaiting since her arrival in London. Now she was passing from an outsider, through the portals of sanction, into final social acceptance! She particularly savored the moment of handing over her voucher and being bowed in. Lady Jersey herself was on the receiving line, and she gave the girl a thin smile and two fingers. Entering with a group of people, Charlette kept her cloak on until they were well inside. Joining Lady Austen's party, she found her ladyship all abubble over the success of Emma Hamilton and Lord Nelson. Charlette was profusely admiring the results. It was then her turn to be viewed, and she gave the nod to Sir Smithers, who took her cloak. There was a collective intake of breath from the immediate party.

There she stood—Venus complete to a shell. From bodice to toe, her costume was all white gauze and tiny shells with mother-of-pearl centers that gleamed like jewels as she moved. The material rose up to her throat and went down almost to the tip of her fingers, so that what at first glance seemed shockingly risqué, on second glance was the epitome of modesty. The dress was so jeweled itself that no other jewelry was needed, except for her two favorite mother-of-pearl shell combs on either side of her head. Most awesome of all, indeed, was her hair, worn loose and flowing to her hips, its golden-red vibrancy like a jewel itself. Here and there it was threaded with the same tiny pearl shells trailing down her riotous locks. And as she moved, her cloud of hair floated and glowed behind her.

" 'She walks in beauty, like the night of cloudless climes and starry skies,' " Sir Smithers was moved to quote.

Charlette thanked him with a nod and handed him the shell she was carrying. Not being able to stand on a shell, as had Venus, she carried this memento shell, found for her on the Isle of Wight, thus completing her message of representing her island to the Londoners.

All about, as she had predicted, there were monarchs upon monarchs—heavily brocaded and petticoated Queens and regally robed Kings. Romeos and Juliets, there were aplenty, as well as Caesars and Cleopatras and Mark Antonys. But mostly, the lords and ladies dressed as their own ancestors, with countless coronets.

Being reassured by Lady Austen that she looked quite delightful, and further having all qualms subdued by being surrounded by many young gentlemen clamoring for a dance, Charlette at last allowed herself to enjoy all. Although she conscientiously observed the Almack's injunction and refused all waltzes, until a patroness gave her leave. While all the other young ladies were waltzing, she waited by Lady Austen's side until Lady Sefton approached, escorted by a pirate with cutlass gleaming almost as brightly as his smile. Introducing Darrel to Charlette, Lady Sefton fulfilled her function of sanction. The two then waltzed off, watched with pleasure by Lady Sefton and Lady Austen, and displeasure by everyone else.

"I thought," he whispered, but with a look of pride, "that I had never seen so many beautiful ladies, until I saw you. And then you made them all seem human, while you are divine."

"Actually, I am tossing my love-child heritage in their faces, while representing the shells of our island," she said with an impish smile. "And you, I see, are also throwing your past reputation in our faces. Outfacing us with your piracy."

"Perhaps we are both merely showing our true selves," he said with a gleam of unholy amusement.

Although Charlette grinned at that, she was mainly occupied with having him acknowledge there was no longer any need for feeling *sorry* for her. "As you can see," she said with deep satisfaction, "the walls of Almack's have fallen before me!"

"You have me to thank for that."

"Indeed, not!" Charlette exclaimed, annoyed at his constant conceit. "Lady Austen procured my voucher!"

"But Lady Jersey would have blackballed you had I not explained that we grew up very like brother and sister. She has a *tendre* for me. Blast me, every lady here is at my heels. I have to be careful I do not trod on them."

"Speaking of trodding . . ."

"I did not, Charle!" he protested. And then laughed. "You are merely attempting to bring me down a peg. But I speak only the truth. You would not believe the letters and gifts that are being constantly sent to me from the most exalted to the sweet little maids. It was rather a lark at first, and then it became rather tedious. Look at all the ladies dressed in harem, hoping to remind me of the veiled Arab lady I have spoken of. And there are some, would you believe, even dressed in naval attire! I shuddered to see it. I have spoken of my being lashed to the bone while on the ship your father imprisoned me on."

She had been about to warn him of Francine's emotions, but the last aspersion distracted her and she defended hotly. "Your father *requested* he give you the honor of joining His Majesty's navy. My father merely complied with his wishes—for your own good! You could have been a captain in the King's navy if you could have kept your exalted sense of worth in check!"

"Why are you the only woman here—when all else are exalting me—who blithely reduces me to the level of a peasant child on the beach, being honored by the presence of me betters!" he exploded. Then whirling her about some more, he watched her pleased face, and groaned. "Yes, you can put me in a rare taking. No one else can do so. Thoroughly dished, I am, me girl. And now what? Shall I bow to you, my goddess, and take you away on my ship to an island of shells, where we shall count them as if they were our wealth?"

"I have the shell you dove for near the cliffs. Sir Smithers is holding it. I kept it on my dresser till Francine arranged for a maid to steal it. But I got it back."

"Francine? Miss Farweather?"

"Yes."

"She would."

"Darrel . . . she is spreading rumors that you have made improper advances and carries a letter from you as proof. If not careful, you shall have to offer for her."

"I'll be blasted first!" He grinned. And then seeing that she was both annoyed and yet still concerned, he explained. "I'll be dashed if I have to offer for every lady pursuing me. Faith then, I'd have to have a harem for certain. Stop frowning, Charle, I'm careful with the really resty ones. Although I lark about with the petticoats, I have more serious hopes."

"Ah, yes, you intend to marry into the peerage."

"I could marry higher than that," he grinned with cocky assurance. "Have supper at my table and watch the women flock round. Look there, at that group of harem ladies, they are all wishing you ill. And yet you make them look ill by comparison. You are a true daughter of Wight, tonight. A treasure scooped up from our many gleaming shores." His grey eyes had darkened with emotion, and he held her so closely they whirled together as one. "Did you wear the gown to remind me that we are linked from childhood—forever?"

His last assumption had her in whoops. "You are quite a bellows-blower, Captain. A cock of the walk with all your chickens running after you! I am not so hennish. Actually, I wore this outfit for Sir Smithers who first dubbed me Queen of Love, seeing me as Botticelli's Venus. If I recollect, he concluded that through her, or rather me, all men shall discover the true meaning of love."

"The Devil he did! Blast him! Where is that gentleman! I believe I have something to say to him on that score."

"What could you say?" Charlette grinned. "He said it all in rhyme, and all is acceptable when versified."

"Oh, one of those poesy fellows. Blast it, Charle, is that what you want! Did you really wear this magical shell dress . . . for him?"

"No," Charlette relented, but when he smiled too quickly she stopped him again. "Actually, another gentleman selects my entire wardrobe. My hats and gowns. He found this one to his liking, for it reminds him of his name as well as the beach where we met." Clued by the incorrigible gleam in her eyes, the name hit him, but too late to share their amusement, for her next partner had claimed her. Yet, he shouted, "Froth, by gad!" and went back to his party laughing his hearty laugh, and having all the women in agonies at his having been so vastly amused by another lady.

At the supper, Charlette was surprised to see a meager spread and further hear it was typical of Almack's. "There is no need to puff off their consequence with viands," Lady Austen explained. "Yes, it is paltry. But one does not come here to eat."

"A real lady rarely eats at any affair," came a cold voice, and Charlette turned to see her aunt. She was dressed as Queen Elizabeth. The ruff cut into her throat and made her voice sound strained. Or was it that her niece was at Almack's, after all?

"Lady Austen has graciously invited me to stay with her for the rest of my Season," Charlette explained.

"Indeed."

"Oh heavens, Priscilla, is that you?" Lady Austen laughed. "I nearly bowed, you are so like the late Queen, one would think one was looking at an effigy!"

Quickly, Charlette turned about to hide her smiles. Her aunt was obviously in capable hands. "Would you believe it," Lady Austen continued, "but no one actually made an effort for a voucher for Lydia's child. Heavens, when you think how far Lydia's family went—to William the Conqueror, no less. They were not one of the families that gained their titles for fighting against Cromwell, as did the Bridingsleys. I told the patronesses that Charlette's family tree goes back to authentic English royalty! And there was an immediate rush to beg Charlette's pardon for the oversight."

"Indeed," Lady Bridingsley repeated in her ruffled voice.

Charlette's evening was complete, having done all she wished. She had been a success, putting several ladies who had cut her in their places, received a full plate of compliments and proposals and propositions, had had the pleasure of seeing her aunt handled by a master or rather mistress of tact and repartee and she had danced with Darrel, warning him about Francine. She could do no more.

At that moment the Duke, dressed in armor for Lancelot, after all, claimed a dance. Though granted, Charlette treated him with some distance, for he needed a lesson. His lack of attendance of late, when she so needed support, rankled. Then too, his armor made any degree of closeness rather difficult.

But as he did not realize that her silence meant disapproval, she had to put it into words. "I have felt an absence from you, your grace, which suggested dismissal?"

He sputtered at the first reprimand he had ever received from a lady. "I say. Ain't meant to cut you, by Jove! Marj needed me. Sailor-fellow too close."

"Fortunately, not all of my escorts are so slighting. Sir Smithers is never cruel."

She said the last with a slight sniff at the end that reached his grace's heart. He was a kindhearted man, but a bit of a fribble—one so concerned lest he step on another person's toes that he backs up and steps on three others. And his being in armor would have made it particularly painful for the three others.

"Made a muddle," he said sadly, referring to more than his dancing.

She excused him, but the more she did so the more he apologized. Yet, he added in his own defense, "Not cruel! By gad, *cruel!*"

"A bit, your grace, for what else is denying your friendship to one who had come to rely on it. And, of late, I was alone, without protection, being on the point of leaving London—if it were not for the kind graces of Lady Austen. It makes one wonder how there can be so many heartless people, and then, others of such kind gentility."

"By gad. Didn't know. Never meant to . . ."

For the first time in his grace's life he was not praised past his merits, not toadied to . . . nor, on the other hand, was he dismissed with sarcasm, as by some of his friends at Harrow, and even later his father, or even his sister. No, Miss Varrick had spoken to him with a touch of surprise, as if she expected him to live up to a higher level, and the Duke realized he would have to go some distance to recapture the friendliness he had so thoughtlessly tossed away.

To recover her good opinion became of essence. In fact, the rest of the evening the Duke remained at Charlette's side, as her flunkey. She treated him graciously, and yet remembered that Sir Smithers was the man who brought her—which meant his grace had to listen to three sonnets and one full poem. "By Jove—" the Duke mumbled, "if this ain't cruelty!"

By the fifth poem, the Duke was looking at Charlette as Froth did when she was not responding to his needs, so the young girl, relenting, suggested to Sir Smithers that a poem concerning her costume, as he suggested, would be most agreeable, but she wished a *written* one. If he only had a quill, Sir Smithers said, with great regret; otherwise, he would be forced to continue verbal declamations.

"By Jove," the Duke interrupted, signaling a footman, "a quill, and sheets, several sheets . . . direct this gentleman to a standish, *immediately!*"

"Your grace," Charlette admonished, but she exchanged a small smile with him as Sir Smithers was led off. The two were chatting companionably when abruptly interrupted by Francine's voice sounding throughout the entire ballroom.

"But you have danced with every other lady here! Why have you not asked *me*—when we mean so much to each other!"

She was addressing an all-suffering captain, who replied, "My apologies for overlooking you, Miss Farweather. But I am afraid my dance card is full. Some other time . . . perhaps." And bowing to her, he turned to Lady Webster.

Francine was not that easily deflected, following him around as he danced, making a third. Lady Webster was bright red in the face, but Francine was determinedly carrying on her protests. "I am dressed as a captain to honor you, as the captain of my soul."

"I am accustomed to a crew that obeys my commands," the Captain said smoothly. "And I order you to . . . sit this one out, if you please."

When she would not do so, the Captain merely shrugged, and taking both ladies by the hand, danced with them both. Instantly, Charlette grabbed the Duke and Lord Austen by the hand and made a similar threesome. In a few seconds, others, seeing it as a new dance, were forming their own threesomes, and soon the entire dance floor was moving three-by-threes.

Darrel had seen Charlette's act and was giving her their usual exchange of secret congratulations. When the music was over, everyone was most impressed, asking to know the name of the new dance.

"What else, but the Triangle!" Charlette exclaimed.

"Slap up to the echo!" Lord Austen exclaimed.

"For many a lady sitting on the sidelines it should be of inestimable benefit," Lady Austen declared with pleasure and some pride that her husband had been part of an innovation. She could not quite credit it. But, subsequently, she herself became part of a triangle when Charlette had her whirling about with herself and the Duke. And then, Lady Austen and her husband kindly accepted the Dowager Viscountess Drummand into their whirling.

Sir Smithers had been in a side parlor writing down his poem when the dance was created, and had just returned to read the first few verses to Charlette. While he was doing so, the Captain asked her, his eyes twinkling, for the pleasure of Triangling with him. Attempting to keep her face composed, Charlette simply took the spouting poet by the hand and included him in their steps. So

absorbed was he in his declamations, he merely stepped along
with them, reciting all the time:

> "And like a shell from Poseidon's deep,
> She glitters, glows, too glorious to spy,
> An island lady whose beauty makes hearts leap.
> Pearlized, foam-born, Aphrodite is nigh.
> Zeus blessed her eyes, her form, her thigh . . ."

"She's got two of them," Darrel interposed, as they hopped
through their Triangle steps. "Thighs," he explained matter-of-
factly.

"Sir! One does not mention . . ."

"You did."

"I mentioned the perfection of her form, her thigh. *One*."

"Blast me!" Darrel exclaimed. "Are you saying it is permissi-
ble in polite Society to mention one of a lady's thighs, but not the
other. Which one?"

"This discussion is indelicate. One does not mention either
particular thigh . . . but one may allude to the general perfection of the configuration of her form, and thus indicate the
thigh . . . or the eye or arm—whichever is rhythmically, that
is . . ." Suddenly, he became aware that he was dancing with a
man as well as Miss Varrick. "I say! What are we doing, the three
of us on the ballroom floor!"

Unable to resist, Darrel said seriously, "You requested the
pleasure of my dancing with you, did you not?"

"*I*, sir? By Jove. We must stop. We are making dashed cakes of
ourselves."

"Look around, Sir Smithers," Charlette said kindly. "We are
not the only ones thus engaged. It is the newest craze. The
Triangle."

Looking about him, and seeing it was indeed true, the
gentleman-poet was somewhat mollified. But he exclaimed, "I do
not like it. By Jove, it is better to be dancing alone with a lady.
E'gad, I hesitate to think what this Triangling can lead to . . ."

"You are putting the lady to the blush," the Captain warned,
and Sir Smithers bowed in confusion and broke away from their
triangle.

"Your pardon, Miss Varrick. I should dashed well rather retire
and wait for a moment when we two can be alone, without
disturbing asides."

And bowing stiffly in her direction, he left Darrel and Charlette to waltz away.

"Actually, the chap is correct. This is much more satisfying," Darrel grinned, holding her closer and whirling her away from the stumbling triangles to the outer corner of the ballroom where there was some privacy.

"We shall always come to each other's defense," he said with satisfaction.

"Indeed, like the brother and sister we are."

"I have a poem for you, if that is what you wish—it is a ditty of Byron's. Listen." And his dark grey eyes captured her wavering glance and forced her into complete close attention.

"For he through sin's long labyrinth had run,
Nor made atonement when he did amiss,
Had sigh'd to many, though he loved but one.
And that loved one, alas! could ne'er be his."

Breaking loose her held glance, Charlette attempted to diffuse the feelings between them by responding, "The dance is over. Supper begins."

He held her back. "Why are you always running from me, Charle?"

"Don't call me that! I am no longer Charle and you are no longer my friend, Darrel. You have become a rip, a rackety loose-screw—strewing hearts about as if they were shells, indeed!"

"When have I ever done anything but been your friend in all things?" he exclaimed, his voice in earnest, although she could not be certain of his words.

"Then be my friend," she responded seriously. "And do not attempt to add me to your list of conquests. Be content with your harem. And, remember, we are merely one-time friends and can never be anything closer."

"Are you so certain of that?" he said with a twinkle of daring.

"I am certain that I saved your groats tonight. Francine would have made a scene that would have finally unmasked you as a philanderer."

Darrel laughed but remained silent.

"You laugh at that and us all, do you?"

"Were I to be defeated by the world and Society, I should have succumbed to many things, years ago. Even on the Isle of Wight,

I learned to laugh at all others hold dear. And yet I hold in my heart one thing dear."

"And that is yourself," Charlette said, and joined the table where the Duke was signaling her.

When her heart had stopped beating, she looked up to see that Captain Huntley had arranged for Lady Marjory and himself to join them.

"We thought we should make a lovely rectangle," Darrel said, with a humor that apparently was irrepressible. "What think you, Charle, shall we start a new dance—the *four* of us intermingling?" He gave her a significant look, and she could not but understand that rather than being grateful to her for attempting to save a social situation, he was contemptuous of her . . . even now, for wishing to preserve dignities. He cared for none of that, challenging her to risk being ostracized from the Society she held so dear, and he so cheap.

"I recollect," he continued, deliberately taunting her, "that those very shells were some of the ones I was wont to throw at your window. Did you save them and make a dress in commemoration of our *closer* moments?"

Lady Marjory gave her brother a triumphant look. "I collect you and Miss Varrick were once quite . . . close?"

"He would have you assume that," Charlette said calmly. "Actually, we were children together. We have not seen each other since we have become adults. The Captain apparently has a habit of exaggeration learned on the wharves of the world. One wonders how much truth there is in all his sailor's tales? Or present brags?"

The Duke, not wishing to be standing about like a stick while they fenced before his very face, brought more food to the ladies, and made a comment that implied the Captain did not know how to serve ladies, or have regard for their comfort or appetites.

"I always attempt to satisfy all ladies' appetites," Darrel said, refusing to be crushed. "As for comestibles, I cannot but feel that it's rather displeasing to see ladies eating so much supper."

They had, at that point, been joined by Lord and Lady Austen. And Lady Jersey, passing, stopped at that comment.

"Is that a criticism on the spread, Captain, you devilish cad?" But she was smiling at him fondly.

He returned the goodwill with a deep bow. "I speak merely from a gentleman's observation, your ladyship. On my world travels, I noticed that in the East the ladies eat very little, and very delicately. One does not have to suffer the affront of watching a lady swallow an entire chicken wing—or, rather, a pork hock!"

"And you gentlemen may gulp down whatever comestible you wish? Surely that is rather hard on our delicate constitutions. Ladies cannot live on air, you know."

"Indeed," Lady Austen inserted, amused. "The Captain would wish us to live on love alone, I collect?"

"That would be the ideal world," the Captain replied. "And ideally if the lady were one of those at our little grouping."

Each lady took that as referring to herself, and was pleased.

"What shall a lady eat? I daresay, one must wonder," Lady Marjory objected, taking him seriously. "One attempts to swallow delicately."

Incorrigibly, the Captain carried on. "Most foods cannot possibly allow of delicacy of swallowing. Therefore, I believe a lady should dine on fruits only . . . and perhaps sweetmeats . . . served to her by an adoring swain; and as for drink, it must be only champagne."

"I agree," Charlette complied, unable not to play along. "I feel myself turning positively plain whenever I eat pork, and becoming an antidote when munching mutton. I have long since forbidden those foods from my diet. One can find nothing reprehensible in seafood, would you not agree, Captain? Oysters have a way of swallowing themselves, without need of much assistance."

"Absolutely unexceptionable!" the Captain agreed, unable not to throw his head back and laugh—the two of them enjoying themselves too much to stop.

"I cannot, however, endorse crabs," she said seriously.

"No, blast them! Turn you crabby in an instant."

"You are jesting with us, Captain," Lady Jersey said, and hit him delicately with her fan, walking away to see to her other guests.

"Were you funning?" Lady Marjory asked, concerned.

"I am never as deadly earnest as when I am funning, your ladyship," he said seriously, and she did not know what to think!

One of his lady-admirers approached, peeking at him through her veils, which were beginning to impede her breathing. Observing her, the Captain bowed, and said, "Arab ladies are vegetarians. And, of course, one never sees them swallow, since they slip whatever they are to consume behind their veils, and *voilà*! it disappears."

And he leaned over and slipped a piece of cheese behind the

lady's veil in the supposed direction of her mouth. It disappeared in there, and a slight gulp was heard.

"You see," he said, toying with the girl, and laughing at her and all of Society jumping to his remarks.

Charlette could no longer go along with his amusing himself at all of their expense. "I have finished with all this," she said clearly, and rose, turning to the Duke. "Shall we walk?"

With alacrity, he gave her his hand and they were off, shortly mixing into the crowd of couples; a bow from the Duke and a nod from Miss Varrick, and they were dancing off.

The Captain watched them, the smile slowly disappearing from his face, his eyes darkening. But then, he took a swig of champagne and turned back to his waiting admiring ladies. "Now, which one of you veiled ones shall risk your reputations by honoring a poor sea captain with a dance?" he said lightly.

Chapter Fourteen

❁ ═══════════════════════════ ❁

SIR Smithers' proposal of marriage came in rhyme. And after the Almack's signal that Society had accepted her, offers came flowing in prose as well. Charlette, having a delightful time at Lady Austen's, allowed her ladyship to peruse the written ones and suggest which were compliments and which must be given the smallest response.

"Ah, do not bother to pen a reply to the Marquis. His estates are so heavily encumbered, he proposes to any lady with deep pockets."

"Then certainly, 'tis no honor to be in that grouping! Not a word of reply shall he receive. Poor Marquis."

"In every respect," Lady Austen agreed, and continued with the listing. "Ah, now, Lord Rothfort: That *is* an honor. He is much in demand. You may pen him a polite negative. What? None from the Duke?"

"Not a marriage proposal. He is a cautious wooer. He has invited me to spend a fortnight at his principal seat."

"That is significant. But a lady should not allow herself to be seen to give such a marked preference, unless she had received more tangible encouragement. You must refuse, with regret."

Charlette did so. Without much regret. Finally, she was enjoying herself being the most sought after young lady on the Marriage Mart and had no desire for seclusion. Lady Austen, often accompanying her, was herself having a time. That evening it was to be Vauxhall for the fireworks. Charlette had accepted the Earl of Warrensby's escort. He was in his thirties and had so far not succumbed to many lures. It was quite a coup to receive his attentions. As for the Captain, he had been good enough to invite her to ride with him in the park of a morning, but Charlette refused. She would not be one of his attendant court.

Nevertheless, they passed each other at Vauxhall, and he kissed his hand to her, while she pretended not to see the gesture.

Routs, picnics, even sight-seeing—whatever she wished, there was always a gentleman honored to be at her side. And none of the ladies were cutting her any longer. Now, she was acceptable to all and invited by all. And then, in the middle of her pleasuring, the outings began petering out. It was the end of June and the Season was closing. Everyone was flocking to Brighton or their own country estates. Lady Austen advised her to accept the Duke's invitation; she herself was to spend at least a fortnight at her father-in-law's manor. "One has one's obligation," she said nobly.

Charlette wished instead that Lady Austen were accompanying her.

"But nothing could be more delightful! I was looking for a reason to refuse my in-laws. This is unexceptional. I shall send my sons in my stead—they shall much be preferred—and Lord Austen can exert himself to travel between both places!" Yet, Lord Austen opted as well for Wingshire. One did not oft have the opportunity to stay at such a renowned castle. Its parks and lakes were much admired. But the main house proved to be a vast disappointment to all three when they arrived.

Wingshire Castle appeared as if a hundred nipperkins had designed it while at play. No symmetry to its style. A red brick center with Tudor towers had shockingly sprouted Georgian wings. Grand of size—a full village of people could be housed in it. The grounds, Lord Austen claimed, were the sites of notable battles between the Cavaliers and Roundheads. The Duke, upon greeting them at the entrance, acknowledged this historical fact with total disinterest.

"Full of history, this. Queens running amuck, sleeping in every room. Kings battling in the rosebushes. Me steward has the straight of it. Ain't my thing."

Lady Marjory, not there to receive them, was riding with her guest.

"Keeping it cozy, what?" the Duke said, explaining no one else was expected.

Charlette was in a pet at not being in the same wing with Lord and Lady Austen. Her rooms were in the unrenovated old part—Tudor airs all about. A massive bed, fully closed in by musty brocade crimson curtains, dominated. The floor was stone and cold, and needed sweeping. Shockingly, there were no signs of welcome at all. It bordered on the uncivil. Only upon stepping onto the stone balcony did she feel reconciled to her rooms. For the vista was overwhelming: Distant hills were changing colors as the sun set and spilled down to a quiet, dreaming lake. She herself changed for dinner into a simple cream muslin gown with blonde rows at the cuffs and neck. Before entering the drawing room, she heard a known voice. In her heart Charlette had expected Darrel to be Lady Marjory's guest, and her heart was not disappointed.

He turned when she entered and gave her an unguarded smile, the kind when one simply cannot disguise one's pleasure. Such was the honesty of it, Charlette could hardly refrain from returning it, and even allowed him to take her hand, leading her to a comfortable settee by the fireplace. Sitting by her side, he immediately inquired as to her comfort, as if the host. Which action had the Duke muttering.

"Pleased to have you in me home," his grace called out, to remind her. To which Charlette instantly responded by giving him her hand, and the Duke politely bowed.

"Captain, I was to show you the changes in the gardens," Lady Marjory reminded.

At that moment Lady Austen and her husband arrived, inadvertently rescuing the Captain. They were delighted with their rooms. The fireplace did not smoke. The French design, much to her ladyship's taste. Especially pleasing was the bouquet of roses.

"And did Miss Varrick approve the bouquet I personally arranged in her room?" the Duke asked, staring at the young girl pointedly.

"My reverie at the view from the balcony was so deep I scarce observed if there was a bouquet. But I must thank your grace for selecting the room with that lake vista."

The Duke gave Lady Marjory a pointed glance from which she hurriedly looked away. What it imparted only they two knew, but Charlette caught it and wondered.

Dinner had been set back to allow the guests time to refresh and rest themselves. Now, Lady Marjory sauntered around the Gothic room with its heavy wooden chairs and velvet scarlet cushions and indicated an innovation she had herself ordered.

"Percy claimed they would ill-fit with the general period of this room. But I had Jeffers' opinion, a disciple of the Regent's own Mr. Nash." She pointed out two glass doors. "From France. At

Jeffers' further suggestion, I added a veranda. Here, the pleasant results." And she passed through and returned, almost as if expecting applause for the feat. "Rather a pleasure now in the summer."

"Early summer and rather nippy," the Duke said matter-of-factly.

Ignoring his interruption, Lady Marjory continued, "You'll note all the iron trellises. Another recent development, Jeffers assures me. And quite the thing for them to be vined." She cut a viney leaf and showed it round.

"Passion flowers," Captain Huntley said, with an air of surprise.

"Yes, quite the most passionate of all flowers," she acknowledged, and blushed fiercely. "The entire veranda is a place for romantic experiences."

The Captain bowed. "Let us hope it has many such."

Lady Austen, unaware of the flirtation going on, or not appreciating being reduced to a spectator, interrupted. "I collect this is part of the growing trend to bring the garden into the living areas. Lady Darlymple's manor house is quite a case in point. She brought her conservatory closer to the house by means of an arched passageway. Most exhilarating walking of a morning between the two."

"That would be difficult here. Conservatory is ten miles by the cottage ornée."

Helpfully, the Duke inserted, "Tilbury take you—just tell me man. Got me a church on the grounds. Pond. Gazebo . . ." He paused, running out of his sights, and then his brain eked out additional places of interest. ". . . Bird cove . . . village with people. Woods, and game . . . and, by Jove, forgot the *stables*!"

Lord Austen's attention was fairly caught by that last, and the conversation soon turned to hunting, and then there was no stopping them. It was all "coming to grief at a rasper," on one hand, and "hunter's points" and "excellent bottoms," on the other. So absorbed were the gentry, they missed the sight of Captain Huntley walking softly behind Charlette and taking her hand, and almost pulling her outside onto the veranda.

"It is quite pleasant, indeed, out here," Charlette began lightly.

"Do not waste our time!" Darrel responded, with a touch of impatience. "We shall shortly be forced to audience the Duke's hunting tale of foxtail being worn under his friend's vest. Heard it above five times. One more rendering and I shall order him to walk the plank!"

"What would you have us do?"

Not bothering to respond, he stopped all conversation by putting his lips on hers, enveloping her into a tight hold from which he would not let her free, the kiss deepening.

"Captain!" came the horn-like voice of Lady Marjory, approaching.

It could not fail but get the Captain's attention, yet he would not be rushed. He finished his kiss as he wished, and then turned round.

"You sounded, your ladyship?" he inquired innocently.

Charlette could not believe the coolness of his voice, especially when her own senses were so disordered. Yet, he gave her a glance which showed his grey eyes were glowing with a lighthouse intensity, following her as she walked from passion flower trellis to passion flower trellis, holding onto each one, and receiving from each a most willing push, until she had reached the entrance and could manage to slip inside one French door, while Lady Marjory was striding out of the other.

Inside, none had noticed her departure. They were all listening to the Duke, who was imitating a galloping pace. " 'Ye gads, old sport,' said I to Willoughby, 'are you wearing that dashed foxtail trophy?' And blast if he were not. Showed it me. And them dogs went wild, turning into a pack and coming right for us! 'Willoughby, dear boy,' I cried then. 'Toss it to 'em, or we'll both be torn to shreds!' He did and we turned our nags' heads toward the stone border. Took the jump easy. Throwing our hearts over. And by Jove, we was free!"

There was much applause for the tale, and the Duke was flushed from his escape. Charlette continued to walk around the room, back now to the French doors; she gave a mere glance in that direction, but it was sufficient to have her stopped where she stood, and even take an amazed step across the entrance-way. The Captain was now embracing Lady Marjory. Even when he spotted her watching, he did not remove his arms from the lady's person; instead, he stared directly at Charlette, in a challenging way. A slow smile on his lips communicated his thoughts. And she could not bear sensing them, immediately stepping backward, away from him and his glance and his triumphant smile and all his thoughts, back, back, into the drawing room, then sat shaking on a huge hard chair with such large carved arms they hurt when she held onto them.

And through dinner, of which she made a very light meal, Charlette could hardly direct her concentration; it was constantly sifted through by thoughts of Darrel's game. Was he such a blatant libertine! Or was he merely teasing her, while his interest in Lady Marjory was quite sincere? A weather vane alone could depict her relationship to Darrel, she realized. At times, they were old friends, at times, competitors, but, of late, he was blowing harder at her, attempting to put her in a proper (or improper) whirl. Obviously, he could not refuse the challenge of her insisting they were just friends, and set out to prove her wrong—by winning one more match.

"Miss Varrick is not attending," Lady Marjory said, while the ladies were waiting for the gentlemen.

Charlette begged pardon and listened. It was a mere commonplace, and she answered in kind.

Subsequently, all were sitting on the veranda observing the moon's patterns on the trees. Lady Marjory and the Captain went for a stroll. The Duke offered to show his weapons collection to the Austens. Alone on the veranda, Charlette kept her eyes focused on the moon; she remembered it on the sea, skimming across the swaying waves. A sense of despondency had nestled within her breast, like a forlorn sea bird. She longed to run across the grounds, letting the wind take her where it would, to wipe out the sensation growing within her. And then she felt a hand timorously touching her bare shoulder. Turning as if stung, she saw the Duke.

"Insect," he said apologetically.

"Pardon?"

"Insect on your shawl. Brushed it off."

"Ah. Thank you. I'm much obliged. I detest, above all, the touch of insects."

"Would do anything to make you happy," his grace said humbly.

She turned back to the moon, feeling he was going to make her an offer, and she held her breath.

But he remained silent.

"Very kind of you to have invited Lord and Lady Austen—I so appreciate having them with me. Her ladyship is like having my own mother at my side. Lady Marjory is gracious, but I believe she does not care for my presence."

"Dashed if I care what she cares. Put you in the wrong rooms. I had you in me mother's rooms. Flowers all over. She went into a snit about me bringing shame into her apartments. Told her, you bring honor. Told her, think of you all the time. Think of you like flowers. Bright gold in the sun. My idea of a lady. Kind, elegant and a dashed beauty."

"Your grace leaves me, as always, with nothing to say."

"Don't want to do that, either. Want you always to have plenty to say. Like your voice. Clear and direct—not all whispery like the girls in their first Seasons. Not loud and brassy like Marj's. And you're pluck to the backbone. Stood up to Society and turned it round. Throw your heart over more than a fence, I should dashed well imagine."

"All these encomiums, your grace. I am much obliged."

The moonlight glowed softly round her cream skin, and Percy put out his hand to touch her once more.

"Another insect?" she smiled.

"Devilishly buggy out here," he conceded.

"Always coming to my rescue."

"Do anything for you. Wish to be your champion. Wear your favor. You are a devilish fine gal. Wish you would stay at me house . . . and never leave."

"Are your proposing?" Charlette asked, making things direct.

"Dashed if I know!"

"Then, let's assume not. That is one thing, I expect, one should be dashed certain of before risking putting into words. I might have accepted you, and then where would you be?"

"Been the happiest man in the world."

"Quite gallant," Charlette approved, and walked hurriedly into the drawing room.

She had had him in her hands and let him go. Why had she done that, she wondered, and answered immediately with one word— pride. If a man wished to marry her, he best make more of a push to get her!

The days at Wingshire were not varied. There were cards at night, and Lady Austen entertained on the piano. Neither Lady Marjory nor Charlette were of a musical bent, but Charlette and the Duke sang along tonelessly when Lady Austen played recognizable ditties. Lord Austen had a fine voice and often did solos. There was riding, of course. His grace had a superb selection of animals. Frequently, Captain Huntley rode off with Lady Marjory. He had made some attempts to continue his flirtation with

Charlette, but she had resolved not to allow that. Rather, her
manner was of the most reserved. The several attempts he made to
take her aside, she avoided, and generally behaved as if they were
hardly acquainted. Even when he removed his watch fob and
revealed within a lock of golden-red hair, she steadfastly did not
react.

Occasionally he looked at her with a wondering expression,
attempting to transmit his thoughts, but she quickly moved away,
refusing to be the recipient, any more than she would accept his
vocal attentions.

He then began his stratagem of speaking to her through other
people. That is, he would say things to others that could be
interpreted as having another meaning by herself, whereupon he
would fasten her with his fierce glance to see if she understood.
Hopefully, she succeeded in maintaining a blank look while
seething at his tactics.

It was a warm midday, and Lord and Lady Austen had not as yet
come down from their rooms. The rest were in the garden, in
desultory conversation. Actually, the Captain had been continually occupied attempting to get Charlette's attention. Of a sudden
he was aided by the flight of a bird from the tree above him.
Reflexively, Charlette turned her head and met his eyes. Both
were recollecting the wood pigeons that shot out of Freshwater
Cliffs, and both knew instantly they were sharing that remembrance. Darrel reeled the memory in for both by softly saying,
"Freshwater."

The Duke, overhearing, summoned a footman. "Fresh water,
did you wish? Ho, there, a glass of water."

With a laugh, the Captain was about to disabuse him when
Charlette said calmly, "I should like some as well. I oft have a
great thirst for fresh *new* waters." Two could play at Darrel's
game of *double entendre*. And by her emphasis she hoped the
Captain understood she had no desire to dwell in the past. Even in
conversation.

The Duke, impressed by Charlette's emphasis, called after the
footman, "Make that two glasses. By Jove, why skimp! Water all
round, my man. Nay, make that lemonade. Not thirsty, meself, but
recollect a time when I was rather parched, and lemonade . . . or,
I daresay, it was orangeade . . . was just the ticket."

Darrel would not permit his opportunity to be deflected into the
Duke's pointless meanderings.

"Speaking of fresh water, there is a ring of white rock cliffs on

Wight, three miles in length, called Freshwater Cliffs. Once seen, they never leave one's memory. During the summer they are the habitat of a kingdom of birds. One lies back on the rocks and looks up at them nesting or lazily sailing by, and tests each other on spotting the different species: gulls, of course, and guillemots, razor-bills, puffers and cormorants."

"Do say! Ornithologically speaking, are we, what?" the Duke responded, unaware of how that connected, but too polite to point that out.

"I am stalking a bird, yes," Captain Huntley said softly, never deviating his eye from Charlette, watching her every reaction. She wanted to remind him that she usually won that contest, but then recollected she was not to be reached anymore by his shallow, obvious tactics. He sensed her reluctance, and yet pressed on, his voice insistent. "The sound of the ocean came over us, and we'd close our eyes and list to its humming us to sleep."

"Nodded off, did you? Hope not while steering your ship," the Duke put in, still attempting to keep apace with the conversation. Lady Marjory was listening intently, but so far had not found a foothold.

"The fire of a pistol!" the Captain shouted, and paused purposely, while his aristocratic listeners reacted in prodigious alarm; the Duke dropped open his mouth, and Lady Marjory, in a relative reaction, similarly opened her mouth, but delicately covered it with her hand. Charlette merely waved her fan, attempting to wave away her attention.

"Or one could sound a bugle or clap hands in succession—any method causes the birds to rise," Darrel's deep voice continued, softer now. And the wild world of the island was now appearing before her: the cliffs, white as a cloud, looming above, and below, the deep blue of the sea, with the wind constantly hitting against the cliffs' sides, scraping off nature's settling in of grass or bush, cleanly cutting to the fresh white chalk. Inexorably, he carried on. "Two children clapped and shouted till, from thousands of ledges, the birds rose and flooded the sky, forming one massive, winged shadow that wiped out the sun."

He had succeeded in drawing the picture for her. Helplessly, she had given him her hand and let him draw her back to that moment on the sand, the two of them standing there, with the birds winging all about them. And the great glee that rose within. She shivered again now, as the birds newly went through her, and Darrel saw her shiver, and smiled, content to have woven one more thread between them that would bind her back to the past and him.

"Shot the birds, did you? Never ate a sea gull meself, but shot many a partridge and pigeon. Need the right size shot for so small a game. The sport is in the speed of their flight, actually," the Duke continued.

Pleasantly, Darrel explained, "It's the birds' eggs that are the real delicacy, your grace. And their feathers are collected as well. The country people drive stakes on top of the cliff and tie a rope to one end of that and a board of wood to the other end to make a seat, and lower themselves over the side." Then smoothly he turned to Charlette and carried on their conversation. "One goes to all limits to pluck an egg another might have thought was safely in his nest." And he gave her a slow smile that lasted as long as their eyes held.

"Poor spirit plucking eggs from a nest! No sport in that!" the Duke scoffed.

"Quite a daring sport, actually," Charlette could not resist inserting. "The cliffs there are several hundreds of feet high, and if one doesn't know how to manipulate the ropes, one could be dashed to the rocks below."

"All for an egg! I say, that's coming on too strong for such a little value."

Darrel was laughing then aloud. "It is not for the egg, nor for a mere feather, but for the challenge of it, I expect."

And Charlette agreed. "Actually, for the moment when one is back on top with basket filled, having overcome the sensible self within that was crying out about risking one's life, not to mention the gross impropriety for a lady . . ." She paused and grinned at that. "The accomplishment, I daresay, is a conquering of self."

Now they were openly talking only to each other. Darrel, dropping all pretense, came closer, and said, "And we gave the eggs to a village lady, Mrs. Dawson, and she said, 'But them's trophy eggs, little miss. You must always eat your victory to keep it yourn.' And we ate one egg raw, right there before her, and gave her the rest."

And Charlette, forgetting all her own warnings, was joyously recalling. "And we each took a feather from the basket to wear behind an ear, feeling ourselves rather something!"

"And we were!" they both said in unison, laughing.

"Oh, I say, are we reminiscing?" the Duke said, in disgust.

"Quite right, old boy," Darrel said, with a grin.

"Not jolly fair, using a lady's past. A lady might not wish to be reminded of certain past occurrences. A true gentleman would not force those reminders on her."

"But a sailor lives on *memories*. Oft, on a long voyage, one has nothing but memories to keep one sane. Especially when having been sent to the masts. Then memories turn punishment into pleasure, as one lays there, under the basking sun, not even wiping away the sweat, lest any disturbance of balance might send one plummeting to the sea."

"I say! Moved along from memory-sharing to boasting of one's sad plights, have we? Not the thing, old boy. Shockingly bad ton. The trick, I expect, of naught but the most rackety traveling . . . gentlemen!"

Not insulted in the least, Darrel merely bowed, replying, "You flatter me, your grace. I have some small claims of being a traveler, but, blast me, I never pretended to be a *gentleman!*"

"Never thought I'd hear anyone brag about that!" the Duke exclaimed, confused.

"Belay that thought, Duke. We don't all wish for your dignities. Know crews of sailors who wouldn't spit on the best part of you—cause you be a landlubber! But if you're claiming my adventures are shams, that does get me hackles up! Although 'tweren't much of an adventure climbing to the mast; children do as much." He looked again at Charlette. "I meself played up there . . . with a companion, and our only problem was we might sweat too much and slip off.".

"Infamous to continue in the way you're going, sir!" the Duke dithered. "A gentleman does not use *that* word! And you have used it twice, and before two ladies!"

"What the devil is he dribbling about!" the Captain exclaimed.

Charlette felt it behooved her to explain. "Not having dealt all your life with ladies, but rather just girls and women, Captain, you are not aware of a principle of nature, and that is that ladies have no bodily functions, and therefore, should find it distressing to hear about a gentleman's . . . eh, perspiration."

"Well, blow me down, is that what all this dither is about? You mean, sweat?"

"I say!" the Duke ejaculated. "You've done it again. One more mention of that word and you shall meet me, sir! I collect you are being deliberately offensive!"

"Certainly not. It is just my nature to be so . . . I mean, my nature to be direct. Your pardon, Miss Varrick . . . and Lady Marjory."

"Granted," Lady Marjory said with hauteur. Yet, unable to check her curiosity and rather annoyed at her brother for challenging *her* guest, she continued the discussion. "But when you were positioned up there in the height of the sails, in such direct access to the sun, surely you should have provided some means of preventing your, eh, discomfort. Indeed, even here in London, I cannot comprehend why gentlemen who use devices for their decoration should feel it beneath their manly dignity to carry a fan!" And to illustrate, she removed her fan from the reticule, hanging on her wrist. "At such an occasion as you described, Captain Huntley, it would have been of inestimable use!"

"Indeed! I wonder why I did not think of it!"

"Perhaps you forgotten it in your reticule—below deck," Charlette inserted.

"Doubtless," Darrel agreed, suppressing his grin. "Although regretfully, on a mast, one lacks a free hand for proper use of a fan. Yet, for other occasions, fans might be most handy. I shall offer a full ration to be distributed to my crew, along with their usual portion of rum, on the next voyage!"

"A fan would be preferable to the rum, Captain," Lady Marjory continued, delighted to be having some effect on his running of his ship, and never loath to tell people exactly how to manage doing things about which she knew nothing whatsoever. It gave her a feeling of scope. "Certainly, during excessive heat, rum would only heat the blood more. If refreshment be needed, I recommend lemonade."

"Fans and lemonade, instead of rum," Darrel repeated seriously, as if logging it in his memory. "Do you have any other recommendations—I, and my entire fleet, shall be entirely at your service."

"Fleet!" Charlette could not help but inserting. Suddenly a great many other memories came flooding back to her, and none of them of help to Darrel's campaign.

"I am always fully equipped with recommendations," Lady Marjory said with unbecoming modesty, fluttering her fan with self-satisfied gusto as she rose. "Let us discuss them on our stroll. It is time for my constitutional."

Rising with alacrity, Darrel replied, "My honor, your ladyship. How far a walk had you in mind? Shall we be back afore tea?"

Lady Marjory was slightly taken aback. "I meant up to that bench and back."

Covering his surprise, Darrel properly extended his hand. Languidly, Lady Marjory accepted it, and they strolled ten feet away; whereupon fatigued by the journey, they succumbed to resting themselves on a farther stone bench for a tête-à-tête.

Turning to the Duke, hovering near, Charlotte said, "Would you care to walk?"

Disappointed, the Duke could only acquiesce, but when he saw that Charlette meant in an opposite direction, he exclaimed, "Jolly good! We shall show 'em what a stroll really is, eh what? Are you up to the gazebo?" He indicated the marble edifice under the willows, not only within walking but calling distance as well. She nodded, thinking of the miles of walks she had taken, and heard the Duke enthusiastically exclaiming, "There we can be private at last! Shall we not, Miss Varrick?"

"If that is what you wish," she replied with a small smile.

"With all my dashed heart!"

At the gazebo, the Duke helped her up the two steps, and after much dusting of the seat with his lace handkerchief, and shooing away a curious, determined bee attracted by its scent, they sat side by side.

"Now, Miss Varrick, I have something of a most particular nature to say to you."

"Perhaps we can all hear it?" a deep voice interrupted. "I always so enjoy hearing things of particular nature."

The Captain and a panting Lady Marjory were ascending the gazebo's stairs. "We felt the sun was too direct, and thought to join you in seeking shelter here," he said smoothly, wiping the seat with his hand, and almost plopping the heavily breathing Lady Marjory alongside of Charlette.

"That was a jolly good run," Lady Marjory finally spoke when she had new breath.

"Isn't it pleasant? All of us here together?" Captain Huntley inserted, seating himself between the Duke and Charlotte, for the Duke, having had too much of a nicety to crowd the lady, had left quite a space between. The Captain, having no such nicety, pushed in, comfortably stretching out his legs. "Jolly cozy, ain't we, your grace?"

"Jolly," the Duke acknowledged politely, but his voice was low.

"Are we to do everything together from now on?" Charlette asked in amusement.

"I cannot think of a more fitting way to spend the fortnight," Darrel agreed heartily, eyeing them all with amusement. "I dare say since we have taught the ton to dance in triangles, it shall not be difficult, in private, to be squaring off."

And so they continued boxed in for a good part of the visit. Then there was the morning when Charlette rose early and went for a ride to the lake. She had just dismounted when Darrel rode up and joined her, standing quietly at her side. The dawn mist was rising over the water, and Charlette said, almost reflectively, "So peaceful."

Keeping his eyes on her, rather than the view, Darrel replied, "Too peaceful. Not for the likes of us. We want wild seas and cliffs that can break a man's back. Just as our women can break a man's heart."

"There you go, playing your games," she said matter-of-factly. "Obviously, you are courting Lady Marjory. Why must you continue these libertine ways! And with me! I did not think you would ever treat me . . . so shabbily!"

"*I* treat you shabbily! You have treated me infernally all my life! And if I have occasionally taken a little of my own back, it is only justice!"

"You are in earnest at last?" she exclaimed. "Is that what this is all about?"

Darrel turned away from her blazing eyes, unable not to tell her the truth.

She moved quickly in front of him, demanding harshly, "Answer me, Darrel! Are you in London merely to revenge yourself on me! *I* who have ever been your friend, and even been your friend here!"

"Blast you, when have you been anything but the grand lady to me—treating me with a degree of kindness, and yet maintaining a distance that one would give a favorite servant! Even your rushing to rescue me from social disgrace was maddening! Do you think I care a whit for this puny, quizzing-glass toting, cravat-choked, dandified Society and its hysterical ladies who cannot keep their hands off me, while pretending to be modesty's maidens! I scorn them all! And you, as well!"

"Scorn for scorn then, Darrel, and as of old, we'll see who can best the other at that game!" Charlette said hotly and turned to leave, when he quickly grabbed hold.

"You'll always win that game, my girl, you are a master of it. And at inflicting pain on me by doing so."

"I never scorned you," Charlette cried. "We were always heart-friends, and I remained so even when you deserted me to seek your glory and scarcely bothered to write or seek me out when you returned, but only sought to injure me and mine."

"Who first played the Society game—putting it up as a barrier between us! Yet, I bested you in that, did I not? Showed you what fools all these Society people be. And still you run after them, ignoring me throughout this visit, turning away." And his voice softened as he continued. "Nay, Charle, I could not injure you one quarter as much as you do me by merely looking away. You need only do that to blast me through."

Feeling his hands almost breaking hers as he gripped them, Charlette stared back at his whitened face and felt herself swept up by the gale of his emotion, allowing herself to be taken along for a moment. Then, she pulled back, and breathed out defensively, "Shall I believe you are in earnest? Or are we playing one more grand game . . . whose loss for me shall be a loss, indeed."

"Play the game out," he urged. "One more challenge! Come, Charle, have the courage to reveal your feelings for me. But I shall dare first. I'll jump first into the sea and wait for you to come along. If I do, will you come?"

Charlette took a deep breath, hesitating, tottering on the rail. Some strong adult sense of self-preservation held her back, and she even stepped back, but he would not allow it, pulling her closely, not loosening her even between kisses. "The devil take these safe, ladylike ways you've learned! Be yourself, Charle! Say what's in your heart and accept what's in mine! Say you love me one particle as much as I have loved you—ever!"

Her senses were so disordered, Charlette could only hear his last sentence, for he'd repeated it several times, until it pierced through her whirl of emotions.

"I loved you . . . ever," she whispered back.

And Darrel, at that, let out a cry of triumph that she could feel hollowly echoing in her own body.

Chapter Fifteen

EVER lasted until Charlette was handed a letter on her return to Wingshire Castle. Much struck by its weight, Charlette opened it in alarm. It was from her father, and not his usual brief note, but three full pages of his large scrawl.

Earlier, her letter revealing her full knowledge of his romance with her mother, and her admiration of both of them for following their hearts had received his usual handful of lines. "Much moved. Knew I could count on our daughter. Mother would be as proud as I am. Carry on, dear child, with your usual pluck. When days become tiresome, come home. Wight and I are waiting to welcome you."

A following missive giving details of her social acceptance, especially at Almack's, and an extra sheet for the kindnesses of Lord and Lady Austen, plus mentions of several marriage proposals, had gone unanswered. Yet, her hasty note upon her arrival at Wingshire Castle in which she merely included that Captain Huntley was also of the party brought forth her father's verbosity.

She was not to trust the scoundrel. She must be fully alive to his various machinations. There was a concentrated campaign by Huntley-Bates to mill him down. And he urged her to cut the blackguard's acquaintance. The Bates brothers were considerably puffed up about Captain Huntley's success in Society, and were using it as an inducement for further investors. Taken in concert with their considerable winnings from the side betting at the London Prize Race, they were presently flush enough to set up a competitive yacht-building firm adjacent to his own on Cowes!

A few years back, her father acknowledged, these maneuvers would not have even concerned him, but, of late, he had been in a devil of a bind due to his excessive patriotism. After the war

there were several captains who had given their all to their country
and been retired on paupers' pensions. Mr. Varrick could not but
engage them, and, similarly, rescue and refurbish the war-surplus
ships. Not wishing to curb her pleasures, Mr. Varrick had not
written about his reversals. Anyone who engaged in trade had to
make arrangements with the East India Company, as he had done,
which generally left him with the short end of the bargain. But
Huntley-Bates refused to follow the old ways, deeming that since
the changes in 1813, monopolies need no longer be observed, and
they were sailing *independent*. Yet, that young jackanapes,
instead of falling on his face as he should have done, had reaped
unconscionable profits and set the pattern for Varricks' own
subsidiaries. Thus, blast it, Varricks was being attacked on all
sides. But Huntley-Bates' most dastardly act was spreading the
rumor that Varricks was collapsing. Which was untrue. They had
a long wait before he should cock up his toes! Admittedly, he was
a trifle cucumberish, but he was hardly in dun territory! Still, to
end this harassment, he'd even humiliated himself by sending a
note warning the boy not to overreach himself with this yachting
enterprise.

In reply, Captain Huntley had returned a two-line note of the
grossest incivility, indicating once set upon a purpose, *old-time
acquaintance* would not deter him! Upon receiving that, Mr.
Varrick was spurred to write to his daughter, to warn her of this
young man's machinations. His every act was not to be trusted, for
everything he did was geared to one end only—the destruction of
the Varricks!

By the time Charlette had allowed the letter to fall from her
hands, she was thrown into a positive quake. It had required
several readings to accept the full import of her father's message.
For, on one hand, there was the devastating news of the instability
of Varricks, which, while somewhat alarming as regards the
comfort of her future, mainly had her concerned for her father. It
was not usual for Mr. Varrick to be the slightest bit overset by
competition, nor about finances, actually. And here she had been
making matters worse for him by her lavish spending all over
London. And not merely her own spending, but now she cringed
at her winking at her aunt's exploitation of her father. Oh, she had
known about the double-billing, and the redoing of a good part of
the house under the guise of preparations for the Season. But in
sympathy for her ladyship's years of deprivations, she had
encouraged her father's accountant to be generous. Now, she

could only chastise herself for being so concerned with everyone else's situation, and her own success, and not picking up on her father's plight until he had been reduced to spelling it out! Infamous of her.

And added to that was the agony of her not having received this letter one day sooner. Before she had made her declaration to Captain Huntley! Good God, on recollecting his manipulation of her, she could only squirm, particularly as she saw again the look of satisfaction in his eyes. Nay, even contempt. Doubtless, she now ranked with his harem girls to be fed cheese under her veil! Ignoble!

Nothing could erase that picture of herself! Her only easement was that there had been no public acknowledgment of her regard, and she was at least saved from that humiliation, as well as her father's ever knowing how she had betrayed them both.

Picking up the letter, she reread it. Now when she put it down, there was calm acceptance of her situation. Captain Huntley had been deliberately gulling her, as he had all the other girls on the Marriage Mart. It was she who had been blindfolded by her own self-confidence and conviction that she was special to him. The additional intensity that had her believing him sincere, as regards to herself, obviously was rather an added relish in overcoming the Varricks—father and daughter!

There was an hour of emotion, during which several scenarios flicked through her head, Darrel denying and she cleverly exposing him. Then, that not sufficient, she changed to Darrel's proving that it all had been a shocking mistake. That last could not be credited, not in view of her father's letter, Mr. Hitchens' warning before the London Ball, and indeed, her own sensing of his reveling in their competition at that very ball and later at his jibes at Society! But she had allowed herself to forget that side of him in the joy of their being together.

Having accustomed herself to facing challenges with an undaunted air, Charlette refused to devote any more time or thoughts to regrets. Therefore, she sent down a message that she was occupied writing letters, giving her a free afternoon to make her plans. Just before the dinner hour, Lady Austen knocked and could not be denied. They discussed the letter her ladyship had received disclosing that her youngest son must needs to London for a tooth extraction. Her ladyship was in a tizzy. She did not wish to be wanting as to her companionship to Charlette, but her motherly emotions cried out she accompany her son to the jaw-breaker, and not leave him to his old nanny. Rarely an alarmist as regards her sons, Lady Austen once had had a particularly shocking extraction which left her with a severe case of dental panic. Seeing her own solution in her ladyship's ambivalence, Charlette announced they must all depart. Obviously, both were called back to town by their duty to their loved ones. She, as well, had received a letter from her father necessitating her immediate return to Wight.

Ordinarily Lady Austen would have inquired further, but so distracted was she by Nanny's note describing the swelling of her son's jaw in such multi-colored detail, that she could only be grateful to Charlette for the solution. Rushing to begin preparations for their departure on the morrow, she kissed the dear girl, who was looking far from well, but after being assured Charlette's teeth were not giving her pain, she had no other fear.

At dinner, Lady Austen's description of her child's sufferings, while not of great interest, at least gave all something to discuss. The Duke was so kind as to recollect that he had had a tooth pulled by a friend at Harrow. "Chap put a string round it and round a doorknob. Next chap entering, pulled the bloo . . . eh, blasted thing out!"

"That form of dentistry is not for general application," Lady Marjory interposed. "Percy has very little sensation of pain. I once dropped a horseshoe on his boot, and he did naught but complain about my ruining the shine."

"Hardy type," the Duke said, with a modest grin.

That called for a round of dentist stories that continued through the three courses and two removes. Not even the most gory descriptions impeded the appetites of the victims, although Lady Austen was finding it quite difficult to chew. Charlette was surreptitiously observing the Captain to sense whether he were the greatest hoaxer or the most misjudged of men. He seemed like neither, while making a good meal and adding graphic descriptions of dentistry aboard ship. And then, when he sent a warm glance her way, over the head of Lady Marjory, she realized with a jolt that he had made quite an art of duplicity. His entire maneuvers at Wingshire had been ones of disguise, deceit and double-meanings. But then, she took a longer look at the face she had known all her life. Heavens! He could not be so complete a sham, and she not know it here!—she almost pounded her heart, but then heard her name.

"Charlette, dear, are you overcome?" Lady Austen inquired, as all eyes turned.

It was immediately concluded that the topic was too extreme, and it was then noticed as well that she had not touched her dinner. Lord Austen introduced a topic that could not possibly disturb one's digestion—hunting.

When the ladies had retired, awaiting the gentleman, Charlette concluded she could not continue in such indecision. Rather, she would meet Darrel in the garden and ask for an explanation. Every man was entitled to be heard before final judgment!

Lady Austen and Charlette were sitting on the settee when Lady Marjory surprised by inching in between them. "Forgive me, pray, but I wish to say something of the greatest confidentiality and do not wish to be overheard as yet by the staff."

Lady Austen encouraged her to speak freely. Charlette moved away, as far as the settee allowed—a dread was overtaking her, like a rising tide swamping over a deck.

"Captain Huntley and I are to be wed," Lady Marjory whispered, hugging herself in exaltation, and that not sufficing, she hugged each one of the ladies in turn.

At the gentlemen's entrance, Lady Marjory made the announcement universal, in front of the staff as well. The Duke was most concerned, emitting a succession of "by Joves." After recourse to his snuff, the Duke announced he was knocked acock! "Here's a facer! A flush hit right in the breadbasket!"

While Lady Marjory was making her explanations to her affronted brother, Charlette looked toward the happy bridegroom-to-be, who had not said a word. It was then Charlette grasped she no longer could sense his feelings. Not a vestige of his emotions or thoughts reached her. The connection between them was cut off. That, more than anything said by anyone else, either her father or Lady Marjory, convinced her that Darrel had been false—false of face, false of tongue . . . and false of heart.

At that moment he grinned and made the victor's motion they usually made when one had beaten the other, and Charlette's heart thudded, indeed. Yes, his victory was total, and she ignored his continuing signal to meet him outside.

The next morning she and the Austens rose for an early departure. While waiting for the approaching carriage, the Captain whispered he had something to say to her.

"You had the opportunity to speak to us all last night and did not take it," Charlette replied, turning to the approaching Duke and thanking him for his hospitality. His grace bowed and offered regrets at her leaving as he handed her into the coach. Inside, she did not look out at either the Duke waving or the Captain staring after.

Charlette did not remain for the tooth extraction in London. Lady Austen assured her that her accompaniment was not needed, and so she departed immediately for her island. When she arrived there, her father repeated the details with more emphasis and such embarrassment she could no longer have any doubts. Great was his relief at her assurances that she was not the object of the Captain's lures, that rather he had been occupied making an offer to Lady Marjory—which had been accepted.

Mr. Varrick turned white at that. "The fellow's going to have additional capital, then. The blighter. Poor lady!" And he was off to Cowes to see what could be done with his advance knowledge, before the announcement came out in the *Gazette*.

It was not a full day later that her butler announced a gentleman calling. Charlette put down her book of poems as he was ushered in. It was not Darrel, but the young poet with whom in the earlier part of her Season she had debated the relative merits of their homes. Foolishly she had promised to show him her island, and in mopes over his reviews, he had made an impulsive return visit. Discovering a purpose, she ceased stroking Froth and set about stroking *his* confidence. At a sequestered glen, he crowned her with a handful of primroses as well as words of such delicacy they were a balm to her spirits; and as he came closer to view the world through her "enkindled" eyes, he was lifted up into the air before those very eyes.

"What are you doing with this sapling?" Darrel demanded.

Ignoring the Captain, Charlette rose, requesting the young poet put down his fists and escort her back to the castle. Which he was pleased to do. She hardly had time to direct the poet into the library and furnish him with a standish, quills and paper, when she was summoned to the morning room to receive another visitor.

"I suppose that man is here, preparing to burst in on us with his ditty, as Sir Smithers did during our Triangling?" Darrel said, seeking a lighter tone between them.

But she did not smile. "He is in the library. You may adjourn there to peruse his work, which I request you do, for it has a sensitivity you are sorely in need of."

"Blast you," he grinned. "I don't know whether to be amused or enraged."

"You are hardly in the position to be either. Have you brought Lady Marjory along to christen your new yachting line?"

"Ah, I collect we have many grievances against me. Yet, beginning with the first, I am not engaged to Lady Marjory. Though if I were, I would have outplayed you by winning a noble, despite your blatant lures to his grace. But I digress. My flirting with Lady Marjory had no more seriousness than with any other lady. Actually, we were discussing my intentions toward ladies in general, and I said lightly that I never made offers of matrimony in the summertime! Which, good grief, cannot possibly be conceived as an offer! By anyone! Indeed, she herself did not take it as such, asking what was the *season* for my offers—which showed she understood we were jesting! And then, by Jove, that afternoon, *after* we had met by the lake, she approached, claiming to have decided to make me the happiest man in the world by accepting my proposal! Immediately, I reminded her that I had *not* proposed, having specified never to propose in the summertime, and she replied she was content to wait until the fall!"

He looked to Charlette to share his laughter, but as she was coldly serious, he continued. "The Devil! I could not disentangle myself! She was deaf to all disclaimers! I intended to tell you about it and have us both leave. But you rushed off!"

"All this is merely funning, is it? Have you always been so shallow?" Charlette asked in a calm, wondering tone. "So uncaring about a lady's feelings? Well, now you have been properly caught, and I am delighted. You have been on the town long enough to realize a gentleman cannot possibly cry off once an engagement is announced by the lady. She alone can do so. Therefore, I advise you to prepare yourself for a long and happy life with her ladyship—through many a summer."

"That shall not happen to me," Darrel said calmly. "I told you—indeed, I told all Society—that I am not a gentleman, and thus, I cannot be forced into marriage."

"Your basic sense of decency shall force you into it," Charlette merely said, wandering away from him toward her open balcony. They could hear the sea from there, and she wished to hear only it and no longer this false man's excuses.

"I have no basic sense of decency," Darrel said, and still she would not smile.

"I expect that is so. Yet, you do have a strong basic sense of profit, and shall not ignore the investment possibilities of her dowry. All of Wight talks of naught else but the new Huntley-

Bates Yachting Enterprise. My father informed me this morning that, due to your inexperience in yacht design, your investors are wobbly. What could settle them down quicker, or rather make them unnecessary, than Lady Marjory's fortune?"

"If you think I plan to marry for money . . ." Darrel cried out in anger.

"Of course," Charlette replied, her face quite cold and distant, "you might not need to go to the expense of starting up a new line. Wasn't that why you were not in earnest in your proposal to her ladyship, because you assumed you already had a fully operating yachting firm, one that set the standard for perfection of design for years . . . not to mention achieving with the same maneuver the entire Varrick Shipping Line?"

Darrel was fully silenced. And then he swore a bit and said in a blast of fury, "How can you so undervalue yourself . . . and so pronounce me as a person of no honor at all! Having known me so long, do you really think I am so false—to the very core?"

"You have played me false. You have played all the women in Society false."

"And you! Are you not equally false! With your Sir Smithers and your Dukes, and now you're scarcely home and already you have a new little follower. Surely, you swore falsely to me about loving me ever! Why not admit that all along you never believed me equal to you? *You* wished a Duke—well, *I* got his sister. Not that I offered for her, and if you'll recollect, Miss Varrick, I did not make you an offer either. Merely wanted a bit of honesty in our feelings. I'm not prepared to be leg-shackled by anyone, for a long time. And when I do propose, it shall be upon discovering a woman like your mother, who risked her position in life for the man she loved. She took up his challenge and was willing to be ruined rather than lose him! But you cannot equal her. Too much of your father in you! Too much Miss Varrick and scarcely any Charle left that I can see."

Miss Varrick remained Miss Varrick as she went to the bell rope, and rang. "Mitchen shall see you out. No doubt you have similar calls to several ladies of fortune to make in the area, and I should not wish to detain you."

"You go to the devil!" he exclaimed and strode out, unescorted.

Recollecting the poet, Charlette realized she could not rush to her room to review the conversation. Rather, she entered the library. Perhaps he could wipe the Captain's words out of her mind with some of his. But he was still writing at a fast clip, and even unaware of her entrance. A page fell off the desk as he completed it, rushing onto a new sheet. Picking it up, she perused it. Two lines echoed through her:

"Feel we these things?—that moment have we stept
Into a sort of oneness, and our state is like a floating spirit's."

She would have spoken to him about the beauty of his words, but feared to interrupt. She could only sit and continue reading— and consider how he appeared like an ordinary person and yet was like a bird, with a song coming out as sweet as a nightingale's. And she felt tears, and knew not whether they were for the rhymes or her own conclusion that people must be viewed for what they were within, and not lightly disbelieved. Darrel had always been unique to her—a man of emotions not obvious to any but her. Heavens, had she been wrong to cease believing in his uniqueness? Had that not been what he was attempting to prove by his flaunting of Society—that neither she nor he need suit themselves to it? Rather, he had made them all turn around and suit themselves to him!

Charlette felt a flush of hope, but it died as she further recollected that he had treated her as he had Society, flaunting, taunting . . . daunting. His very pointing out that he had not made her an offer proved, rather, how little he believed in *her* uniqueness! For then his offer became one of a temporary and shameful liaison, a *carte blanche*! Obvious now why he urged her to believe in the unimportance of Society's rules! No, she would not look for the unique in him if he could not see it in her. Ah, Darrel, she cried within herself, he was still her puzzlement and . . . torment.

She heard the voice of her poet, and realized he was waiting for her reaction to his poem. Upon her praising it so warmly, he flushed. His eyes had the look of a man coming from another land, and she wished with all her heart she could be he!

"Miss Varrick," he whispered, "this island and you, both fill my heart with soft and glorious music." That was a comfort at the moment, and later when she heard that Darrel had left the island and herself, she recollected Mr. Keats' words and poem, and felt there was something of beauty still on earth.

Subsequently, her father made her acquainted with the particulars of Darrel's actions. Captain Huntley had set sail to meet his ship due from the South Seas. That proved he wished to go for the

South Sea Island trade by winning *that* London Prize as well. "Never been done before, taking over for two of one's captains! Never such a thirst for prominence! Curse him. I'd hoped that with Captain Holland at our helm, he being with Nelson at Trafalgar, we had a shot! Now that cold-blooded devil is after another chunk of my hide!"

So much for the puzzle that was Darrel. Clearly, he was after his pleasure and profit first, and no matter whom he sailed over.

That conclusion was more than affirmed when Jem Barker paid her father a hurried visit. After being closeted for awhile, Jem exited, shaking his head at her. "The boy's done it again. That scapegrace . . . that shuffling rogue."

Jem had uncovered a Huntley-Bates spy placed aboard the Varrick ship *Winged Angel* going for the London Prize, whose object it was to encourage Captain Holland's tendency to drink. "This noa be a fair race with one captain ape-drunk and the other, the champion—Darrel Huntley, hisself."

More in sorrow than anger, Jem was, but Charlette, out of countenance, cried out in high dudgeon, "What is Father doing about it?"

When Jem bemoaned there was nothing to be done, she insisted, "But we cannot wait for him to win and then cry foul! We must prevent it from happening beforehand!" And when Jem, suspicious of that look in her eye, moved to leave, she stopped him. "You and I can do it, Jem. Father need not be the wiser. We shall meet the *Winged Angel* passing by here *before* she hits the Channel's turn, and board and warn the Captain of the treachery aboard. And then we shall sail on to victory! Wouldn't that be a lark! And we shall just be assuring a *fair* race!"

But Jem cried, "Noa! Your father'd make me walk the plank. Noa, missy! Noooaa!"

Continuing to urge him on, Charlette reminded him of all the times she and Darrel had made the trip up the Channel with old Captain Huntley, assuring him she would get the authorization from her father. "We'll catch the blackguards and turn the race fair!" she finished, and Jem, watching her excited face and her confidence spilling over on him, was left with nothing to say. She could always make him do what she wished, for he felt her to be the child he never had, as he had once felt toward Darrel. Proud of her, he was, for her pluck and daring. And the Varricks had to do something! "We're in for a sea change," he grinned toothlessly at her. "We be so, by gum."

Charlette made Lady Austen her excuse for her sudden absence, and had her father sign a note to her, which he did without looking, and thus signed their authorization. Mr. Varrick's list-lessness was even more of an incentive for her act. She would save him from one more blow; her mother would wish her to! And, she admitted to herself, of a sudden, with a grin, "I shall dashed well enjoy being a lady-at-sea. I haven't been sailing like this in ages! Ah, we shall beat that havey-cavey Captain, and show him what it means to come to grips with a Varrick who isn't a gentleman either!"

Chapter Sixteen

AT the rail Charlette watched the ship's surging leaps and the waves flying white before her; above, the shrouds strained as the *Winged Angel* flew, and that motion, after so long being landlocked, filled her with unspeakable joy. She was dressed as a gentleman in pantaloons, boots and a large coat that gave her a more dominating form. With hair pinned up under a cap and a last minute inspiration of the addition of a Duke-like quizzing-glass, she was regarded as quality, especially since she so strictly kept her distance from crew and officers.

Barker and she, with use of their paper, had shown themselves as Varrick representatives and taken over without the slightest opposition. Indeed, Captain Holland was three sheets to the wind and easily locked in sick bay. His known companion in his drinking bouts was placed in irons for further official interrogations at port. Lieutenant Waters, in control, had done a credible enough job to have the *Winged Angel* in the Channel at the same time as Huntley-Bates' *Porpoise*. But the latter was clearly ahead.

Positioning herself on a long chair lashed to the rail on the poop, and screened by a canvas, Charlette rested there, consulting a paper, often jumping up to check course and the trim of the yards. Through Lieutenant Waters, she gave all the orders. Her first ruling was half pay for all who refused to put their hearts into the race, and bonuses for all if they won. But when the role of Bates' spy was revealed, all hands on the ship were united into a team—eager, cheering for victory.

Yet, it might have come too late. The *Porpoise* was still ahead, even though the *Winged Angel* was moving at a fast clip of fourteen knots. A disagreement between Waters and Jem was decided by Charlette on Jem's side. They were to risk hoisting a foretopmast stunsail. Though closing in, every advantage had to be taken. For the *Porpoise* not only had a disciplined crew and its competent original captain, but now boasted of a superb new captain and previous race winner. On their side was only a superior ship, the pride of the Varrick Line, and the incentive of the crew to work its heart out. And they did so, until a mere hundred yards separated the two ships, and still, relentlessly, miraculously, the *Winged Angel* neared.

On the poop deck of the *Porpoise*, Charlette saw Darrel, his large frame relaxing against the wind, a big grin of victory on his face. He turned and strode to the deck rail just as the *Winged Angel* began pulling alongside. A streak of daring, characteristic of Captain Huntley in all his actions, whether in Society or on sea, had him laughing at his competition and ordering his ship to luff to get windward, actually about to cross the bow of the Varrick ship. Unable to resist, Charlette pulled off her cap, and the wind pulled out the pins till her long golden-red hair was caught up and on the rise, forming a sail around her head.

"Charle!" he called. But she did not hear it, for the wind had taken his word away with it, yet she saw her name on his lips and smiled back, removing her long overcoat as well. Perhaps it was being on the sea, or the heightened joy of competing with each other, but they were communicating again. And when he understood what she was suggesting, even before the pointing to the masts, he grinned at that challenge and took her on. Ignoring Jem's cries, Charle climbed. All her concentration was on that, discovering with each step her body was not as limber as when a child. Or the wind was too strong for their contest. Yet she climbed, slipping once but refusing to back down. Rather fall into the sea! When she reached the masthead, Charle gracefully stretched out along the cross-trees, and only then glanced at the *Porpoise* and saw Darrel. Curse him, he had bettered her by walking to the extreme end of the topsail yard, and at that dizzy height had stretched out nonchalantly between the yard and studding-sail boom. The roll of the ship was making it difficult enough for Charlette to hang on where she was; it was not possible for her to go higher.

For a wild moment, she was considering challenging him to jump into the sea. It would be less of a fall for her than from his height; yet, even from where she was sailors had drowned. But from the topsail yard, Darrel would break every bone in his body. Still, she was tempted, feeling they could do anything at that moment and succeed, till she felt his warning and stopped. A gust of wind had her laughing, wondering if she were going to fall, after all. Better if she had jumped. A heavy roll of the ship brought her close to a crest of a wave, and Charle reached out and patted it with a toe as it passed below her, leaving her arms stretched almost out of joint, holding on. And before another wave tested her again, Charlette was making her way down. The wind escorted her to the rail. He was there, already waiting, waving, laughing in relief to see her safely down. Intent in their communication, both ignored the further rise of the wind. Even as the ships pulled apart, the two old friends held on through their eyes, and to the last blended their sights on each other.

Yet Darrel would not relent. Forgetting the race, he ordered his ship to come round and head straight for the *Winged Angel*. The two ships, so close, seemed as if they would merge and sink together in an embrace, becoming one pile of destruction. And the wind, whistling in the riggings, was the only winner over all. Charlette, closing her eyes, felt him reaching across and embracing her, using the wind as his surrogate. But with Jem Barker and Waters in charge, the *Winged Angel* got the best position and went past—pulling ahead before Darrel could be reached by his staff and brought to the realization that they were being left behind. Still bemused, Darrel watched the *Winged Angel* sail away. He had to close out the after-image of Charle before he was finally able to fully bring himself back to the race.

"We're ahead!" Charlette was shouting, and the crew, some recognizing her as Miss Varrick, some seeing her as a Sea Goddess, all concluded, with the miracle of their lead, that she was their good luck.

When the night came on, it brought with it a thick fog that clouded out all competition. No visibility fore or aft. They were close to the Strait of Dover, near the Downs, where many a ship had becalmed, and so Charlette, nursing her arms, took this intermission to rest in the now-vacated captain's quarters. Jem's words of warning interrupted her ease. "Blister me, but his pa had cat's eyes, and the boy the like. He'll navigate his way up, while we're stuck waiting for dawn's light. Mark me, if it noa be so."

At dawn, Charlette, back on deck with her spyglass searching the horizon, saw it was so. Darrel had risked the foundering of his ship and crew just to pull ahead.

She'd be blasted if all this was for naught! Ignoring Waters's warnings, she ordered all sails unfurled, including the addition of

those rarely used little light topmost sails—the "trust-to-gods."
They must trust to the gods, indeed.

Once more this maneuver brought them within sighting distance
of the *Porpoise* as the two ships reached the end of the Channel
and rounded at Ramsgate. London was directly ahead. "At least
we made it a close race," Waters said, as the *Porpoise* moved on,
sailing up the Thames toward a second London Prize.

Was it possible for foul tricks to succeed! Charlette thought.
Should not God and the sea be on the side of the angels? And then,
a sign appeared that God had an angelic preference, after all, when
from nowhere a barge came out, blocking the *Porpoise*'s path. By
the time the barge had been maneuvered round, the *Winged Angel*
had taken the lead.

Charle was hanging over the rail, eyeing the dock gate dead
ahead. Just aft, the *Porpoise*, unobstructed now, was making up
its lost yards. Last minute, the superiority and grace of one ship
made the difference. Keeping her eyes on the figurehead of the
angel, Charlette flew with her, urging her to spread her wings, and
it seemed as if she did. One last graceful dip, one last leap, and the
Winged Angel passed through the gate—first. Winning by a wing!

From the wharf came sirens and bells and marlin spears being
beaten. The sounds lifted Charle along; she was sailing on the
rising sensation of victory, felt it spreading throughout her body as
a glow of pure joy. And then the signal cannon fired in
acknowledgment, and Charle came to herself and quickly covered
her hair with her hat. When the dock gates locked behind, she
turned. Darrel and the *Porpoise* were closed out.

From all round the docks and decks was heard the shout: "Long
live Varrick—champion of the seas. Three cheers, mates, for
Winged Angel!" At the bow, Charle stared aft. She had beaten
him, she mused with a smile. And strangely, she wanted him there
to celebrate with her. Lieutenant Waters was at her side with
tearful congratulations; she gave him a smile, but, urged by Jem's
signal, put on her cloak and followed the old man over the side
and down to the waiting boat below, disappearing into the crowd
while the shouts of victory were still being sounded.

In a sennight Charlette had become accustomed to congratulations—both of the self and others variety. Mr. Varrick, while
giving both Jem and his daughter a rare trimming, could not quite
remove the smile from his face long enough to make his stern
words effective. Although Charlette's participation was not dis-
closed, there were whispers throughout the sailing world of her

appearance aboard ship, but not the smallest hint had as yet reached the ton. The official version of the *Winged Angel*'s victory was that Captain Holland had been taken ill and the first mate had taken over.

As so oft, her thoughts returned to Darrel and that moment during the race when they had looked into each other's souls—sharing the joy of the challenge and being each other's competitor. Thus absorbed, she doubly flushed when Mitchen entered and announced none other than the Captain himself. And actually, when she saw him stride in, she had the distinct sense of having conjured him up.

Attempting to crush a rush of inexplicable happiness, Charlette's thoughts were that he had learned his lesson and was come to apologize for his dastardly act. She was prepared to forgive him, as long as he promised most sincerely to mend his ways.

Finally, he spoke, grinning at his own recollection. "I defeated you on the masts, at least. Not much of a consolation, that. But your . . . shall I say . . . delaying tactics, were masterful. You're so delightful a girl. One is always on the jump to keep up to you! Even afterward, I could not blink away that image of you on the mast, with the wind making a spinnaker of your blazing hair . . . and the sun haloing your every motion. My heart was in my mouth following you."

"Not enough not to challenge me to go higher," Charlette exclaimed with a laugh. "Nearly did . . . In fact, actually, I nearly . . ." she hesitated and did not say it.

"You nearly had us both winding up in the sea."

"Yes," she admitted, awed by his knowing it.

"We could have swum to land and told the rest of the world to go to the devil!"

"Yes. We could have done that. But there was the race. It meant so much to you, after all. Considering all you had done to win it. Indeed, subsequently, you risked the foundering of your ship by sailing in the fog of the night."

"Who I? Not a bit of it. There was no risk," he concluded immodestly. "I'm like Froth. I see in the dark. Knowing the Channel so well, I could sail it without use of my eyes." He came closer to her. He was wind-tanned from his days on ship; it made his grey eyes glow like a cat's. He lowered his voice as he continued, "You leave your imprint on my eyes, so everywhere I look, I see you before me, even when your ship sailed on . . . even when I am alone in my cabin."

Catching her breath, Charlette looked about. The familiarity of the Varrick morning room, with its sea paintings and her father's scrimshaw collection in the étagère, brought her to her senses. She realized they were both awkwardly standing, and signaled for him to be seated, then seated herself on the Grecian settee. He sat on the mahogany chair at its side, pulling it closer to her, to continue their confidences.

"The barge came out of nowhere," Charlette conceded, but could not restrain a bit of a laugh. They were enjoying reliving the adventure; it was more amusing seeing it once more through the other's eye, as if one had seen only half the picture and was joining it to its other half—and making it whole.

"That blasted barge," he exclaimed with a whoop. "Admit you called that up!"

"I merely reminded God of his special relationship with winged angels."

"Meaning yourself as well as the ship?"

"I? I am hardly an angel!"

"Are you not? I should say you are. I wished you had wings when on the mast."

"You thought I'd fall? Actually, I nearly did when the wind came up. My body has become a good deal stiffer than when we last climbed."

And so they stroked each other, with memory upon memory, bathing in the glow of that, until Mitchen appeared.

"You rang, Miss Varrick?"

"No, Mitchen, I did not. Unless the Captain wishes some refreshment?"

He shook his head, and Mitchen departed.

"I gather he does not wish you to be alone with me. I remember that old gaffer, he never let me in the front door. Neither did your father." His voice had lost its amused glow and was rather harsh.

"Ah, infamous of us to have treated you so! I collect you have been brooding about it all these years. And with the results that the Varrick Line must be destroyed," Charlette exclaimed. "Even if you have to resort to the most odious means."

From the moment Darrel had entered and pulled her back into their shared world, where no one or nothing else could interrupt their mutual absorption, Charlette had forgotten all he had done to her father. Again and again, she kept seeing Darrel as her playmate of early times, till he himself reminded her of the vengeful Darrel, and she could no longer continue their playful fencing. She rose, and he rose.

"The Darrel I knew would ne'er use dishonorable tactics in a race," she said sadly.

"What are you saying? I scarcely need to be dishonorable to win any race. I am the best sea captain in all of England, nay, say rather Europe . . . and America."

"With all this confidence, why place aboard the *Winged Angel* a spy to incapacitate Captain Holland? I expect you felt you needed an advantage, after all."

Darrel's face was a mixture of the ancient Greek masks of comedy and tragedy as both these emotions played across his visage. "You are not jesting!" he exclaimed. "Ye gods, you are in earnest. You seriously believe that gammon. It is total fustian! I neither sent spies nor encouraged that noted sot, Captain Holland, to revert to his natural inclination. Everyone knew what would happen upon your father's hiring him! He was generally half-sprung on shore. Bound to become completely jug-bitten on a voyage!"

"I myself saw the instigator aboard and had him in irons. He admitted all to Jem."

"Ah, that knock-in-the-cradle! If you took sail on old Jem's words, you're not as needle-witted as I recollect! He called me a traitor and a pirate for sailing under American colors!"

"You taunted us all with that possibility. You even dressed as a pirate and implied it was your true self!"

"Merely gammoning those who dared believe such stuff! Although, at times," he winked, "I might have been a bit of a privateer. Noticeable difference between the two—one being illegal and the other ill thought of. Still, I own, I fought some out-and-out pirate frigates. Also, took on a British naval vessel once—after the captain attempted to impound my crew, thinking we were still fighting the War of 1812. Times had changed, and I was forced to remind him of that fact." Darrel was remembering his triumph with a smile, until Charlette's cold voice brought him back.

"I'll not be the audience for another of your tales of adventure! One would think you had used that tactic sufficiently on London's social scene. It won you several impressionable admirers such as Lady Marjory. My advice is retire on those laurels."

"There's only one lady I would win!" he said softly, reaching out to take her in his arms, but she stepped back quickly.

"You've played this game too often! It is becoming tiresome!" she sputtered, moving back until hitting up against the marble fireplace, knocking acock the ormolu clock. It complained with a jangled chime. Both looked at it.

"The bells," she exclaimed. "Your time on watch is over. Dismissed."

"I am the captain. I give the orders . . . especially to my first mate!"

"If you believe that is effective, let me inform you, you are grossly offensive! You have become a stranger—a man whom your own father, as a respected sea captain, would have disapproved. I recommend you and the Bateses commiserate together at not yet having destroyed the Varricks—not while there are some sailors willing to sail their hearts out for us, not while I and Jem were there to foil your ramshackle attempts."

And all this she said while he was inches from her face, attempting to enrage him enough to step away, for she was feeling in a serious state of unease.

Effective. He stepped back, removing his hands from her bare shoulders.

"It appears you must needs find excuses for the disintegration of your father's empire. Rather, I should say, you are pitching this gammon to disguise the humiliation of no longer being the empress of our isle! Not being able to bear *that*, you assume others are playing havey-cavey. You are doing it too brown with all these stories. As for my father and what he would or would not approve, I expect I should know better than a young chit who never went to visit him when he was pensioned off before his time in order to bring in all these war heroes!"

Charlette was relieved that her way was now clear to walk around him, and back to the Grecian settee. She sat down like a lady of Miss Smidgeon's school. "I paid many a visit to your parents, Captain. Your father was quite pleased with the double-pension he received. He often told me as much."

"My father, like everyone else on this island, was in awe of the Varricks. He thought the sun rose and set on that line, but he suffered for being put to pasture before his time . . . as I did. What a cawker I was, coming to your father, hoping he would keep his word and take me on in my father's place . . . and even offering him all my savings as an investment. He threw me out with such disdain! I'll ne'er forget it. Nor would he tell me your whereabouts—just ordered me not to dare approach you!"

"Yet, you did more than that. You had me in your arms. That should have been sufficient retaliation without your needing to destroy the Varrick Line . . ."

"Is Varrick's so frail it cannot take fair competition!"

"Is Huntley-Bates so dishonest they cannot offer fair competition!"

Almost face to face again, both heightened with emotion, they threw words about.

"Speaking of dishonest tactics! The *Winged Angel* could easily have been disqualified on several counts. Count one: that a landlubber with no sailing history stepped in for a sailing captain. Count two: most blatant grounds—the presence, nay, the direction of a woman! Therefore, you should be grateful I have not informed the Committee of those counts against Varricks, or it would not only take back the prize and award it to the second place, or the *Porpoise*, but indeed, rule the Varrick Line ineligible for all subsequent races as well. Nay, all I had to do was ope my mouth, and you should have been in the suds! And think of how the ton would react to your escapade, Miss Varrick! How they should be saying you are quite like your mother! Even Lady Austen's good graces could not prevent you then from being labeled 'fast.' "

Abruptly he was silenced by the stricken look in Charlette's eyes.

"You . . . you wretch! Oh, heavens, that I should ever have thought you my friend. You speak thusly of my mother and my position, when you saw how it destroyed me in Society. You ramshackle loose-screw! You waterlogged, pea-brained, rackety knave! You . . . . blasted *pirate*!"

Darrel grinned at that. "You can curse with the best sailor, Charle, my girl. I have a parrot I should wish to put to school with you! One day we should have a contest to see who knows more, shall I say, colorful curses!"

Breathing deeply, Charlette's frozen blue eyes refused to melt into laughter. "I play no more games with you, Captain. You shall no longer be allowed admittance into my home . . . nor shall I ever even acknowledge you elsewhere. I intend, henceforth, to cut our acquaintance."

She said the last with full solemnity, as if she were excommunicating him.

"You can't cut me out of your heart, Charle," he whispered, "because we long ago gave each other half of our own." And saluting her with a grin, he turned and left.

Putting her hand defiantly up to her heart, she attempted to order it to stop beating so quickly. "Blast you, blast you, blast you!" she began, and her words were swept over by a sudden squall of tears.

But in a few moments she had wiped her tears with her sleeve and swore to the empty room, "Those are the last tears the Captain shall ever get from me. Henceforth, he is wiped out of my mind and heart forever!"

Chapter Seventeen

BUT naturally Charlette could not keep her vow of banishing the Captain from her thoughts. He intruded almost immediately with the announcement that the Varrick win had been challenged. Huntley-Bates had issued the challenge before the Sailing Committee. Thus, Mr. Varrick's view of Darrel was verified. For the very charges were the ones Captain Huntley had so proudly praised himself for not using.

Immediately, her father departed for London to be present himself at the hearing and bring forth his own charges of the Huntley-Bates spy aboard the *Winged Angel*. To defend herself and her course of action, Charlette wished to accompany him, but Mr. Varrick was adamant in his refusal.

"There is still a slim chance that no one, outside of the Committee, is aware of your being aboard. I may have enough power to prevent your name being officially used, and thus prevent rumors from reaching London's Society. If not, I shall curse that boy, for it shall be repetition of your mother's plight. Ostracized. In disgrace. You do not know how it hurt her. And to think I should have to live to see the same thing occurring to her little girl. And all because that young man could not wait to have it all. Hell's bells, he is young. He has years to win both prizes. Why couldn't he be decent about it? Or at least discreet. I'd hoped your friendship would make him hold his tongue."

"There is no longer a vestige of that friendship remaining," Charlette said firmly.

"If it were not at such a cost, I should be rejoicing," her father replied, and left for London.

But the storm cloud on their horizon did not dissipate. It came on wet and developed into a full downpour. The *Winged Angel* was disqualified, and Mr. Varrick's countercharge of incapacitating their captain was dismissed, resulting in the *Porpoise* being given the prize. The same mailing that brought the news of the verdict from her father brought a letter of commiseration from Lady Austen, dashing all hopes that her escapade would not be known to the *beau monde*. Her ladyship wished a round story—every detail. For the rumors were simply not to be believed! Had she really dressed in pantaloons and lived amongst the roughest crew members, unchaperoned by a single other lady, or even a male relative or guardian! Heavens, nothing else was being discussed! Lady Austen was totally occupied in the defending of her young friend. One could not believe how many people were affronted by her actions. Even Lord Austen, much as he cared for Charlette, felt she had gone too far for decency. Nevertheless, her ladyship swore to stand buff and invited her to her home from whence she could face Society with the truth, promising, "Together, my dear child, we shall stare them all down!"

Charlette, overcome by her friend's kindness, sent a reply by the next post, explaining she had worn a large cloak over the pantaloons, which was so fully a covering as to be the height of decency and respectability! Nor had she mingled with the crew. That was a gross lie, a positive rapper. She had kept as much distance as a captain would. And there could be no wider separation, except perhaps of King and subjects! Further, she'd been chaperoned by an old family friend and protector in his *sixties*! But it was pointless to defend herself against *on-dits*!

For her ladyship's own good, Charlette decided against accepting Lady Austen's invitation, much as she wished to take on her challengers. And then Charlette had to laugh philosophically, as she concluded to herself, "I have recovered from mother's disgrace only to have my own; and it is scarcely likely that even I can overcome *two* such, and in succeeding Seasons!"

One man was responsible for this, her final fall from grace, and while walking through the woods they'd run through as children, she wondered how he could have cared so little as to totally sink her beneath all reproach.

Froth, always loyal, rolled about to entertain, momentarily diverting her, till he raised a paw and struck at a passing beetle. "Ah, consider," she addressed the unfeeling feline, "it might have a family waiting. How can the world be so cruel?" Unintimidated, Froth scampered ahead to the beach below. She warned him against the waves, but he rushed on, till his feet were touched by the sea's froth and he cried out. She ran toward him, but someone was beforehand.

On the same beach as he had, years ago, Captain Huntley handed her Froth again.

Recollecting her vow not to recognize him, Charlette was in a quandary. She wanted to take Froth in her arms, for he was complaining about his sand-covered paws, but she did not wish to acknowledge his rescuer. A compromise suggested itself: Without looking at Darrel, she reached for Froth. But Darrel refused to let go, so that when she reached out, he simply held her hands as well, and they were jointly holding Froth.

Turning her head aside, she muttered menacingly, "Let go, you varmint! I am not recognizing you!" She grabbed the complaining cat, and rushed on.

"Charle," he whispered.

But she was running ahead. Jumping out of her hands, Froth climbed up the cliff path to the woods ahead. Charlette let him go, knowing he would be home before her. Her sprig muslin gown was the exact shade of her hair, and she was holding a leghorn straw bonnet with a fashionably wider brim and a satin bow in the same golden-red tone. While walking, she placed the bonnet on her head and resolutely tied the bow. It gave her a sense of being Miss Varrick, and she needed every defense as she heard him climbing up behind her. At the peak of the cliffs, he pulled her down on the promontory where they oft had sat to look out over the sea.

She shook her head at him, not communicating except through struggling.

"It's too late, Charle," he said softly. "You've already broken your oath. You've spoken to me. You called me a 'varmint'!"

"You are!"

"That makes twice."

"Oh, why didn't you drown on one of your voyages, before you ever came back to destroy my life!"

"I didn't destroy you. Listen to me, Charle, I was not part of the challenge. In fact, ask your father, I appeared at the hearing and said that since you were known to me, I would have recognized if you were on board. But there were members of your own crew there describing your climbing up the mast. And questioned under oath, Lieutenant Waters admitted that Jem Barker and you were running the ship."

"Then why didn't you confess to your spy aboard our ship!"

"I told you, I never placed a spy aboard any ship. I dashed well don't have to win that way! And I questioned my partners and was assured of their innocence as well. And any part they may have in rumor-mongering, I scotched."

Charlette struggled to get up and away from him again.

"You have to listen to me, Charle. Your father is in a devil of a fix. You have to persuade him to accept my offer of combining Varrick's and Huntley-Bates into one company. He can hang on for several more years, becoming second-rate and losing more and more of his ships until you and he have nothing left. This shall prevent that. I may not have been ready to marry yet, but a merger would be in both our interests. We can make it a family organization. And, then too, you know, I'd always come to your rescue. You must marry straightaway, considering what Lady Marjory writes me is the general reaction to your . . . walk on the masthead."

Enraged, Charlette cried out, "Are you implying I need the protection of *your* name to give *me* respectability! I'd sooner marry Jem! Spare me your grossly demeaning offer and presence."

"Reef your sails, Charle, my girl, you're caught in a storm and should be heading for the nearest port . . . and that is me."

"You underestimate my ability to sail out a storm," Charlette said coldly. "You always underestimated me . . . and mine."

And she decidedly removed his hand holding hers, scratching him in the effort.

"I trim my cat's nails," he said with a laugh, and the laugh grew louder and followed her as she ran into the woods, losing her hat on a branch, yet not stopping to retrieve it, going on—home to Sea Castle.

Captain Huntley picked up her hat and held it against himself, stroking the golden-red ribbon. "Charle," he whispered. "That's a devil of a way to respond to a gentleman's first attempt at proposing."

And he walked about on the beach. In his heart he'd known all along that he had not come back to Wight only to fulfill his dream of running a sailing line or to gain the London Prize. He'd returned to claim Charle herself. Good God, she was the dream itself! That had become particularly clear when she was on the masthead and the race became secondary to just watching her and his fears that she might be hurt.

"Said it wrong," he muttered—too shocked by finding himself suing for a lady's hand, after having held himself above such romantic twaddle. And he'd attempted to include in his proposal all the practical reasons for her marrying him so she could not possibly refuse, even putting her father's interest first, when he cared not a jot what happened to old Varrick or his blasted business! But she'd taken it amiss.

He should have asked that poet to put words in his blasted mouth, he groaned. A plain, rough sailor was all he was, after all. "I really made a mull of it all," he whispered and sat down on the sand.

At that precise moment another gentleman of Miss Varrick's acquaintance was feeling so materially out of sorts, he was actually down-pin. The Duke of Wingshire's solution was to take more than his usual amount of snuff. Very delicately he flicked open his enameled box and took two pinches of his latest mixture, soaked with attar of roses, and sneezed profusely all over his rose-embroidered brocade vest.

"Ain't my sort," he said aloud, and put the offending snuffbox on the mantel, pushing it behind the ormolu clock, out of his sight. Everything of late was not up to his specifications. His French chef that had been the pride of his London establishment was lately offering him paltry provisions. He had visited him in his kitchens and received the information that the man was off his feed because he was homesick. Dash it, he did not need to hear the troubles of his staff—not the thing. But he was a kindhearted man when things were shoved under his nose and he was not allowed to look away. He suggested a month's vacation to return to his homeland, and the man's spirits rose prodigiously. He himself considered the possibility of taking a trip to get out of his dismals. But the only place, dash it, he wished to travel was the Isle of Wight.

He had written several letters to Miss Varrick, but she had not responded. The more he wrote, he realized with a flush of humiliation, the more he sounded dicked-in-the-nob. His last one was all denunciation of Society for its treatment of her. Got it all out of his system, not having to worry about franking.

Never felt so akin to a lady as when I heard you'd won the race. Often feel that way meself when I'm shouting on one of my horses at Newmarket. Feel the urge to jumb on the nag's back and bring him across! Any doubts that we would not deal famously together were done away with by that very revelation. Told Marj when she joined your cousin in brewing up the scandal-broth about you that she should take a damper. Nose out'a joint, I expect. Told her a real lady ain't ashamed to show her feelings—for animals, people *or* races. Dash it all, told her you are a real lady and a perfect Duchess. And, stab me, if you would only return my feelings, I should dash well be the proudest peer in the realm! I offer you my heart, my wealth, my position, my title and all its attributes and attending honors— humbly dump the dashed lot at your feet, and hope you would care to walk across them and become my Duchess. Already see your portrait in my Hall of Portraits, as the pick of the lot!

> Percy Langford, Duke of Wingshire
> Your most humble servant and admirer

Charlette received this latest epistle of the Duke's just after being informed by her father that he was selling off his yachting line, and several ships, especially the navy surplus that had brought on his difficulties. Further, he was close to cutting out the China trade. Varricks would be half of what it was, but it would come about. Bit of a bumble broth now, but he would leave for Portsmouth for a fortnight to settle things. Some auctions should see them through; she was to disregard any dunning notices till he returned.

Charlette was afire to be of use. Admittedly, her last attempt to assist her beloved parent had scarcely improved their circumstances. A great many creditors that would have waited had panicked by the condemnation of Varricks by the London Committee. That explained her father's last remark, "I'd as lief handle matters on my own. Just stay here like a good girl, and all shall blow over. That's my darling," he finished gruffly, and left with such a pucker between his brows, Charlette was convinced he needed her help, after all.

All would have been well if she just had not removed her cap and scarf and played that silly game with Darrel on the masthead. Still, the two had always been prime for a lark, especially if it had a hint of challenge to it. Yet, only when the crew knew she was Miss Varrick did the tongues begin going like fiddlesticks—which led to her father paying the piper. Darrel had been correct: Her father's line was diminishing. Marrying Captain Huntley might have put a stop to that erosion, but at what cost! A humiliation her father would scarcely be able to bear. Actually, it was a question of being swallowed whole or going down piece by piece. A whale's meal or sharked to death! Scarcely a choice.

And then, of a sudden, Mitchen brought her a third way. In truth, she had been keeping the Duke in the back of her mind, on reserve, so to speak, and now he pushed forward. She had even kept Sir Smithers back there, so less discriminating was she become. Yet, she kept hoping, rather, to reach shore safely on her own. But the storm was hard upon, and she could no longer wait for a clearing. She had to jump ship.

Taking up a quill that needed mending, she tossed it down and found another. Then opening her crystal standish, dipped her point into the ink and wrote a fateful reply to his grace. She held off sealing it for half a day. Then, Mitchen asked if she wished the epistle on the desk posted? That was the needed sign. She walked quickly to the desk, found a wafer, applied it and handed it over. When her butler walked out the room, she had a momentary mad desire to call after and retrieve her letter. But she kept herself still. And it was gone.

The Duke of Wingshire received her letter with such a blast of joy throughout his constitution that he emitted a very uncharacteristic yell. Half the staff of his establishment came running. "Wish me joy," he said to them all. "I have been accepted by the most beautiful lady in the world! Blast me, I'm to be wed!"

There was no hesitation on anyone's part to give their heartiest congratulations. Rather unorthodox of the Duke to announce his marriage plans to his staff at all, but to announce it to them before notifying even his sister was clearly outside of enough!

Lady Austen, first to be informed of the news by Charlette, almost repeated the Duke's exuberance—running to her husband's dressing room in triumph! Now he should see how correct she was about Charlette. All of Society should be eating her words.

Her father received the notice from his daughter just as he was about to sign away his entire yachting line. With tears in his eyes, he turned to one of the Bateses, waiting for his signature, and said, "I am delighted to inform you that Varrick Specialty Yachts is no longer on the market. I have just received news that puts a different color on all future negotiations." And with his face all aglow, and savoring the questions being asked and ignored, he picked up his malacca walking stick and sauntered out.

The notice in the *Gazette* soon made the matters clear to all. His creditors, considering the vast fortune, not to mention the prestige, of the Duke of Wingshire, not only recanted their requests for payment but were quite anxious to offer further investments. The Duke was ordering a yacht and a new ship as a wedding present to his daughter, Mr. Varrick was pleased to announce. Yet, he would continue the sale of the war-surplus ships in order to streamline the operations to equal the quality of his daughter's new position. Further, Mr. Varrick immediately invited his grace for a visit to Cowes, where, quizzing-glass in hand, the Duke's appearance was enough to awe any doubters. Next, arriving at Sea Castle, his grace had the pleasure of a few private moments with his intended. She appeared more subdued than he recollected, but she was even more beautiful than ever. He had the pleasure of finally being able to kiss her perfect lips, and was overcome by her closeness. She was completely ladylike in her shyness, and yet totally herself in the way she held onto his hand and asked a question only she would ask, "We shall be happy together, shall we not, Percy?"

"I shall do all within my power to make you happy, my love. For myself, there is no question, I am already in alt."

About Lady Marjory's reaction, the Duke was hesitant to transmit anything beyond civilities, which left Charlette without the desire to press for anything further. Actually, Lady Marjory was not in London when Charlette and her father arrived to visit Lady Austen, so Charlette had to wait for her blessing. As for Lady Austen she was in her element. Every day people were calling to express their delight. Charlette, her ladyship felt, had matured noticeably. She accepted every good wish with graciousness but none of the old twinkle that used to tweak all Society. There was to be a special Engagement Ball in her honor given by the Duke himself, to prepare Society for his fiancée's future dominance of it, he had said seriously.

"*My* dominance!" Charlette had echoed, and momentarily her old laugh had surfaced, but when he looked surprised, Charlette inclined her head. "Doubtless, that is my future."

"Dashed well 'tis. Duchess, you know. Lots of responsibility that. Mother was busy all the time telling everybody what to do. Don't have to do that. But a dash bit of interest is actually expected."

"I see. Obviously, I shall soon be quite interested in all this." But her voice lacked conviction.

"No need to fret, my pet," the Duke said, thinking her frightened. "I shall be by you. Ain't nothing you can't do with grace. Going to be 'her grace,' after all, what?"

And she smiled at his jollity, receiving a passionate kiss upon her hands. His grace had developed a habit of kissing her on the palm she found rather endearing, if not humorous. Nevertheless, she restrained her giggle, merely smiling at his scented head bowing beneath her nose. Mr. Varrick found his grace rather endearing as well. Especially when during a discussion making the Duke aware of the full Huntley-Bates perfidy, his grace had waved to his man-in-charge and promptly ordered a sizable investment in Varricks as a wedding gift. "She likes ships. Planned to give her one or two estates, but she'd jolly well like this better, what?" Mr. Varrick agreed, and realized while dressing for the ball that Charlette, his gift from his wife, had not only provided for her own future, but for his comfortable one as well. Reverting to strictly shipbuilding, he need never again concern himself about cargoes or about outmaneuvering anyone. Indeed, people were already treating him as a bit of nobility himself. And after all the years of being held accountable for his wife's fall from Society, his own darling daughter had reestablished them both. E'gad, it was even possible, he thought, in a golden dream, that he would be hobnobbing with royalty. He laughed aloud as he joined Charlette and Lord and Lady Austen in their coach on their way to the Engagement Ball.

It was the Duke's decision to give it himself at his home. And he was delighted to give vent to all his own fantasies, without anyone to take over and ruin it for him. It was his moment, and he and his man, Perkins, had planned it all—down to the color of the silk napkins. All ruby. He liked brightness of color. That had been the first thing that took his eye about Charlette: There was nothing pale about her. Her blazing golden-red hair had him following her about as if she were a flame. He liked the red brick of his Wingshire Castle, and had been quite put out when Lady Marjory had stuccoed the sides, in keeping with current Nash fashions. Now, waiting for his fiancée, the Duke perused the ballroom. It was a blaze of ruby satin—festoons of it around the chandeliers and over the pier glasses in the entrance. Red satin roses decorated the banisters of the stairs leading to the ballroom, and wishing for alleviation, his artistic eye had added touches of golden braid. On the balcony of the ballroom hung a shield-sized golden heart with ruby stones forming the initials P and C, setting the theme, he felt proudly.

The engagement ring he had already given his wife-to-be was the prized ruby ring his grandmother wore on state occasions—to match the family ruby coronet. As well, he gave her the rest of the ruby collection, including a heavy gilt and ruby necklace, and matching bracelet and earrings.

"Your grandmother wore these in her portrait, if I recollect correctly. And with it, a rather ornate gown of golden material as the background to her rubies, did she not?" The Duke agreed, delighted by her remembrance, so Charlette instantly decided to pattern her own gown after it. And put it all in Madame Fanchot's hands.

Percy was overcome at the final vision. A blaze of golden sunlight, she appeared, made even brighter with the ruby collection showering all over her. The jewel of his heart, he thought, and rushed to call her so, before the guests arrived.

As part of her willingness to forgive all past insults and arrange for her smooth acceptance into Society, Charlette had invited everyone she knew, including Lord and Lady Bridingsley, Francine and, to assure the latter's happiness, Mr. Buckston.

That party, approaching Miss Varrick in her blaze of rubies and gold, had tears in their eyes. His lordship because he had never seen so much wealth on one person and was overcome thinking what a stake she would make at White's. Lady Bridingsley because, as she told all, she had pushed for this happy marriage. And now her fondest dream had been accomplished. She was to be a close relation to a Duchess! That her niece had sent a kind reply to her note of congratulations also boded well for the future. Her dear, dear Charlette! Approaching, Lady Bridingsley kissed her niece's offered cheek, her lips sliding to the glowing ruby earing, kissing that stone with trembling reverence. As for Francine's tears, they were of rage. She could not bear that her cousin was to be a Duchess. Yet, she kept herself in control and listlessly curtsied before Charlette, who gave her a warm smile. Francine, without the igniting presence of Captain Huntley, had retreated back into her silent and colorless self. Mr. Buckston had been put off by the wild Francine and ceased to call. Yet, this evening he arrived having new interest in the soon-to-be Duchess's family. He needed only one look at the pale and prosaic Francine to see her back to her old tolerable self, and he stepped up to ask for the first dance, which turned both Lady Bridingsley's and Francine's tears into smiles of joy.

The guests had almost all been welcomed when Lady Marjory arrived with her escort. She had just put off her ermine wrap and was being led up the stairs, where she bestowed a kiss on her brother and gave a nod to Charlette. Her escort was unsmiling. He had lost the secret grin that had been his trademark at all of his past social events. Nor did he have the daring challenge in his eyes, often there when sailing. Captain Darrel Huntley was grim as he stepped up to the bride-to-be.

"You are a riot of rubies, Miss Varrick," Captain Huntley said, staring at her fixedly. "One wonders how much you are worth, standing there a testament to your fiancé's wealth. Amazing how the rubies tend to wipe you out."

"You're out there, old boy," the Duke interrupted. "She is the only woman who has more brilliance than all the baubles . . . puts 'em to shame."

"She perhaps should know best about shame. I came to wish a happy life to an old friend . . . There seems to be nothing else I can think of," Darrel concluded in a slow, languid manner, yet his words seemed weighted with added meanings.

"I perfectly comprehend how sincere your well wishes are, Captain, and am most obliged to you," Charlette replied, and turned her head and extended her arm to greet the next person entering.

The dancing had been continuing for nigh unto an hour, and Charlette had danced with all the Dukes present—from the Duke of York on down to her own Duke of Wingshire. She had danced with her father, who could not contain his happy grin throughout the evening. Lord Austen had his turn. And Sir Smithers took his dance time to read her his just-composed poem, that ended with: "Salute the glorious rubied face—of our new, our sea-sailing her grace!"

The rubies were beginning to weigh on Charlette. Especially those several rows around her neck.

More dances. Occasionally she paused on the side of the ballroom and received the good wishes of the elderly ladies who felt themselves beyond dancing. They fluttered round her; all their lace caps converging into one giant, multi-petaled flower around the golden-red center that was Charlette.

A heaviness in the air slowed Charlette's motions. If she had been aboard one of her father's ships, she would have deduced from the atmospheric onus that a storm was brewing.

The table was set with the finest gold plate. Two rows of footmen in livery stood behind it, ready to serve the massive spread. Fowls of every kind. Five porks complete with their heads. And several flanks of roasted beef stood red and bulging in the center.

Charlette was unable to partake of any of it. The music in the background also had a ponderous note. Again, she felt a need of air. When the dancing began once more, she excused herself to her partner, explaining she should be returning shortly.

When she stepped into a small saloon that was unoccupied, she took a moment to rest her head against the white marble mantel, looking down into the red fire, but it reminded her of her rubies, and she shook her head and went to the window. The view was of a small garden with evergreen bushes and a small stone fountain, topped by a dolphin spewing water from its mouth. Dolphins brought good fortune; they had been known to rescue sailors adrift on the sea, she recollected, needing a dolphin at this moment. An overpowering desire to be by that fountain fought her decorum: One did not leave one's own engagement party. Further, to reach it, she would have to go out of this room, and should then probably encounter her guests.

The window was large and would scarcely be a challenge to a girl who had oft climbed down from her own second-floor balcony—although never dressed as she was now, and with the weight of so many rubies. Yet, one shove of the lower sash, and in a flash she was over the sill, running down the stone walk to the garden. There, she touched the water and splashed a few drops onto her face.

"What delayed you?"

Whirling about, she spotted him standing nonchalantly against a pine tree. He came forward and put his own hand under the dolphin's snout and drank of it. Cupping his two hands, he offered her some as well, and she accepted a sip.

They waited, watching the dolphin. "Why are you doing this to us?" he asked intently; and the words seemed to be wrung out of his soul. "You know—Jem wrote you, I proved to him I had naught to do with a spy aboard the *Winged Angel* or its disqualification. Never in my life have I sought to hurt you. I merely returned home seeking a ship to captain, as my father before me, wishing to sail for the Varricks. Since that was denied, I accepted the next best offer and did my best."

"You wished for the London Prizes, do not deny upon having them. You wished to revenge yourself against my father. You've been wishing that since a child, when we were forced to hide our friendship," she said without emotion, speaking merely the truth.

"Aye, some of that burned within me," he admitted with a gasp. "It gnawed, being constantly considered beneath his daughter's touch, doubling the pleasure of my beating old starched pants. His sinking to the level at which he wished me to remain might be considered justice, but his humiliation meant *your* humiliation, and so I stayed my hand. It does not help me to give you pain, for I must then feel it, too. No, you stood between him and any attempt I should make to unfairly challenge him. But a fair challenge we always believed in. The devil take it, you must know me well enough to know I never won unfairly! My own sense of worth assured I should only wish to win on merit! You must know that!"

Charlette, after a moment, shrugged her shoulders, causing the rubies to gleam in the moonlight. "Even if I do, it is no longer relevant," she said tonelessly. "Earlier perhaps it would have mattered . . . altered our circumstance, but now I can no longer even think about what might have been. It is over. We are over."

"We shall never be over," he insisted. "You know that. I know that! I only did not immediately ask you to marry me because I had to rise to your level, afeared you would refuse me else. And when I did offer, I said it all wrong. But good God, you know we were always meant to be one. Blast all to hell who tries to stand between us—for they shall not prevail . . . not Dukes . . . not ladies . . . not your father."

"It is too late," Charlette said, stepping away from him. "I have given my word. And more, the Duke has saved my father's reputation, if not his dream. I could not possibly cry off—for both their sakes! All this, whatever feelings you think lie between us, must be suppressed. They are best left with most of our relationship—back in the past."

"No," he said, pressing her hands so tightly, and then pulling her into his arms and not allowing her to squirm away, holding her against him, until their hearts were synchronized, and they stood there, joined. She breathed with him silently for awhile, feeling a sudden awakening from her stupor of the evening, nay, a stupor of the last months.

"Be as daring as your mother, Charle, run away with me now. Throw father and everyone else to the winds! This moment! We'll sail to the South Seas and live there together, and never look back on anyone here."

"You're talking to me as if I were Charle, but I am no longer that wild, willful, unthinking child, running off with you, not caring for aught but the wish of my heart. And . . . my mother's position and mine are not equivalent. She ran from a cruel forced marriage: My word has been pledged to a gentle, kind, decent gentleman I could not possibly disgrace! Further, my mother owed no love to her parents who had forced her into that untenable position, while my father never requested I do anything but allow him to cherish and protect me. No, it should be infamous of me if I allowed him to fall once more into his recent peril. Why could not you have challenged someone else and risen at another's expense, and come to me then? But because you could not see how deep my feelings are for those I love, that is why we are at this point of separation. I will not have him hurt! Nor shall I seek my own happiness at so many's unhappiness. I am committed, and shall never of my own volition break that committal. Oh, this is intolerable, even discussing it. Pray, return to the ball. Why did you come out here! How did you know I should be here?" She stepped away from the fountain, and looked toward the window. ". . . When I myself do not know what drew me out."

"Your heart did. You say all those words, and they mean nothing. You know it would be hurting others more to continue this pretense." Suddenly, he was silent, looking up and then to the side. His next action was done so quickly Charlette was just able to sadly respond with all her heart to his kiss, saying her good-bye that way, and then whispering, "Darrel, Darrel . . ."

"Bit of a squeeze within, ain't it?" came a voice behind them.

Darrel let her go, and she turned to see her fiancé staring at them.

"Bit of a squeeze going on out here, as well," his grace continued.

"More than that!" Darrel spoke up. "I have been making advances to your fiancée!"

"Quite understand, old chap, often feel the same way meself. Childhood sweethearts, eh what? Good thing to say adieu to all those infantile inclinations."

Then turning toward Charlette, the Duke said smoothly, "May I escort you within? Our guests, and I, have been missing you."

The stupor took over again, and Charlette, seeing that nothing had changed after all, merely nodded and gave him her hand.

"I have seriously compromised your fiancée," Captain Huntley insisted, stepping between the engaged couple. "Surely, you, as a gentleman, cannot accept that! It is not in your code!"

"Odd's life, are you challenging me?" the Duke exclaimed.

"Must I knock your foppish grin off your face to make my point? I challenge you, indeed. Charle is mine—you cannot buy her, you cannot win her, you cannot keep her."

The Duke had recourse to his final weapon. He raised his

quizzing-glass and eyed the Captain with a contemptuous magnified eye.

Not only was Darrel not intimidated by that eye, but he brushed the glass aside impatiently, as if it were an insect.

Feeling it knocked off his eye, the Duke could no longer take the situation as something too beneath him to notice. "Very well, Captain, if a challenge you want, a challenge you shall have. But recollect, since I am the injured party," and he stooped to retrieve his fallen quizzing-glass, as if that were the cause of the argument, "I have choice of weapons. But gentlemen do not themselves discuss these minor details. I shall send someone to act for me. Certainly, one does not discuss it before a lady!"

The Captain nodded, appeased.

"I shall not permit this," Charlette exclaimed, looking from one to the other. "This is unconscionable! Neither of you has the right to decide for me with this Gothic exhibition! I have made my own choice, and both of you must accept it without creating any more gist for Society's bumble broth!"

Both men merely bowed, but she was certain they were not bowing to her wishes. The three of them returned to the ballroom, where fending off Lady Austen's questions, she turned, seeing the Duke and the Captain exiting toward the gaming room together. Half-relieved, half-disappointed that they could so frighten her and then forget it all over a game of whist, she whispered, "Blast 'em."

"Who, dear?" Lady Austen asked pleasantly.

Unable to explain, hoping she had scotched it, she just mumbled, "Men."

"Indeed. Blast 'em. But whom would we have to dance with else? I fear we must accept them with all their shortcomings—until one can teach Froth to take a turn for the gavotte." And that picture had Charlette grinning, as both ladies accepted an offered hand and danced away onto the ballroom floor.

Chapter Eighteen

THE wedding was to take place in a fortnight. Since the Engagement Party had been such a grand social event in London, the wedding was to be a more private affair on Wight. Charlette was preparing to depart for there when the Duke visited her, at Lady Austen's, requesting a few moments.

"Did we not say our adieus last night?" Charlette said.

"If your feelings were as strong as mine, you would wish for every opportunity for us to be together," he said seriously.

Charlette said what was ladylike and proper when the Duke interrupted. "Marj and I are planning a tour of Europe. Did the Grand Tour on me own, but Marj wants to see the old buildings before they fall down."

"Are you . . ." she paused to catch her breath. "Are you giving me a slip on the shoulder? Crying off?"

The Duke looked pained at her plain speaking. "Postponing it. Marj fell into such a state I feel she needs a while to adjust. We shall pick up where we left off on my return, what? Otherwise we'll be in the suds—poor girl has been crying on my sleeve since the announcement. Thought I could push through, but she had the doctor to her, and he advised me to take her away or the poor dear will come apart. In a decline, don't you know? She's a total watering-pot. Can't let her continue to mope herself to death. Fond of the old girl."

"Well, of course, if that is what you wish."

"Don't wish it, dash it. Must do it, for the old girl. Sister."

"Yes, I know. But what about your investment in Varricks?"

"Oh, that. Piddling sum. Gave it all to you. Good-bye gift. No need to get yourself in a quake over that. Always mean to see you are taken care of."

"Thank you, indeed!" Charlette said in a huff. "But if you do not wish to marry me, I shall certainly not keep you to any of your obligations . . ."

He waved her silent. "Already done. Spoke to your father. If when I come back in a year or two, you are still not wed to someone else, I shall claim you for my own. But don't wish to keep you on the ropes. Dash it, too beautiful a gel. What? And even if you should wed someone else, perfectly willing to be your cicisbeo for life," the Duke said sadly. "And if that blighter should ever go sailing and fall off the edge of the earth or take up a life in the South Seas, I shall nip in and have my chance, what?"

"Heavens, did you and Captain Huntley arrange this? Are you tossing me to him as if I were a Hatcherd's lending book, Percy! How dare you! What is going on, exactly?"

"Breaking my heart," the Duke said humbly. "But must do the noble thing. Nobleman, you know. Besides, played cards for you—that was the weapon I chose, and I lost. And then Marj had her fit, ain't a gel for vapors, so I was worried. Knew you and the Captain were in love, just hoped you'd stopped caring for him. Hoped you'd care for me. But you been moping around ever since we've declared ourselves. Knew your heart wasn't in it. Didn't have the pluck to ask you—thought you'd tell me the truth. Didn't want to hear the truth. It is the truth, ain't it? Don't have a *tendre* for me."

Charlette took a deep breath. He was eyeing her so directly she could not face him, and had to turn away to admit her feelings were not totally engaged.

"Ought to be . . . to be engaged," he said simply, hopelessly.

"Yes," Charlette agreed. "But I do care for you—quite a bit."

"Obliged," he said softly. "Knew that, too. Hoped it would be enough. But you were too much in the blue dismals. Didn't even like the rubies. My mother didn't either. Always said they weighed too much. Like you to have them, anyway, to remember what for me was the happiest night of my life."

"Percy," Charle began turning back with concern in her eyes, but he waved her silent.

"No need to fuss. I'll always be your sincerest admirer. Happy to have had you as my own—for this brief time. Besides, can't do anything but give you up, what with Marj flying off the hooks. Then too, only gentlemanly thing to do. The Captain won you off me, fair and square!"

"I am not a stake, your grace. I make my own decisions. And

since you have been kind enough to give me Varricks, I intend to devote my time to running that. I believe I have had enough of gentlemen making decisions for me."

Lady Austen appeared to inform her that the coach had arrived for her departure from London, and Charlette thanked her, allowing his grace to hand her in.

"Adieu, my island girl," he whispered, "I shall always wear you in my heart."

Charlette, barely able to return a civil answer, quickly signaled the footman to close the door. Although she waved at both the Duke and Lady Austen, and smiled at them through the window, when she sat back her face showed how out of countenance she was. "That odious wretch," she exclaimed. "Both of them—playing for me." And yet, although refusing to admit it, she, nevertheless, was feeling quite a good deal of relief.

In the weeks back at Wight, her father, although concerned that her marriage was postponed due to Lady Marjory's sudden indisposition—for that was the story being given to Society—was not displeased that he would have his daughter for some time on his own. Nor did she seem as out of whack as she had during the engagement period. "Needed a breather," he concluded. And she agreed.

The letters she received from Darrel, she returned—unopened. It was at least the fourth one in a row she had done so, and was considering writing him a note to explain her awareness of his dastardly act of playing for her, as if she were some doxy, when she decided not to give him the courtesy of even that much attention.

The Captain next sent her a large box, which she was also set to return, till hearing noises within. And Froth was making rather odd noises while circling it. Dismissing the footman, she opened it herself. The cries had given away its contents, but she was still astonished at the duplicate Froth jumping out. Two Froths faced each other, as if performing a dance before a mirror. She could not help but laugh.

Picking both up in her arms, she attempted to negotiate a friendship between them, but they were too busy spitting at each other.

"Oh dear, you remind me rather of your master and mistress, after all," she said with a giggle, and let them alone. In a few moments they stopped circling each other. Her Froth settled before the fireplace, ignoring the stranger. But the latter was adventurous, and jumping beside him. Froth, warily, then happily jumped alongside. And as Charlette watched, she recognized she'd been manipulated by a master strategist.

At this very moment, she heard the seashells on her balcony window. Unable to resist finally having it out with him, Charle went down. No longer did she pull up her skirt to descend the balcony. Now, like a lady, she walked out of her own morning room and slowly continued to the path in the woods and down the chalk cliff to the beach. As of old he was waiting for her. Behind him, there was a new sailboat.

"We're off for a sail, Charle!" he called as she came close. And before she had time to say anything about Froth and the duplicate Froth, or indeed about the Duke, he took her by the hand and showed her the name: *Charle*.

Picking her up in an instant, he had her in the sailboat and they were sailing through the waves. The wind obligingly filled their sails. When they reached far enough, he reefed, and they paused to exchange a happy look, whereupon he said calmly, "You see, out here, we have no disagreements. Nothing to stand between us. Out here, we are one. You must admit that. Isn't it time you stopped playing off your games and admitted we are only half a person without the other?"

"But to use me as a stake in a game of chance!" she exclaimed, still unable to quite forget that humiliation.

"That was the Duke's decision. I just as soon have shot the bloke."

"Shoot kindly, gentle Percy! How could you?"

"He dared to try to take you away from me," Darrel said calmly. "Besides, I would have chosen swords and merely pricked him. Just to get him to let you go! But he was decent enough to realize we belong together. Thus, if *he* knows it, and *I* know it, when, blast it, shall *you* admit it? You must know, and feel . . . that we are one, as I know and feel it. And shall do so for the rest of my life."

"If we could live for just these moments—together," Charlette agreed, relenting.

"These moments have always been with us," Darrel whispered. "No matter how far away I sailed, and no matter how high in Society you rose. Our hearts were always here on the sea—bound together."

And as Charlette did not respond, looking out at the horizon, he began to press her with his words, pulling her close to himself at the tiller. "I sailed through all the seas, and when I came back, I knew the prize I always sought was you. That you were not only part of my dream past, but the dream itself. Or the heart of it." Charlette remained still silent, listening to him as if bemused. Running out of words, Darrel turned to oaths. "I swear you have always been the star of my destiny. I can set my sights by the star you are and come home to you from whatever distance. For without you, I am becalmed . . . adrift . . ."

"Very nautically put," Charlette cut in, with a twinkle in her eyes, the old Charle in her rising up and taking charge. "However, I notice I am the one who must remain in place—as a fixed star to guide *you*. There as an inspiration, while you sail away, till you eventually deign to come back to me. Forgive my incivility, but that is a load of rather overdone gammon, for what you really are saying to me is: '*I* sail—*you* stay put.' Yet, actually, I, too, should quite prefer taking flight. You might jolly well try being *my* fixed star for awhile. I've taken it into my head to go for a prodigiously long voyage."

Highly diverted, Darrel replied, "But you mistake me. I spoke of the past, when we were apart. The pattern of one-going-somewhere-and-the-other-staying-put is exactly what I am objecting to. I would bring us back to our pattern when we were growing up and did everything together. Indeed, that is what I am proposing while I am proposing to you—that we, henceforth journey *together*. Blast it, we were always best as a team. I've had enough lone travels. We must be together from now on, whether on land or on sea."

Allowing that he was now making a more attractive offer, Charle admitted she was actually quite close to accepting him.

At that point the sailboat contributed to the discussion by lurching, and both put their hands on the tiller to steady it. And looking at each other, they sensed each other's thoughts—that they were pledging their troth in a way that they, as sea creatures, would most respect.

"With the wind at our backs, and both our hands thus pledged on the tiller, we shall be *one*—riding the sea together," Darrel whispered, sweeping her into his arms and concluding gruffly, "I vow by the sea we both love, it shall be smooth sailing for our union from here on out."

"Indeed," Charle said with a nod, freeing herself enough to make a movement of the tiller that had the Captain jumping to catch the swinging boom, as she laughingly concluded, "But not without an occasional, obligatory bump."

"Aye aye, my captain," he acknowledged with a grin and a teasing, albeit loving, salute.